FOREVER PROTECTED

FOREVER BLUEGRASS #18

KATHLEEN BROOKS

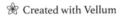 Created with Vellum

Bluegrass Series

Bluegrass State of Mind

Risky Shot

Dead Heat

Bluegrass Brothers

Bluegrass Undercover

Rising Storm

Secret Santa: A Bluegrass Series Novella

Acquiring Trouble

Relentless Pursuit

Secrets Collide

Final Vow

Bluegrass Singles

All Hung Up

Bluegrass Dawn

The Perfect Gift

The Keeneston Roses

Forever Bluegrass Series

Forever Entangled

Forever Hidden

Forever Betrayed

Forever Driven

Forever Secret

Forever Surprised

Forever Concealed

Forever Devoted

Forever Hunted

Forever Guarded

Forever Notorious

Forever Ventured

Forever Freed

Forever Saved

Forever Bold

Forever Thrown

Forever Lies

Forever Protected

Forever Paired

Shadows Landing Series

Saving Shadows

Sunken Shadows

Lasting Shadows

Fierce Shadows

Broken Shadows

Framed Shadows

Endless Shadows

Fading Shadows

Damaged Shadows (coming Oct 2022)

Women of Power Series

Chosen for Power

Built for Power

Fashioned for Power

Destined for Power

<u>*Web of Lies Series*</u>

Whispered Lies

Rogue Lies

Shattered Lies

<u>*Moonshine Hollow Series*</u>

Moonshine & Murder

Moonshine & Malice

Moonshine & Mayhem

Moonshine & Mischief

Moonshine & Menace

Moonshine & Masquerades

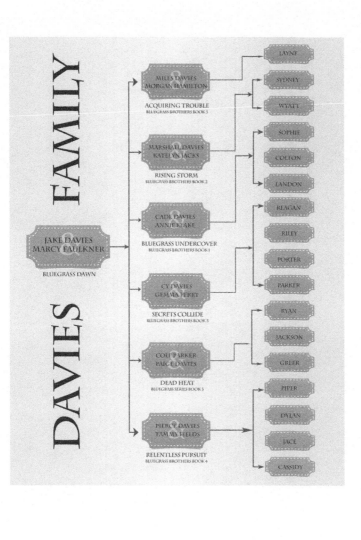

DAVIES FAMILY FRIENDS

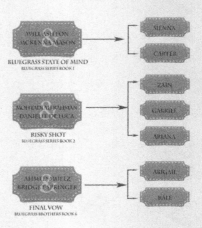

WILL ASHTON &
MCKENNA MASON

BLUEGRASS STATE OF MIND
BLUEGRASS SERIES BOOK 1

SIENNA

CARTER

MOHTADI ALRAHMAN &
DANIELLE DE LUCA

RISKY SHOT
BLUEGRASS SERIES BOOK 2

ZAIN

GABRIEL

ARIANA

AHMED MUELZ &
BRIDGET SPRINGER

FINAL VOW
BLUEGRASS BROTHERS BOOK 6

ABIGAIL

KALE

PROLOGUE

Lexington, Kentucky
   US Marshals Joint Task Force
   Four months ago . . .

Parker Davies tightened the strap on his US Marshals' bulletproof vest as the commander finished running down the facts of the case. The US Marshals had worked with the FBI and local law enforcement in five different states to orchestrate a simultaneous hit on known sexual predators.

It was a far cry from the days of strapping on his vest and hoping not to be gored by a bull when Parker was on the pro rodeo circuit. However, he had seen the writing on the wall. Any more hard falls, a kick to the head, or another broken bone, and Parker wouldn't have a future. His twin, Porter, was learning that lesson now. He was injured after winning two championships and trying to figure out what to do with the rest of his life. For Porter, it had always been about the rodeo and rodeo life, but not so for Parker.

It had started out that way, but then in college he and his

brother had been recruited to join the CIA. They'd found out earlier in their life that their father, Cy Davies, had been a spy for the CIA. While that didn't tempt the Davies brothers to follow in their father's footsteps, it had inspired Parker to start looking beyond the rodeo world to find his next passion.

He'd been named after his parents' close friend, FBI Agent Cole Parker, who'd helped them with a case. So, Parker had turned to Cole to talk about his life in the FBI. Cole had told him about the FBI, but then also had discussed the other law enforcement agencies. There had been something about the US Marshals Service that resonated with Parker.

Maybe it was because it was so hard to get into and he liked the challenge. Or maybe because it was the nation's oldest law enforcement agency. Or maybe it was because it was his nature to be a protector and that's what the US Marshals did—they protected. They hunted down the worst of the worst and protected those who were brave enough to stand up to them, whether in WITSEC or temporary protection for government attorneys, judges, and witnesses.

"You know to expect more than just some scrawny drugged-out traffickers," his boss, Deputy Newman, was saying. "Human trafficking is big money and they use big guns to protect it."

"You must be a Davies."

Parker turned to the woman standing next to him with POLICE emblazoned across her bulletproof vest.

"Yes, ma'am. Parker Davies. How did you know that?"

"You all have the same hazel eyes. Detective Andrea Braxton. I've worked with Ryan before."

Parker nodded down at the woman, her dark hair in a tight ponytail and several guns strapped to her. "He's my cousin with the FBI." He was also leading a raid thirty miles away.

Braxton looked up at him and shook her head. "Do you all decide which branch of law enforcement you go into by size? You Marshals are giants."

"Better to shield witnesses with," Parker joked as he gave her a wink. He was a bit over six feet two inches, and his rodeo days had made his legs thick and strong, his shoulders wide, and his chest had women doing a double take. Just like Andrea Braxton was doing.

"If only I were a little younger," he heard her mutter and grinned in response.

"What does age have to do with sex?" Parker asked and watched Andrea blush at being overheard.

"Davies. Braxton. You with us?" his boss snapped.

"Yes, sir," they both answered.

"Good. You two lead the teams at the warehouse in the industrial park," Agent Newman assigned. "Everyone get into position. We kick the doors down at three sharp."

"Want a ride? Think you can handle me being in charge?" Braxton asked and Parker grinned again. He enjoyed verbal sparring as a means of foreplay. He'd had enough buckle bunnies to satisfy him for a lifetime. Someone who made him think was a major turn-on.

"I've ridden bulls my whole life. I think I can manage a little detective."

"I like a challenge."

Parker kicked the door down at three in the morning, sharp. Detective Braxton and an array of state and local police stormed into the building behind him. Parker didn't flinch when the shots began to ring out. He'd been shooting since he was old enough to steady a rifle and he rarely missed. Especially when he saw what he saw. Cold rage filled him as he took out any man who fired on him. Women and children were in cages. Some were in dog cages and some were in chain-link kennel runs. All appeared drugged and had been beaten.

Parker kicked a man trying to flee in the back. He went sprawling to the ground as Parker dropped a hard knee to his back, yanked his arms back, and zip-tied his hands before practically throwing the man into one of the empty kennel runs and locking him in.

By the time all was said and done, fifteen men and two women had been arrested. Two had been killed in a shootout. A state trooper had been wounded and Andrea Braxton had bloody knuckles after beating the crap out of a man who tried to attack her.

Fifty-three victims had been rescued. Nine pallets of illegal firearms had been confiscated. Pounds and pounds of meth, fentanyl, cocaine, and heroin had also been confiscated.

"I'll talk!" the man Parker was dragging by the arm shouted. "But I want protection, man. Don't put me in with them. They'll kill me."

Parker stopped dragging him toward the bus they were using to transport all the detainees. "Why would they kill you?"

"I'm the new guy. They always throw the new guy under the bus. I ain't going down for this. I just thought I'd be selling a little weed, man."

Parker looked down at the scrawny, obviously stoned patsy who couldn't weigh more than a hundred and thirty pounds. "Okay, you want to talk. Let's talk."

That's the thing about US Marshals—they were always

after the bigger fish. The deadlier, the more connected, the more violent . . . that's who Parker wanted. This guy wasn't it. There was always someone bigger pulling the strings, and the instinct to hunt them down had Parker nodding goodbye to Detective Braxton and settling into an interrogation.

Parker didn't want to brag, but he knew women liked him. He'd had his fair share of them too. However, standing outside the arena in Lexington watching his brother in the reining event and meeting Tilly Bradford was an experience all to itself.

The woman was mesmerizing. Her blonde hair was pinned into a fancy bun at the base of her neck. She wore makeup, but not so much that it stood out. It seemed this firecracker of a woman was full of endless energy as her mouth ran on and on and out came way too much information. Such as finding him incredibly hot. The feeling was mutual. Parker was a big guy, but there was something about this curvy woman who sat on horses twice her height and jumped six-foot fences that had him totally infatuated.

His brother, Porter, was a temporary CIA asset charged with watching Willa Aldridge, Tilly's best friend, to determine if she was a traitor or not. Willa clearly wasn't and Parker enjoyed watching his brother trip over his feet and land flat at Willa's. But then Parker had met Tilly and damned if he didn't completely understand Porter's goofy grin.

It also had Parker going toe to toe with two silver-spoon-fed brats trying to bully Willa, Tilly, and everyone else at the horse-jumping event. Parker wasn't even mad when one swung a haymaker. It amused him greatly as he slammed his fist into the man's stomach and threatened him with assault on a federal officer. The dumbass had mistaken him for Porter. He'd been lucky because Porter wouldn't show nearly as much restraint as Parker.

"Willa, I might have to marry that man," Parker heard Tilly whisper to Willa. Normally the *M* word would have him running for the hills, but this time it made him puff up with pride.

"Davies!" Newman shouted and Parker looked up from his desk the first time back to the office the day after his brother's show and falling head over cowboy boots for Tilly Bradford. "That interrogation you did on the pot dealer yielded results. The man who financed the operation is from Florida. He didn't directly deal with the gang, but instead there was a go-between that secured the money from the man in Florida and presented the loan to the gang."

"So the main money man in is Florida?" Parker asked, picking up the file his boss had tossed on the desk.

"Yes. We don't have any information on the person who secured the money, though. The pot dealer was right to take the deal and enter WITSEC," he said of witness protection. "He might have been new, but apparently the leader of the group mistook his pot chillness as being stupid and freely talked business in front of him. The money man has been narrowed down to several men in Florida. Take a look."

"What did the gang leader say?" Parker asked as he opened the file.

"He was killed during the operation, but we're

questioning the rest. So far they've all lawyered up and are pinning everything on the dead guy."

Parker opened the file and read the first two reports and then froze after turning the page to read about the third possible subject. Theodore Edwin Bradford V. Wife, Celina. Daughter, Matilda, also known as Tilly.

Crap.

"Right now, investigators are doing their thing, but we might be called in to close this out. They want to give you credit for your generation of this lead. The Florida office will be in touch. Good job, Davies."

Parker stared down at the file and felt the goofy smile fall from his face. Tilly's father was a suspected criminal Financier now under investigation by the government. No matter how much he liked Tilly, he had to back away and fast.

Parker took out his pent-up frustration on the various assassins coming after Willa. Porter was handling it well, but when a Chinese assassin had come to their small town of Keeneston, Parker took advantage and helped clean up the mess.

When he looked up, the object of his lust-filled dreams that he could never have was walking toward him with her arm clinging to Ben Jacobs's muscled one. Tilly batted her eyelashes up at Ben and, Catholic priest or not, Parker wanted to beat the crap out of him for daring to touch Tilly. She was *his*. Only she couldn't be. Parker took a deep breath. Her father was still under investigation, which meant Parker couldn't touch Tilly until he was cleared.

"He was former Special Forces," Tilly said to Parker

when he asked her what she was doing with Ben. Parker wasn't touching her. He was just trying to keep anyone else from touching her—including a priest. It wasn't until Tilly said Ben had offered to come over for one-on-one time that Parker realized two things. One, his sweet little Tilly didn't realize Ben was a priest. And two, she wanted him to be jealous.

Parker was ashamed to admit he *was* jealous, especially of a priest. Father Ben was a man who would never be with a woman for the rest of his life. However, it also felt damn good that Tilly liked him enough to try to make him jealous. He'd have to see Father Ben himself and say a special prayer that Tilly's father would be cleared so he could finally claim her the way he wanted to. Parker could just imagine her blue eyes going wide when he picked her up and kissed her senseless.

"What are you two going to do?" Parker asked, pushing Tilly to answer what she had planned to do with Ben. He was being an ass setting her up like this, but dammit, he was mad he wasn't able to get her out of his mind.

"I can think of all kinds of things," Tilly said, dropping her voice and suddenly the joke was over. Would she really go that far to make him jealous? Tilly brushed off Porter who was trying to warn her that Ben was a priest as she strutted over toward Parker.

Parker's breath caught as Tilly laid her small hand against his chest and rose up onto her tiptoes. Parker went hard the second her breath caressed him as she whispered into his ear. "I wanted you. You didn't want me. Now I'm done waiting," Tilly whispered. "I'm going to go down on my knees and worship a man brave enough to go after what he wants."

Parker's jaw clenched. His hands went into fists and he

had to remind himself it wasn't Ben's fault. Hell, it wasn't even Tilly's. This torture was all her father's fault. "Darlin', the only thing you're going to be doing on your knees with Ben is praying."

Parker couldn't take it anymore. He couldn't stand the thought of Tilly with anyone but him. However, until this case was wrapped up and her father cleared, he was going to stay far, far away from Tilly Bradford.

1

Washington D.C.
   Present day...

What is the saying about best-laid plans? Parker knew better than to glare at Grandma Marcy or he might never get another apple pie. But months after learning about the Bradford investigation, Grandma Marcy was now forcing him to dance with Tilly at his cousin Greer's wedding to Sebastian Abel. Parker had thought very hard about denying his grandmother's request. However, good manners won out and now Parker was on the dance floor with the object of the investigation—and his desire—in his arms.

One hand curved around her small hand while the other pressed against the small of her back. She didn't even reach his chin, but still had the power to bring him to his knees.

The delicate floral scent of her perfume. The soft skin of her hand. The way her blue eyes narrowed as if she wanted to kick him in the balls. It was almost too much. Parker wanted nothing more than to pull her tight against him and kiss her until she knew she was his and only his.

The trouble? Tilly's father was looking less and less innocent and the investigators had now turned their attention to the entire family—Tilly included.

Parker kept his eyes looking out over Tilly's head as the slow song seemed to go on forever. He just needed to not talk to her until the song was over and then he would leave and not come back until she was either cleared or in jail.

"Why do you hate me?"

The soft whisper of Tilly's voice almost didn't reach his ear. She'd been determined to be tough around him and it had made it easier for him to walk away. But when Parker dropped his gaze down to her face where Tilly let the hurt show, his dedication to his career waivered.

Saved when the song finally ended, Parker dropped his hands from Tilly's body. He could have answered her. He could have told her he didn't hate her. It was quite the opposite, in fact. However, he didn't. He simply walked away, grabbing a tumbler of bourbon as he went to the far end of the patio.

His phone buzzed and as he took a large sip of the bourbon, he answered the call from his boss.

"Where the hell are you?"

"Wedding."

"Oh, that's right. Look, this Bradford case is evolving quickly. We issued a warrant for his arrest, but haven't been able to serve him since he's out of the country. His attorney was notified and he is supposed to turn himself in Sunday evening. But now we think it could be a family affair. His wife is spending a fortune over in Europe this past week and his daughter is putting dirty money into her charity to launder it. The investigative team is working on getting warrants now to better follow the money and see who is a willing participant or if either of the women is in the dark. The Florida office has requested your assistance. You'll work as the lead interrogator on this case with their agents. I'm sending you down there to go over all the evidence our team has and assist them with the roundup and interrogation of any or all of the Bradfords. Report to their office Monday morning. Good work, Parker. This is the kind of case that can make you a legend."

"Dammit," Parker cursed after hanging up. He shoved his hands into the pockets of his tuxedo and glanced around the room. He found Tilly talking to Grandma Marcy. They were both smiling at each other as his grandmother patted Tilly's hand. It looked like not even Grandma Marcy would be powerful enough to get this relationship to happen. Arresting someone and their parents tended to not go over well when trying to woo a girlfriend.

Tilly was exhausted. It wasn't because she'd taken a private jet from Washington, D.C., to their farm in Florida at four in the morning either. It was from the riot of emotions of seeing Parker looking so handsome in his perfectly fitted tuxedo at Greer and Sebastian's wedding. When Marcy Davies had forced them to dance together last night, Tilly had thought she'd be able to handle it. For most of the endless song, she'd kept her armor in place. She'd narrowed her eyes and stared at the base of his throat. But even his throat was sexy. When the song wouldn't freaking end and the heat of his hands on her body and the way he probably didn't even realize he'd pulled her slightly closer to him, Tilly reached her breaking point. She'd asked Parker the question that had been on her mind since things had suddenly changed months ago in Kentucky.

Why do you hate me?

Tilly closed her eyes and remembered when she'd first met Parker in Lexington, Kentucky. Willa was in love with his twin brother, Porter. Others couldn't tell the Davies twins apart, but neither Willa nor Tilly had that problem. To Tilly, Parker was completely different. He was a little more serious. A little differently built. A little . . . *more.*

Most women with her wealth and background didn't have trouble finding dates, but Tilly always had. She'd been a painfully shy child who grew up in a life defined by strict social protocol. She was *the Bradford heir*. As if that mattered to a four year old. She had to go to the best schools, have the well-to-do, well-connected friends, and be seen at all the charity galas. And then she had to be in the right sporting circles. At six, she didn't know there was such a thing as sporting circles, but the boys had to be in the right squash or sailing clubs and the girls had to ride. Royals rode in equestrian events and so would she. Especially since their family dated back to the Norman Conquest and was intertwined with royalty throughout the centuries.

Most of her circle growing up had been naturally confident and outgoing. They were secure in their wealth and privilege while she had always been the shy one. She was the target picked on by the snobby elitist jerks she was forced to befriend. Then one day she met Willa Aldridge and finally found a real friend. Willa was "new money" and while Tilly's father and mother might look down on that, Tilly didn't care. She had a real, true friend for the first time in her life and that was all that mattered.

Tilly dated sporadically during boarding school and then college, but it was mostly boys who were doing their parents' bidding to form a connection with the Bradford family. That did a number on her confidence when it came to men. That, and the fact she didn't develop curves until she was sixteen. By then, Tilly had been hurt enough that she preferred to watch movies or ride horses with Willa rather than date.

However, as Tilly got older, she found confidence not only in riding, but in charity work. Something that had been a chore at first turned into a passion. Then she'd met Porter and his brother, Parker. Sure, it had been lust at first sight, but she realized that it was so much more. There was something about being around the sexy lawman that had made her feel free to be herself. Maybe because she felt protected from the bullies in the horse world, or maybe it was just his quiet confidence that inspired her.

Even as she said too much or acted too silly in her attempts to not be so shy, and even as she felt invisible among his gorgeous cousins and friends from Keeneston— some of whom were literal princesses and models—Parker always made her feel noticed. She wasn't invisible to him.

Until suddenly, she was.

Tilly sighed as she shoved off the covers of her bed in her parents' house and padded downstairs. While all her dating insecurities had come rushing back after getting the cold shoulder from Parker, she'd also found a new path in her life when Willa moved to Keeneston. Tilly stepped out of her parents' overbearing control of her life to stand on her own two feet. She'd taken some of the money from her trust fund and invested in a distillery in Keeneston. Cady Woodson, the owner, was just a little younger than Tilly and was breaking glass ceilings in the bourbon industry as one of the few women owners and master distillers in the industry. When Tilly invested in Cady's distillery, her whole world opened up. Tilly might not have a dating life, but she now had a career that merged her love of charity with the business degree she'd gotten. She was helping fund small, women-owned businesses and she loved every moment of it.

Tilly wished the house cleaning staff a good morning as she walked through the entranceway, down the hall, and into the dining room. Chef Joel came through the hidden door and set down a plate of delicious-smelling food just as she took her seat.

"Good morning, Joel." Tilly smiled at the man who had worked for them for the past eight years. He'd become one of her closest friends even though he worked for her family. Her father and mother believed there should be a mutual kindness but never friendship between them and the staff.

"How was the wedding?" Joel asked. His hair was dark brown, but a few gray strands graced his temples, giving him a very distinguished look.

"Mrs. Davies forced me to dance with Parker."

Joel cringed. "How was it?"

"Torture." Tilly picked up her coffee cup and took a sip as if it would chase away the feeling of Parker's strong hands on her body. "I don't want to talk about it. How are things coming along for the big day?"

Joel's daughter was turning sixteen this week, and he and his wife were throwing a big surprise party for her at the farm. Tilly's parents were supposed to be out of the country for the next month so Tilly had offered to have the party at the estate.

"She has no idea. Everything is in place," Joel said with a huge smile.

"Who has no idea?"

Tilly dropped her fork in surprise at the masculine voice

with a hint of a British accent. "Father! What are you doing here? I thought you were at the Derbyshire house."

Tilly stood up and hurried around the table to kiss her father's cheek as Joel silently slipped into the kitchen to prepare another plate for him. Her father was in his late fifties and she'd never seen him out of a suit before.

She smiled and kissed his cheek. "You look dapper today."

Her father kissed her cheek in return before taking a seat across the table from her. "I flew in from England last night. Unfortunately, it's only a quick trip. I'm flying back out for business after breakfast. I smelled Joel's cooking and couldn't leave without it. I thought you were in D.C."

"I got back a few hours ago," Tilly told him before launching into a recap of the wedding of billionaire Sebastian Abel and her new friend, Greer.

"He's new money, but you could have landed him." Tilly rolled her eyes and her father winked at her to let her know he was joking. "When I was in London, I heard that Marguerite Borghese tried to land a prince of some small country, but it turned out she didn't realize Crusina had turned into a democracy so she left mid-date."

"And you used to make me be friends with her," Tilly reminded her father.

"We live, learn, and evolve. I hope you can settle down soon. Is that what you and Chef Joel were talking about?"

"Nice, Father." Tilly laughed at his not-so-subtle way of trying to remind her she was almost thirty and it was time to settle down and produce the next Bradford heir. "That's not what we were talking about. He's having a surprise sixteenth birthday for Emilia."

The door opened and Joel came out with a plate filled with her father's favorites. "I can't believe little Emilia is going to be sixteen. It seems like just yesterday Matilda was running around in diapers. They grow so quickly, Joel."

"They sure do, sir. Is there anything else?"

"No, this is just right. I'll be out of the country for the next several weeks and Mrs. Bradford won't be returning until next month as well. Matilda, what are your plans?" her father asked, calling her by her full name instead of the nickname everyone used.

"I'll be here." Tilly smiled at Joel who gave her a wink and headed back into the kitchen.

"You should go to Vanuatu. I heard a lot of your friends are heading there. You know several of us have recently bought houses near the resort there. You kids should use them. Spend a couple of weeks at the beach house with our friends. Drink, get some sun, find a husband."

"Father!" Tilly rolled her eyes at him.

Tilly spent the next twenty minutes talking with her father about her next show and Greer and Sebastian's wedding. When they finished their breakfast, her father asked her to drive him to the private airport where their plane was waiting.

As Tilly got out of the car at the airport she hugged her father. "Goodbye, Matilda. I'll tell the pilot to have the plane ready for Vanuatu tomorrow."

"Father." Tilly kissed his cheek and shook her head at his joke. "I'm not going to Vanuatu. It's in the middle of the ocean. Willa is my friend and she's not going, so I'm sure I'm not friends with anyone there."

"Willa is married now. You need a life of your own, Matilda. I'm serious. You don't have anything big on your calendar for the next month. I want you on that plane tomorrow or you can say goodbye to your little pet project." Her father didn't give her a chance to argue at the words that felt like a slap to the face. "I say it because I love you, Matilda. You need to move on with your life. Find happiness. Find a husband. Find your own life."

"And you think I'll find that in Vanuatu?"

"I'm sure you will. I love you, my dear. Be on the plane tomorrow."

Her father kissed her cheek, leaving the "or else" unsaid, and then he was gone.

Tilly slammed the door to the car and hit the steering wheel a couple of times out of frustration. The hangover from hell had nothing on the anxiety of facing the horrid people her father called his friends. Marguerite was sure to be there along with the rest of the gang that had bullied Tilly for years and the "right" sort of husband material like that jerk Callum. But, if it meant she could keep funding her new entrepreneurial business, Tilly would do it. She's come up with a reason she didn't marry any of the men there later. Maybe a volcano would erupt and take out all the single men in her father's inner circle, that would be nice. Well, a girl could dream, couldn't she?

2

Parker arrived at the US Marshals' Miami office at eight in the morning to find the place packed with Marshals. They weren't working at their desks and Bradford wasn't in interrogation. Instead, they were gearing up for a raid.

"You must be Deputy Marshal Davies."

"No, that's my uncle," Parker said with a chuckle. No one laughed. "Sorry, my uncle's name is Marshall Davies. But, yes, I'm Parker Davies from the Lexington office."

"I'm Chief Deputy Castras. We received notice that Theodore Bradford's private jet landed after an eighteen-hour absence at the private airfield near his estate. It's set to fly out again with one passenger, Matilda Bradford, at ten this morning. Theodore Bradford did not turn himself in at the agreed upon time and his attorney is claiming he hasn't come back into the country yet, but will turn himself in when he does."

"Do we know if Theodore was on the plane when it landed?" Parker asked.

"It's doubtful. This morning we learned that the attorney lied and that Matilda drove him to the airport yesterday morning, but we don't know where he went. By the time we heard the plane landed early this morning, we went to meet it only to find it empty. The maintenance man said it was a new pilot he'd never seen before who flew Mr. Bradford yesterday. When the plane returned, the pilot left without a word to anyone and Mr. Bradford was not seen getting off the plane. The name of the pilot on the flight plan for later this morning is the Bradford's regular pilot. But from the filings last night, it said the pilot's name was Johnson with a bogus address. One passenger listed, unnamed. The destination was also bogus. The airport code used doesn't exist. Bradford is now a fugitive."

"Where is the plane scheduled to go later today?" Parker asked as someone handed him a bulletproof vest.

"Vanuatu."

Parker wanted to curse. He didn't think Tilly was involved in this, but this flight plan had just signed her arrest warrant.

Castras finished laying out the plan to breach the Bradford home to arrest Matilda Bradford and any other members of the family at the residence. They also had warrants to search the entire property and were going to execute them immediately.

"Ride with me," Chief Deputy Castras ordered. "Your chief deputy said you're one hell of an interrogator." Castras nodded to Parker as the other eight men walked to their various government cars.

Parker slid into the front seat and waited for the follow-up question he knew was coming. "How did you become so good at interrogation? From my understanding, there's not much talking in riding bulls."

"I have a degree in psychology, but that didn't teach me

squat on interrogation. My family did that," Parker said even as his mind was still on Tilly's deception.

"I read your family has some law enforcement in it." Castras had checked him out. "Sheriffs, FBI, DEA, military..."

"My father was CIA, but they didn't teach me how to interrogate. It was my grandmother who taught all of us how to do it." Castras laughed. Parker didn't.

"You're serious?"

"You don't get anything past my grandmother. She'd been asked to join top-secret intelligence networks, the CIA, and the FBI. She just blessed their hearts and sent them away with one of her apple pies."

Castras laughed again, but this time a little hesitantly as if he thought Parker should be joking. But based on Parker's lack of laughter in return, Castras stopped. He cleared his throat and then asked the other question Parker had been waiting for. "Your chief also disclosed the connection you have to Matilda Bradford."

"Her best friend is married to my brother," Parker said. There was no way he could or would try to hide it.

"How well do you know Matilda?"

"I know her well enough to know she hates the name Matilda. She goes by Tilly. However, the second the file crossed my desk I disclosed all facts and conversations to my chief." And he hated every time he had to do it, but it was the right thing to do.

"Think you can break her?" Castras asked and Parker hated him for asking. The last thing he wanted to do was break Tilly.

"Yes."

"You really think you can slap the cuffs on her, interrogate her, and break her?" Castras seemed dubious.

"Without hesitation, sir."

"I guess we'll find out. Get your cuffs ready, Davies."

Tilly eyed the clock and frowned. The pilot had already called, waking her up, to confirm her departure for later this morning. She had packed, reluctantly, and now had slightly over an hour to spend before the car was to pick her up.

She was tired, she was pissed, and while she was used to flying around the world, she still didn't like flying. She always got nervous as the plane was taking off and landing.

Tilly picked up her Bluetooth earbuds and connected them to her phone. It was going to be a very long trip with lots of stops to refuel the jet. She'd take a relaxing bath to calm her and be ready to start the long journey she did *not* want to go on.

Tilly turned on her favorite playlist and began to hum as she took off her pajamas and ran the water in her tub. She brushed her teeth, laid out her travel clothes, and finally sank into the hot water. Her muscles relaxed and her nerves began to calm.

She could do this. Two weeks in a tropical paradise. She would just hide in the house and stay on the private beach, far away from Marguerite, Callum, and their friends.

The property's gatehouse guard sat in the back of one of Castras's cruisers as a deputy pressed the button to open the large metal gates.

They drove up the driveway in silence. The mansion came into view and Parker blinked. He knew the house was only twenty-five years old. However, it looked to be two hundred years old. It was built as a replica of one of the great European houses of royalty and quite frankly looked a little silly in the middle of Florida.

"We should have brought more men. It'll take forever to go through the house," Parker said as the caravan stopped along the massive circular drive with the largest fountain Parker had ever seen in the middle.

"Most of these houses are filled with rooms that are never used. Let's go, Davies."

With a silent flick of his wrist, Castras sent his men running. Parker, Castras, and two Marshals would enter the front. One man was placed on each side of the house and two men at the back.

Castras rang the doorbell. A maid opened it. Her eyes widened in alarm at the sight of them standing there. "US Marshal Service. We have a warrant for the arrest of Theodore Bradford, Celina Bradford, and Matilda Bradford. We also have a warrant to search the premises. Please step aside."

"I'm sorry, Mr. and Mrs. Bradford are not home."

"But Tilly is?" Parker asked.

The nervous maid nodded. "She's in her room upstairs. Last door to the right."

Parker shoved passed the maid and took the stairs two at a time as the other Marshals began to clear the first floor. The house reminded Parker of a museum as he strode down the long hallway to Tilly's room. Ancient oil paintings and marble busts of old men lined the hall. Apparently, the Bradfords were too weak to walk down the hall without resting because he passed no fewer than six silk-covered benches before getting to the closed door at the end of the hall.

Parker's heart beat faster. His hands were sweating. And he was mad. Mad that the woman he liked was a criminal. Mad that he hadn't seen it. Even when he had flown to Miami, he didn't think Tilly was guilty. But this trip to Vanuatu in combination with the money laundered by her charity changed everything.

Parker gripped the ornate handle and turned it. He pushed into her room and stopped at the sound coming from somewhere deep inside the cavernous room.

Tilly's bedroom had cream walls with one wall in a light-blue silk damask. An enormous king-sized canopy bed, which looked to be from the royal court of Elizabeth I, was in the middle of the room set between a pair of large windows. There was a separate seating area and even a fireplace, rather strange since they were in Florida.

But Parker zeroed in not on the clothes laid out on the bed, but the three suitcases sitting at the foot of it.

There were some thumping noises and then he heard Tilly's voice. He paused in his stride toward the closed door she was behind when he recognized the pop song she was singing. It had taken him a minute to be able to recognize it since Tilly was probably the worst singer he'd ever heard. He realized the thumping was her trying to tap to the rhythm of the song.

Some of the anger faded as amusement took its place. Parker slowly pushed open the door, giving Tilly time to see that someone was there, before walking into the massive marble bathroom suite.

At the far side of the room, under a giant window facing the back of the property, was Tilly. She was chin deep in a bubble bath. Her eyes were closed and the water was sloshing in the giant claw-foot tub as she tapped her foot to music only she could hear.

"Tilly," Parker said, hearing men coming up the stairs to begin searching the other rooms. Tilly didn't respond. Instead, she sang louder and somehow even worse than before.

Parker moved well into the suite until he was standing next to the tub. He took a seat on the edge and took a moment to soak her in, knowing he'd never have her for his own. The one chance of a happy, love-filled future like his brother's was now gone. Not only would he not have Tilly in his life, he would be the one to take her freedom away.

Parker smiled faintly as Tilly scrunched her closed eyes, tried to hit a high note, and failed. Badly. But she didn't seem to care. A smile played on her lips. Parker had never wished bad things about bubbles before, but he did now. They obscured his view of her body as she bopped along to the song.

He'd be happy to stare at her forever, but this was not the time. He didn't want other men coming in and seeing her naked. If anyone was going to slap cuffs on her while she was naked, it was going to be him. Parker reached out and tapped her on the shoulder. Tilly's eyes flew open. Her mouth dropped open in a scream as the same sharp song-voice echoed through the room.

Tilly ripped the earbuds out and threw them at him. "What the hell are you doing here, Parker?"

"Matilda Bradford," Parker said, standing up from where he was sitting on the edge of the tub to hold out a large fluffy towel in one hand and holding his cuffs in the other. "You are under arrest. You have the right to remain silent."

3

Tilly thought she'd scared herself to death and was now in hell. She was naked in her bathtub with Parker inches away. But it wasn't one of her dreams that had him getting undressed and joining her in the oversized tub. No, this was worse than one of the dreams you had about showing up to high school naked.

One, this wasn't a dream.

Two, she was really naked.

Three, there were handcuffs and they were definitely not for fun.

Four, Tilly now heard the sounds of men filling her house and she didn't want them all to come in while she was in the tub.

Five, she was under arrest.

"Wait? What?" Tilly asked as she sank deeper in the tub and prayed the bubbles didn't move. "I'm under arrest? What for?"

"For now, it's accessory. You helped a wanted fugitive escape. Now, unless you want the entire Miami Marshals' field office to see you naked, you might want to get out of the tub."

Parker didn't turn to let her out of the tub in private. Instead, he stared impatiently and somewhat angrily at her.

"Turn around," Tilly ordered as she reached for the towel in his hand.

"Sorry, sweetheart, but I have a warrant for your arrest. I can't take my eyes off of you for one second. You won't be on the run like your father under my watch."

Tilly couldn't compute what Parker was saying. Her father? He wasn't on the run. He wasn't a fugitive. She'd just assumed it was something to do with the horse world. They were constantly going from country to country for shows. The sound of the bedroom door being kicked open caused Tilly to flinch.

"Hurry," Parker said, shoving the towel at her and moving to block her from view if they came in the bathroom door, which they did the second Tilly had the towel wrapped around her.

Tilly squeaked at the two men with weapons drawn and tried to hide behind Parker's large frame.

"I have her. Get out," Parker ordered without taking his eyes off hers.

"We'll be in the bedroom," one of the Marshals said.

"No, wait in the hall and close the bedroom door behind you. I'll call if I need you. Miss Bradford is cooperating and will be treated with dignity and respect."

Tilly's mouth had gone dry with the deep command of Parker's voice and the way he protected her had her swallowing hard. She couldn't let her stupid emotions win out. She had to keep her head to figure out what the hell was going on. This had to be a mistake and she wasn't going to make it worse by throwing herself into Parker's arms and begging him to protect her.

Parker didn't talk and she didn't move until they heard the bedroom door close.

"Get dressed. Quickly."

"What is going on, Parker? My dad—"

"Tilly, shut up. Don't say another word to me or anyone else until you've called your lawyer," Parker snapped.

"Lawyer? It's that bad?" Tilly asked as she climbed out of the tub.

"Your house is filled with US Marshals and you're under arrest. What do you think?"

She thought it was nice to see him. Well, until two minutes later when he slapped the handcuffs on her and led her from her house like a criminal. Then she wanted to castrate him.

Tilly was still handcuffed as she was put into the back of an unmarked SUV. Parker had carried her purse and her phone out in one hand and her in the other. Now she sat in stunned silence as the head of the Marshals' office drove them to Miami.

By the time they arrived at the office, Tilly was fuming. Gone were the shock and fear and in its place was anger. She was going to kill Parker Davies for this embarrassment. She wasn't a criminal. Her father wasn't a criminal. Yet here she was, yanked out of the bathtub, handcuffed, and now arrested.

"You have five minutes to make a phone call," Parker told her as soon as he set her in an interrogation room. A phone was placed in front of her, but her cuffs were not removed before Parker took a seat across the table from her.

"Can I have my phone?" Tilly asked.

"No, it's evidence," Parker responded.

Asshole.

She only knew a handful of numbers by heart and none of them were her attorney. She tried her father first. It went to voicemail, but before she could leave a message, Parker hung up the phone with a shake of his head. "Can't have you tipping him off."

Tilly's eyes narrowed as she tried her mother second. It went to voicemail, and just like with her father, Parker hung up before she could leave a voicemail. The only other number she knew was her best friend Willa's.

"Hello?" Willa answered as if expecting it to be a spam call.

"It's me, don't hang up!" Tilly cried with relief at hearing Willa's voice.

"Tilly? What number is this?"

"Parker handcuffed me, Willa!"

"Kinky! And about time. Was it as good as you hoped for?"

"No, because he arrested me and now I'm being interrogated." Tilly glared at Parker who wasn't even trying to pretend he didn't hear Willa's comment.

"That's commitment to role play. I'm so excited you two finally got over all that sexual tension and just did it."

Parker couldn't hide his smile anymore. Tilly's eyes narrowed. "No, Willa. He literally kicked in my door, arrested me for aiding a fugitive who happens to be my father, and now I'm in the Miami Marshals' office being interrogated. Parker is saying I need a lawyer."

"Wait, you're serious?" Willa wasn't laughing anymore.

"You can ask him yourself." Tilly turned the phone around.

"We had a warrant for her arrest. I've made the arrest and advised Tilly of her rights," Parker said calmly and as if they didn't have a past together. A past where she'd even hit on a freaking priest to try to get Parker's attention.

Willa leveled some very impressive threats against her brother-in-law that had Tilly loving her best friend even more. "Tilly, don't say a single word. I'll get a lawyer there immediately."

Then the call ended and Tilly was left holding the phone in her hand. Well, until Parker took it as if it were a deadly weapon and carried it from the room. He shut the door and Tilly took in the cold, sterile room with the two-way mirror, metal table, metal chair, and her metal handcuffs.

Tilly thought she was strong, but even this was too much. She took one shaky breath, turned her back to the two-way mirror, and cried.

Parker felt like the biggest asshole as he watched Tilly's shoulders shake as she hugged herself and cried.

"Good job, Davies," Castras said as he turned on the speaker to hear her cry for a moment. The sound broke Parker's heart. His instinct was to race into the room, pull Tilly into his arms, and protect her from all this pain.

Instead, he didn't move as he watched the woman who had bopped her way into his heart cry. "Her friend is getting her a lawyer. She's said she won't speak until they are here."

"Well, whoever she called moves fast. We already got notice from the top criminal law firm in town that Miss Bradford's attorney is on the way and we are not to speak to her to even offer her a tissue until they are here."

Parker's cell phone vibrated with a message. He pulled

out his phone and glanced at it. It was his twin brother, Porter. *Do what's right, even when it's hard.*

Their mother had always told them that growing up. He needed to hear it because what was right was doing his job and hunting down a wanted fugitive even when it was hurting more than getting thrown from a bull.

Castras looked down at his own phone. "The lawyer is in the building. Let's go."

Parker followed Castras out of interrogation and into the offices. Before they made it to Castras's office, the door was opened and a fiftyish woman with graying dark hair slicked into a bun and wearing a black pantsuit strode in as if she owned the place.

"Crap," Castras cursed. "That's Isabelle Perez. She's a ball-buster."

Perez cocked her head to Castras as if he were a little boy being called to task. "Chief, chief, chief. Seeing you again so soon makes my Monday." Parker's lips twitched in amusement and Perez's eyes snapped to his. "Does arresting an innocent woman amuse you, Marshal?"

"Only when they're guilty, ma'am."

"Ma'am? Castras, your Marshals are learning manners," Perez said sarcastically.

"He's from the Kentucky office," Castras snapped out, annoyed. Parker couldn't tell if the annoyance was directed at Parker or Perez but knew he wasn't going to ask.

"Ah, you're the one. Well, Mr. Davies," she said, already knowing Parker's name. "Take me to see my client."

"Right this way, ma'am." Parker stepped back and held out his arm to direct her down the hallway to interrogation.

Perez didn't speak until they were alone in the hallway. She pulled up short outside the door and Parker stopped to see what she wanted. "You're my client's friend and you arrested her."

"Yes, ma'am."

"Why?" Perez asked.

"If anyone was going to arrest Tilly, it was going to be me. It was the right thing to do."

"You don't flinch," Perez stated after a moment of blatantly evaluating him.

"No, ma'am."

"You always do the right thing?"

Parker gave a slight nod. "Even when it's the harder path."

"You good Southern men. You're my favorite thing about this country. Now, tell me the charges my client is facing."

Parker gave her a copy of the arrest warrant and watched as she kept her face neutral. Perez was good, but she wasn't Keeneston good. He could pick up the subtle clues of her heartbeat rising by the flutter of her pulse on her neck, the way she unconsciously pressed her lips together as she read the evidence, and the way she seemed to center herself for battle a moment before raising her gaze back to his.

"Why are you smirking?" Perez demanded.

"I like you, Ms. Perez."

Isabelle looked surprised, but then smiled back at him. "That's a first. But it won't stop me from destroying this little arrest of yours."

"Trying to destroy it," Parker corrected. "It was a legitimate arrest. But I look forward to it." Parker opened the door and didn't look in at Tilly's tear-stained face before closing the door after Ms. Perez.

"Think she'll cut a deal?" Castras asked a moment later.

"We'll have to see what she comes to us with after she's talked to her lawyer. My boss in Lexington knows this, but you need to know it too. I don't go into an interrogation with the aim of putting a person away. I go into it with the aim of getting to the truth." Parker waited for the pushback he'd received from some other chiefs, but Castras just nodded his agreement.

"Our job is to uphold justice. I like your way of thinking, Davies. Do what you need to get the truth."

Castras walked into the observation room, and several minutes later Perez knocked on the door indicating she wanted out. Parker opened the door and Perez looked seriously at him. "She's ready for you."

Parker followed Perez inside and knew Castras would have started the recording. It was standard procedure to record every second a Marshal was with a witness.

"Does your client have a statement?" Parker asked as he sat down across from the two women.

"First, can you take off the cuffs?" Perez asked. Parker reached across the table and unlocked them. He tried to ignore the guilt he felt when Tilly rubbed her wrists. "Now, my client is innocent and as such she wants to cooperate. However, she doesn't know how she really can since she doesn't know anything."

"Thank you for wanting to cooperate." Parker leaned forward as he rested his elbows on the table and clasped his hands together. "Tilly." He waited until Tilly's big blue eyes looked at him before continuing. "Why were you going to Vanuatu?"

Tilly looked to Perez who gave a single nod as if telling her to answer the question. "My father insisted. He told me if I didn't go to our house there, he'd stop me from continuing my small business initiatives."

"You own a house in Vanuatu?" Parker asked for clarification.

"My parents do. We have houses all over the world."

"Where?"

Tilly looked up as if she were thinking. "Miami, New York, L.A., Hawaii, England, Switzerland, Grand Cayman, Italy, the Emirates, and Vanuatu. Oh, and the Maldives."

"Are your parents in Vanuatu waiting for you?" Parker asked.

Tilly sighed. "No. My mother is in Europe and Father is away on business. He didn't say where."

"Is that normal for him not to tell you where he's going?"

Tilly nodded again. "Yes. He travels all the time for business."

"What business is he in, Tilly? I don't think you've ever said."

Parker waited as Perez leaned over and whispered to Tilly. "Investment banker," Tilly finally answered.

"What kind of investments?" Parker asked, watching Tilly for every reaction she made. What he saw confused him. She looked as if she didn't know.

"Just investments. He manages my trust fund and also the family money. Then he started handling others' since he was making so much on ours. That's all I know. He never talked business at home. We mostly talked about my school, my shows, and the family."

"No business parties at the house?"

Tilly shook her head. "Not when I was there. Is this what this is about? My dad's business?"

Parker didn't answer. Instead, he pivoted. "Why did he want you to go to Vanuatu?"

Tilly visibly shrank. "Marguerite and that bunch are there. All our parents bought houses close to each other near the Paradise Resort, which Callum's parents own." Parker now understood why Tilly shrank. They were the bullies Parker had met at the show. He'd had the satisfaction of punching Callum.

"Why would your father send you to an island with people you hate?" Parker noticed Perez's slight reaction to that news. Tilly hadn't told her.

"He wants me to marry one of them," Tilly said softly. "He said I need to grow up and get married to someone in our circle and all his cronies' kids were going to be there."

Parker was going to say something, but there was a knock on the door. Parker got up and cracked the door to find Castras there. "We found Mrs. Bradford. She's in the Maldives and is refusing to leave or allow anyone to contact her again while she's there upon the advice of her husband. I told her we had an arrest warrant for her and she laughed. She said she didn't do anything to be arrested for and that her attorney would handle it. I told her we had her daughter in custody and that got her mad. She said she'd see about that and hung up on us."

Parker closed the door and sat back down. "Tilly, tell me about your relationship with your parents."

Tilly looked back up at him and frowned. "We aren't super close like Willa is with her dad or like you and your family, but we *are* a family. My mom is the perfect wife and mother. She plans the right events and is always available to escort my father to some charity event or business deal at a moment's notice. She was active in planning my debutante ball, made sure I always had the right clothes, went to the right school, and encouraged me in riding. My dad also supported my riding and even came to some of the shows. I think we're the typical old-school British family even though we've lived mostly in the States since I was six. See, both my parents are from very old English families with historical ties to the Crown, so they were raised differently from your parents, and I was raised differently from you. We're close and they're supportive, but we're also not overly involved in each other's lives."

"Could you explain it a little more?" Parker asked, feeling as if he knew the direction Tilly was going.

"Your family is very casual. You went to school at home, your parents cooked your dinner and bandaged your scrapes. I was raised at boarding schools and with certain expectations. I studied business, but by the time I was five years old, I knew every old-money family in Europe and their family trees. It's just the way it is with families like mine, Callum's, and Marguerite's. But that doesn't mean we weren't loved and we weren't a family."

"Tilly, we found your mother." Parker hated having to say this next part. "She's at your house in the Maldives."

The surprised look on her face told Parker everything he needed to know. She hadn't expected that.

"You were supposed to be in Vanuatu, your mother is in the Maldives and refuses to leave . . . you see how this looks." Parker saw the quick press of Perez's lips, but before she could whisper to Tilly, Tilly's brow crinkled.

"So? Why is that important?"

"I'll let your lawyer tell you," Parker said as he sat back.

Perez turned to Tilly with sympathy. "Those countries don't have extradition treaties with the United States."

"Well, crap."

Parker wanted to laugh, but the look on Tilly's face had his heart breaking. She might not be the smoothest socially, or with the opposite sex, but Tilly was incredibly smart. After all, she had the best education money could buy.

"I need a moment with my lawyer." And like that, Tilly dismissed him. The sweet, nervous, energetic Tilly was gone. In her place was a polished, poised woman with an Ivy League degree who was used to getting her way.

Parker stood and gathered the papers, but Tilly stopped him by placing her hand on the papers. "Leave those."

Parker understood. She was over the shock and the reality of the situation was sinking in. She needed to fully evaluate the situation. The only glimmer of hope was the fact that Tilly had been so completely shocked by hearing the evidence, he hoped like hell that meant she didn't have a part in this.

4

What the hell was happening? Was any of this real? Maybe she was in a horrible nightmare and still tucked safely in her bed at home? Tilly wanted to believe that, but everything from the hard chair to the weight of the cuffs she still seemed to feel told her it was very, very real.

"I'm your lawyer, Miss Bradford," Isabelle Perez said calmly. "Tell me everything. Don't leave any detail out. I don't care if you're guilty. I just need to know so I can best counter any evidence they find."

Tilly's eyes snapped up to Isabelle's. "I'm not guilty. I don't know what any of this is."

"I don't have very many innocent clients, but I do believe you are one. Okay, let's go over this evidence and see how we can get you extricated from this situation."

Tilly listened as if she were outside of her body looking down at the table from above as Isabelle walked her through the evidence against her family. Disbelief turned to fear and then finally to anger.

"My father used my charity to clean his dirty money?"

The words came out slowly as if it took Tilly time to force them through her lips.

"That's what it looks like to me. See, here's a two hundred thousand dollar donation and then three days later a two hundred thousand dollar grant to a business."

Tilly shook her head. "I didn't make that deposit or that grant."

"Is your father on your account?" Isabelle asked gently.

Tilly nodded. "And my mother. Isabelle, who can I trust?"

"Me. You can trust me." The woman who was old enough to be her mother reached out and clasped her hand.

"What do I do?" Tilly asked in a whisper.

Isabelle's lips flattened. "I normally would never suggest this, but do you trust this US Marshal?"

"Parker?" Tilly asked, knowing that was exactly who Isabelle meant. Even through all the uncomfortable situations, the flirting, and then the complete shutdown of said flirting, Tilly answered immediately. "Yes."

"Then let me do my job and get you out of this mess. It might mean testifying or handing over evidence against your parents. Would you be able to do that?" Isabelle asked.

That took longer to answer. "I could only do it if they really are guilty. Otherwise, I won't use them to get my freedom. I'll find another way to prove my innocence." Isabelle patted her hand and the look of pity made Tilly feel crushed. "You don't think they're innocent, do you?"

"What I think of them doesn't matter here. *You* are my client and I'm going to do what I need to do to keep *you* out of jail."

Isabelle rose and knocked on the door. A moment later Parker walked back inside.

"Let's make a deal, Mr. Davies."

Parker looked over at Tilly as Isabelle laid out her demand. Tilly swallowed hard as Isabelle finished and Parker leaned forward. "You will help us gather evidence to prove that your father and or mother committed these crimes?"

Tilly shook her head. "Or the evidence that will prove it wasn't them. I want to get to the truth, Parker. You know how important my charity is to me. I can't have all these women lose everything because of this . . ." Tilly didn't have the words for it. What was all of this? How deep did it go? Did her parents really do all the government was saying they did?

"Criminal enterprise," Parker supplied her with the words she couldn't say. "Let me see what I can do."

Parker left and met Castras in the surveillance room. A man sat at the desk and had lawyer written all over him. Parker looked back into the interrogation room. Tilly looked broken as she slumped in the chair with her head down as Isabelle talked to her. Since Parker wasn't in the interrogation room, their conversation was muted, but he could read the defeat on Tilly's small frame.

"She wants immunity in exchange for helping us," Parker said even though Castras and this unnamed lawyer had heard the entire exchange.

"This is a big ask, Davies. We have evidence of her involvement." Castras glanced at the attorney. "This is Patrick Arnold, the US attorney assigned to this case."

Parker glanced at Patrick and then back to Castras. Parker knew there was evidence, but he also knew Tilly. "Let me hash out the terms with Isabelle. Do I have approval?"

Arnold finally stood, looking bored. "She's small

potatoes. Immunity if she provides evidence of her parents' participation. Otherwise, jail."

Parker shook his head. "No. Provided she assists with the investigation, I won't have her life dependent on the outcome you want. Justice is the ultimate end goal. Not finding evidence that may not even exist on specific people."

"I don't know who you think you are."

Castras interrupted. "That's what we both want, right? The criminals, whoever they are, held accountable?"

"Fine. I'll write something up. Now, get your ass back to whatever hick office you're from and let us do our jobs." The attorney dismissed Parker, who clenched his jaw, ready to argue back.

Castras grabbed Parker's shoulder and pushed him out the door before Parker lost his cool. "Thank you for your help, Davies. I promise I'll watch out for her and I'll keep you updated on the case."

Parker wanted to argue, but he'd been dismissed. Castras was already back in the room with the attorney. Parker stopped and stared at the closed door that stood between him and Tilly. He should do more to help her. She was his sister-in-law's best friend. She was the woman he couldn't get out of his mind and now he was just leaving her when she needed him the most.

"Davies, I heard you're done here. It was great working with you. Castras asked for me to drive you to the airport." A Marshal whose name Parker couldn't remember came up to him and jingled his keys.

Every instinct Parker had was to stay and protect Tilly, but there was no way he could. He was being pushed out by everyone. Parker nodded and followed the Marshal to the elevator where he launched into a Florida vs. Kentucky sports history lesson. Normally that would fire Parker up, but he didn't hear a word of it. His mind was on that last image of Tilly sitting in interrogation with her head down.

Parker had his hand on the door to the SUV when he heard his name. "Davies!" Castras yelled as he jogged through the parking garage toward them. "Glad I caught you. You have a new assignment. Newman signed off on it already, too."

New assignment. Great. Where was he off to now?

"A joint assignment with your office and mine," Castras explained when he stopped in front of Parker and placed his hands on his hips. There was a smirk on his face and Parker hoped he wasn't being sent on a wild goose chase.

"What kind of joint assignment?"

"I told you Isabelle Perez was a ball-buster. She made Miss Bradford's cooperation contingent on you being the Marshal assigned to her. You, Davies, are on witness protection detail. You are not to leave Matilda Bradford's side until trial."

Parker had never felt two warring emotions so strongly before. He couldn't wait to get to Tilly and make sure she was protected, but he also didn't want to get near her. He'd only survived this long because he'd avoided Tilly at all times. How was he supposed to stay professional when he was with her all the time?

Tilly was pissed. Parker had left her and she had to face down a giant dickhead in a suit alone. Well, not alone. Isabelle had been glorious. "No," was all she said. The man had blinked and sputtered and acted like an intimidating buffoon, but Tilly and Isabelle had remained quiet in the face of his sputtering.

"Parker Davies will be the only Marshal assigned to Miss

Bradford or there will be no more cooperation." Isabelle had stated exactly what Tilly had wanted without her even having to tell her attorney.

As angry as Tilly was about how Parker had been acting, she trusted him. She didn't trust this dickhead across from her. Parker might be cold. He might glare at her. But he'd never mistreat her. He'd protect her. And he wouldn't stop investigating until he got to the truth. He wouldn't frame her or finesse the evidence to go a certain way. The US attorney across from Tilly couldn't say that with a straight face. Well, he probably could, which made him even more of a dickhead.

Tilly had to admit that there was a good chance that the truth they uncovered wouldn't be what she wanted. However, Parker would find the truth and not manipulate the facts for his own purpose. She trusted him and right now she needed him.

The attorney had slammed the door and Tilly took a deep breath. Isabelle grinned. "I forgot what it's like to have an innocent client. It's fun. So, you and this Marshal Davies have a thing, right?"

"Yes, no. No, definitely no." Tilly looked with surprise at Isabelle. "How did you know that?"

Isabelle rolled her eyes. "I deal with criminals literally every day. I'm practically a walking lie detector. They teach you in law school that everyone lies, and it's your job to discern the lies your clients tell you. And my clients tell me a lot of lies. If I don't want to be blindsided by opposing counsel, I have to find the lies, determine the truth, and be prepared to counter any attack that comes from the opposing counsel or testifying witness. You, *mi ángel*, are a horrible liar. Now, Mr. Davies on the other hand is a terrific one. That's what threw me for a second. However, everyone has a tell, including your Marshal. Now, *mi ángel*, what did I just get you into?"

Tilly found herself blurting out all the embarrassment of the past months. She started with how she met Parker at her show jumping competition. How she thought they had a crazy chemistry. Then finally how Parker suddenly changed and became irritated with her and practically ghosted her.

Isabelle patted her hand and gave her a smile that showed she knew something Tilly didn't. "Do you know what is going on?" Tilly asked.

"I'm surprised you do not, but sometimes it's like impressionistic paintings. It's hardest to see what is right in front of you, but when you take a giant step back, it all becomes clear."

Tilly didn't get to ask her more questions before the door opened and Parker filled the doorframe. "Come with me, please."

Isabelle didn't argue for once as she grabbed her briefcase and stood to follow behind Tilly. Tilly wanted to roll her eyes at the order, but she was so thankful to be leaving this horrible room she didn't care where she went as long as it was out of this building.

They didn't talk as they rode the elevator down to the first floor. They didn't talk as they followed Parker out the front door and into the night air. They didn't even talk as they walked two blocks to a twenty-four-hour diner. It wasn't until they were tucked in a booth in the back of the diner that Parker finally spoke.

"The US attorney wants you to go down for fraud and then some. He has a list a mile long of charges he wants to file against you and he's waiting for you to give him any reason to do so."

Isabelle cursed in Spanish and Tilly finally cracked a smile. "I agree. He is a dumbass with the face of a donkey."

Isabelle looked surprised when she saw that both Tilly and Parker were laughing. "You both speak Spanish?" Tilly saw Parker nod and then she did, too. Isabelle rolled her eyes and laughed along with them. "I guess I can't mutter under my breath anymore."

"I speak French, too, so you might want to try German." Tilly felt some of the tension fall from her shoulders as Isabelle laughed and she even caught Parker giving her one of their looks they'd shared before he had turned into a jerk.

"So, Marshal, what do you need from us?" Isabelle asked.

"Tilly, what is going on?"

Damn Parker. He actually sounded concerned. Tilly took a shaky breath. She would not cry. Yes, she wore her heart on her sleeve, but she wasn't going to let Parker see her cry. "I don't know. I swear I don't understand what's going on. You know me. I'm not one to break the law. I feel bad if I take too many ketchup packages for my fries. I would never steal money."

"Your father's name came across my desk right after I met you. I couldn't say anything, but now? Tilly, it doesn't look good for him or your mother."

Dammit, she was going to cry. Tilly took a deep breath and pinched the bridge of her nose to try to stop the tears from falling. She cleared her throat and finally looked back up at Parker. "Isabelle showed me the evidence. I can't believe it's true. Why would my father deposit that money into my charity? Who did it go to? Was he forced to do it or is my father really some criminal? Does my mother know? I have all these questions and no answers. I can't even begin to describe how frustrating and hurtful this is."

"I thought you were close to your family. Maybe you overheard something?"

"I told you. My family's definition of close is not *your* definition of close. Your family is next level close. I'm ancestral British peerage close. Our occasional family dinners are formal affairs where we're 'dressed for dinner' and seated at opposite ends of a perfectly set table. I was seen and not heard while they talked about society gossip. However, I never thought my parents would do this. And maybe they didn't."

Parker nodded. "I understand. I've seen Zain and Gabe's family in Rahmi. It's very much that way, even though they're trying to change after seeing Mo and Dani's relationship."

"Let's hurry this along," Isabelle said with a roll of her eyes. "You think her parents are guilty. You, *mi ángel*, are afraid they are but are trying to tell yourself they aren't. There's only one way to settle this."

"What's that?" Tilly asked her.

"Find the truth yourself. If you leave it to that donkey-faced dumbass, you'll never have an unbiased answer to the questions you both have."

"That's actually why I brought you here, away from the office. I want to find the truth. Will you help me?" Parker asked her.

"There's no one I trust more to get to the truth. How can I help?" Tilly replied instantly.

"Let's start at your house. The Marshals tore the house apart but didn't find any evidence. I'm hoping they missed something."

"Let's go." Tilly didn't even want to wait for the coffee they'd ordered. She was filled with determination and didn't want to waste a moment.

"You go. I've got this." Isabelle made a shooing motion with her hand. "Call me if you need anything and keep me up to date with what you find. Oh, and Mr. Davies," Isabelle smiled up at him, "give Henry my best."

Tilly saw the surprised reaction on Parker's face. He normally didn't show emotion, so this made that comment even more interesting. "You know Henry Rooney?"

Isabelle smiled widely again. "Of course I do. Who do you think recommended me for Tilly? I meet with him and his wife every year when they come to town."

"They come here every year?"

Tilly would have laughed at the way Parker was parroting Isabelle if she wasn't interested as well. Henry Rooney was Keeneston's defense attorney. He loved bad pick-up lines and was rather memorable in his horribly tacky suits.

"Kentucky doesn't make those shiny suits of his. He gets them here in Miami every year." Isabelle slid two of her business cards to them. "Now, keep me in the loop. This is a war that will consist of many battles. Keep fighting, *mi ángel*. My one innocent client better not end up in trouble or I'll be coming for you, Davies."

"Yes, ma'am."

Parker stood and Tilly instantly followed. They were on a mission. Together. Her feelings had no place here. She took a page from Parker's playbook and hardened her heart. There was a lot more at stake here than her feelings. Her freedom and her life were on the line.

5

"Tilly!"

A large man ran from the opened front door in the early morning light, down the steps of the mansion, and across the manicured drive to the truck Parker had just parked in front of Tilly's home. They'd left the diner, got a couple of hours of sleep in his hotel, in different beds, of course, and then headed to her house before the sun was even up.

"It's okay, Joel. I'm not hurt," Tilly said with a fondness for whoever this Joel was.

Parker didn't like it. It was clear this man meant something to her, even if he was a little older than Parker imagined she'd date.

"I'm glad you're okay, but it's the house, Tilly. It's been ransacked."

Tilly nodded as Joel wrapped her up in a hug. "I know, Joel. It was the Marshals. They arrested me, but I'm free now. They're looking for my parents. They think my father is a criminal."

"I always did wonder. When you weren't here, some scary dudes would come by. But this wasn't the Marshals.

We cleaned that up the best we could yesterday. I came in early just in case you came home last night, and the house was destroyed again."

Parker pushed forward, his gun already in his hand, as he walked up the front steps. He noticed the doorframe had been tampered with. Shards of wood had splintered off when someone used a crowbar to force it open.

"When did you arrive?" Parker asked Joel, who had followed him up the steps along with Tilly.

"Not five minutes ago."

"Stay here with Tilly," Parker ordered before slipping into the mansion. It looked completely different after just twenty-four hours. Every painting was off the wall and tossed to the ground. Some were torn, some statues were shattered, and there were more holes in the walls than Parker could count.

Theodore Bradford's office looked as if a bomb had exploded. His desk was shattered. All the books were thrown to the ground, some with pages ripped out. Cabinets were open and emptied. His leather chair had been slashed and the filling pulled out.

Parker kept his breathing steady as he kept his gun raised and calmly scanned the room, categorizing every area that seemed to be focused on more heavily during the search.

"Parker!"

Parker didn't hesitate when he heard Tilly's scream. He was running full speed out of the office and down the hall as he heard Tilly shriek in pain.

Parker heard a struggle as he approached the large entranceway and slowed. He pressed himself to the wall and slowly looked around the corner. Joel was down. His head was bleeding as he sprawled half inside the house and half on the porch. However, the man who was dragging Tilly across the marble floor by the arms had all of Parker's attention. The man was looking down at Tilly as she was half dragged on her bottom and half trying to scramble to her feet.

Parker's instinct was to race forward and kill him, but instead he waited and listened.

"Where is it?" the man demanded.

"Where is what?" Tilly cried.

"You know what I want. Your father hid it and now we can't find him or it."

"I don't know what you're talking about," Tilly yelled frantically.

Parker saw him stop pulling Tilly's arms. He dropped her to the ground and leveled his gun at Tilly's face. "I'll only ask one more time. Where is it?"

There was no time to learn more. There wasn't even time to shoot to injure instead of kill. With the gun to Tilly's head, Parker could only do one thing. He fired his own gun. Tilly screamed. The man and his gun dropped to the ground.

Tilly tried to scramble away, but the man landed on her, pressing her onto the floor. "Get him off me!"

"I got you, Tilly. You're safe." Parker was instantly there. Tilly was shaking and crying as he rolled the dead man off, and then Tilly was in his arms. "I've got you. I've got you, sweetheart. You're safe."

Tilly suddenly gasped and pushed from Parker's hold. "Joel!"

Parker followed her to where the man lay on the ground. Tilly had her fingers pressed to his neck and gave a sob of relief. "He's alive."

Parker went into action. He'd had enough hits to the

head when he was on the rodeo circuit to know what to do. "Call an ambulance while I get his neck stabilized and find the source of the bleeding."

It didn't take long for Parker to see the man had been hit on the back of the head and then had fallen onto the ground, face first, hitting the front of his head again when he landed on the marble floor.

"We have to find whatever that man was looking for before the police come. I don't want you seen here. It'll only slow us down," Parker told Tilly after doing all he could for Joel. He moved to take a picture of what was left of the man's face he'd shot and then connected a small scanner to his phone.

"What's that?" Tilly asked.

"Mobile fingerprint scanner. I'll know who he is in less than a minute."

Tilly bent down and pulled out his wallet. "Or you could just look in his wallet."

"Juan Campos," they both said at the same time.

"But what your wallet can't tell you is he's a Mexican gang leader," Parker said, reading the incoming report. "Wanted for all sorts of crimes."

"What would my father be doing with him?" Tilly asked.

"That's what we need to find out."

Parker watched as the emotions played out over Tilly's face. First was disbelief, then she was thinking, and finally her face tightened in anger. "I don't know what my parents are doing, but I'm going to find out."

"Where would your father hide something important?" Parker asked, knowing the ambulance would arrive soon and with it, police who would muddy the water with their jurisdictional pissing contest. "His office is trashed."

Tilly shook her head. "Everyone always keeps important

things close to them. Offices, bedrooms, but Father never did. He does the opposite."

Tilly took off for the upstairs leaving Parker to chase after her. Instead of going to the right, toward her bedroom, she turned left. "These are all extra rooms. The master is on the first floor. This wing has a ballroom, a sitting room, a billiards room, and a cigar lounge." Parker took in the giant ballroom as Tilly walked into it. It seemed very out of place.

"I know. My parents and their set like to think they are still peerage in nineteenth century London. They host several charity balls every year, full court dress." Tilly rolled her eyes and crossed the giant open room under the massive chandeliers. In the back of the room was a door built into the wall and covered with the same silk wallpaper as the walls. Tilly turned the handle and opened it to reveal a broad staircase. "This goes down into the kitchens." She took a couple of steps down to where the evenly spaced wall sconces cast a shadow and dropped to sit on one of the stairs. "This is a fake panel. See the decorative woodwork along the crown molding? Can you push the crest above me?"

Parker looked up at the crown molding. There were alternating carvings down the entire back staircase of a tree and then a crest. Parker looked directly above Tilly and found that the crest for this panel of the woodwork was the only crest present. He pressed hard and the crest moved just a fraction, however, it was enough to hear the click of mechanics behind the wall. Then the three-foot-by-three-foot panel next to the stair was pulled back a half inch and slid to the right. Tilly reached inside and a second later a light filled the shadowy stairwell.

"My father has places like these in every house. The idea originated from old priest holes in the original family estate in Derbyshire." Parker watched as Tilly pulled out large stacks of cash, jewels, and finally a small fireproof box.

"I hear the ambulance," Parker said.

"I'll get a bag and put all of this in it. I don't have the combination for the safe." Tilly stood and stuffed cash into her pockets.

"I can probably pick it. Don't let anyone see you. Stay hidden and away from windows until I come and get you."

Tilly nodded and shoved a tiara that had belonged to some great- great- great-aunt or something onto her head before clasping a stunning sapphire necklace around her neck and carrying out the fireproof safe.

She pressed herself to the wall when she approached the stairs. She heard Parker below her and was thankful to hear Joel's voice. Interestingly, Parker gave his name as one of the gardeners who worked for her family. As the EMT and police handled Joel, Parker reported the robbery and attack. Tilly kept to the wall as she headed into her mother's salon. It was used as a women's reprieve during galas. There were far more backroom deals accomplished here than in the billiards room the men liked to pretend was where they did business.

Once inside the feminine room, Tilly pulled off a pillow cover and dumped the cash and jewels into it to make it easier to carry. Then she hid behind a sofa and waited. It seemed forever, but finally she heard Parker call out to her.

"Tilly! We have to move. The cop is checking the property before coming back to the house."

Tilly raced down the hall to her bedroom and tore through her closet. She had a large suitcase packed with clothes, shoes, jewels, cash, and the fireproof case in hand before Parker even made it up the stairs. Tilly dragged the heavy suitcase behind her as its wheels struggled to keep up on the plush carpet and met Parker in the hall.

"What did you pack?" Parker asked after he grabbed the suitcase to carry it down the sweeping stairs.

"Everything. I don't know when I'm coming back, do I?" Tilly didn't wait for him to answer. She was always the fun, happy friend, but that joy had all been dashed, destroyed, firebombed, and shot to hell over the past twenty-four hours. "I need to call Joel's wife."

"I already did. I let her cry and reassured her Joel was okay. He was just going to have to take it easy for a couple of days. I also told her it was still okay to have her daughter's party here if she wanted. If she didn't, I could arrange to have it at Willa's farm down the road. I hope that was okay."

Tilly reached out and placed her hand on his arm, then wished she hadn't. Hard muscles bunched under her touch and suddenly all the laughing she did at movies where people had sex on the stairs didn't seem so funny. Parker had kept her safe, taken care of Joel, comforted his wife, and made sure a girl he didn't know still had a party. That was even sexier than the muscles tensing under her hand.

"Thank you."

Tilly didn't have time to think about stair sex, though, when Parker grabbed her bag and ran down the stairs leaving her to follow.

They leaped into the SUV and were driving out of the estate when a phone call came in over Bluetooth. Tilly saw Willa's name on the display and was relieved when Parker answered it on speaker.

"Hey, Willa. I have you on speaker with Tilly."

"Tilly! Oh, sweetie, are you okay?" Willa's worried voice filled the SUV.

Tears threatened to burst forth, but Parker's calm demeanor helped keep her focused. "I'm okay. The lawyer you sent got me immunity so long as I cooperate with the investigation and had Parker assigned to me. But, Willa, my house was trashed, some criminal just attacked me, Parker killed him, Joel is on the way to the hospital with a concussion, and I found a fireproof box in my dad's hiding space that we have to figure out how to open."

"Oh, Tilly. It'll be okay. Parker will get to the bottom of this. Are you hurt?" Willa asked.

"Not physically."

"I'm here in town at the private airfield." Willa was about to say more, but then another voice came over the line.

"I'll get the box unlocked. My brother was never good at that."

Tilly looked over to find Parker smiling. "You wish, Porter. Thanks for coming, bro."

"Oh please. You know I'm the master lock picker in this family."

Parker laughed out loud when another woman's voice interrupted the debate and Tilly had to admit that calmed her more than having her best friend here.

"That's true, Reagan. You were always the best at it. I'll concede that point. What are you doing here, sis?" Parker asked.

"I had a scheduled flight to transport a race horse to Ocala. When Willa told me what was going on, I took over the flight from the other pilot so I could give Willa and Porter a ride down here. We dropped off the horse and flew straight to you."

Reagan and her twin sister, Riley, were the elder set of twins in Parker's family. They were already married with children. Tilly knew them, but not as well as she knew some of their cousins.

"We'll be there in ten. Thanks, y'all," Parker said before hanging up.

The smile faded from his face and then Deputy Marshal Davies was back. Tilly wanted to talk about how great his family was, and how relieved she was to see her best friend, but she didn't. She turned her head to look out the window while she silently chided herself for still wanting nothing more than for Parker to take her in his arms and love her.

6

Parker wanted to reach over and take Tilly's hand in his more than anything. He wanted to tell her it would be okay. He wanted to tell her he would keep her safe, that he was sorry it was looking more and more as if her parents were guilty, that it still didn't change his feelings for her . . . but he didn't. He drove in silence as he went over the evidence in his mind.

When he pulled up to the private airfield, the large cargo plane with Keeneston Air on the side looked out of place among the sleek private jets. As soon as he turned toward the plane, he saw his family. His twin brother, Porter, had his arm around his wife, Willa, while their sister Reagan stood with her arms crossed and a frown on her face.

Tilly leaped from the car the second Parker stopped and ran toward the group. Willa broke free of Porter's hold and they clashed in a tangle of hugs, tears, and love. They were as close as he was to his siblings. Parker was glad Tilly had the support she needed right now.

Porter and Reagan let Willa and Tilly have a moment as they approached him.

"You know she's not some criminal, right?" Reagan asked.

"Yeah, I know that. But I have to find out who is so she doesn't become the easy target for an ambitious US attorney."

"Then let's see this box." Reagan held out her hands as Parker lifted the firebox. "Oh, this is easy. It's just your standard lockbox. Even you should be able to open it."

Parker rolled his eyes at his sister, took the box from her, and set it on the hood of his car. "But I have my lock picks and you don't."

Parker began to pick the lock and Reagan used her hip to shove him out of the way as she held up a monogrammed lock-picking set. "Of course I have mine. You think Dad would let any of us go anywhere without this and an obscene number of weapons? Now, let me pick this lock."

"No, I'm picking it." Parker hip-checked his sister and sent her stumbling. She snarled at him and Parker knew the hit was coming as he focused on the lock. The Marshal's service wondered how he was always calm under fire. This was why. Try having a father who was an ex-spy, twin older sisters, uncles who were Special Forces vets and thought it was fun to surprise attack you, and then a little shootout or a ticking timer on a bomb was nothing.

Reagan rammed him with a body check, but Parker was ready for it. He absorbed the hit as his fingers gently twisted and "Got it!"

Reagan rolled her eyes at him. "I finally get time away from everyone and you take all the fun from it." Then she stuck her tongue out at him.

Parker laughed and kissed the top of her head. "Thanks for helping me, sis."

"Carter has Ryder for the day. He's happy as can be, kissing horses all day."

"Good job, Reagan," Tilly said as she joined them. Reagan smirked and Parker gave a huff.

"I'm the one who got it open. She's getting rusty in her old age." Reagan punched him. Hard. Parker laughed as he rubbed his shoulder. "Practically geriatric."

"Do not make give you a wedgie. I'll do it in a heartbeat." And Reagan would. She and Riley used to tackle him and Porter and practically rip the hair from their heads for misbehaving. And they did misbehave. Porter and Parker would sneak into their slumber parties and steal the girls' clothes. They'd find them in the horse trough or freezer. Or they'd spy on them and then tell the embarrassing preteen and teen stories they overheard to their parents at dinner the next night. "Now, what's in this thing?"

Tilly came to stand next to him as he opened it. Inside was only one thing. A notebook.

Parker reached inside and pulled it out. When he opened it, he found it filled with words that didn't make any sense.

"What is this?" he asked Tilly.

Tilly was shaking her head as she looked at it. "I don't know. Can I see it?"

Parker handed it over to her as everyone crowded around to look over their shoulders. Pages and pages of one word, maybe even two or three, each followed with shapes and symbols, but that was all on each line. *Red Bird. King. Scorpion. Blue Bayou. Rock Song. Catherine the Great.* None of it made sense.

"Look, it changes," Tilly said as she reached the halfway point in the book. There had been at least ten blank pages and then there were longer phrases.

The pawn was sent to the King. Catherine the Great likes to sail Pirate Ships. None of it made sense, but then Tilly stiffened next to him when she reached some of the last pages of writing.

Parker looked at where her finger was resting. "The Poppet feeds the Demons," Parker read out loud. "Does that mean something to you?"

"Maybe. My father always called me his poppet. It's a term of endearment. He also complained about some of the charities we worked with. There are certain national and international charities that are flashy, but only a penny of each dollar donated actually goes to the people or things that need it most. They buy ads, have special days, and huge parties that you must be seen at socially. My dad would say, 'We must be seen feeding the demons' illusions.' He meant it as a slur to the people running the charities who were pocketing the money as if they were in need. They were the true demons in his mind, not the actual charity. The illusion was that the people running the charity actually cared for anyone other than themselves."

"So, he's saying you are one of those people? What an asshole." Willa wrapped her arm around her to show support for Tilly's charity work.

Tilly shook her head. "No. I don't think that's what he's saying. The next line. The Demons then feeds the Scorpion," Tilly read. "I could be totally off base here, but I think he's saying I have donated money to whoever the Demon is and then the Demon gives that money to whoever the Scorpion is."

Parker took the book back and flipped to the front where names were listed. "Here's the first mention of Demon. There's a symbol here. What is that?"

"It's a chess piece," Tilly answered instantly. "It's the king."

"The king of demons? That's the devil." Parker flipped another couple of pages and found the Scorpion. "There're multiple symbols next to Scorpion." An *L* on its side so it looked as if it were to be used for long division. Then there was 10¢ and a triangle.

"He reuses those symbols under the Scorpion, but I don't see another king like he used next to demon. I see some pawns, but not another king," Parker said after doing a quick search. "I see the pawns, the 10¢, the long division sign, stars, a triangle, and upside-down triangles. Sometimes a word has just one symbol, sometimes several, but never the king."

"The demon must be important and I must know who they are," Tilly said after everyone fell quiet.

"What do you do now?" Porter asked. "Want me to get some spy contacts for you?"

Parker rolled his eyes. "You were a spy for two weeks. Let that go."

"Doesn't mean I don't have the connections."

"Derbyshire," Tilly said suddenly. "We need to go to the country estate. This has to be a list of names he was involved with criminally. I know where the hiding place is in the Derbyshire estate. He wouldn't put all his records in one place and my dad had just gotten back from there when I saw him over breakfast."

"That's a little outside my jurisdiction," Parker pointed out. "There's no way the government will let you leave the country."

"Then it's a good thing I have a big cargo plane that flies into private airports."

Parker turned to Reagan and shook his head. "That's too

much. You'll be away from your family for over a day. Plus, you and your business could get in trouble for illegally sneaking us in."

Reagan rolled her eyes. "Bless your heart. Why would you ever think I would get caught? Come with me and bring your bags." Reagan marched toward the plane. They went up the wire mesh staircase to the empty plane filled with fancy horse stalls for the transportation of very expensive horses. "Each stall has a rubber pad under the mountain of hay. Under several of them I have hidden compartments. I can store you and your luggage easily upon landing and while we get through customs."

Parker watched as his sister weaved her way through the tight walkway where he had to duck his head and lean to the side slightly to avoid hitting the curved side of the plane. Reagan kicked back the hay, and while it took some work, she got the rubber mat up. Parker stepped forward and looked inside. "Cozy."

"I also just so happen to have a horse I need to pick up. I was scheduled to do so in three days, but I can call and rearrange it. I already have the paperwork to make it legit."

Parker looked at Tilly who looked a little nervous. "Your call."

"When can we leave?" Tilly asked.

Reagan had the plane in the air in no time. Parker's rental car would be picked up and returned by Joel's wife whenever Joel began to feel better. In the meantime, Willa and Tilly were scrunched close together in two jump seats while the Davies family was in the cockpit.

"You don't have to go to England with us, but I'm glad you're with me."

Willa took Tilly's hand in hers. "You were there for me when I needed you the most. I'm here for you now."

Tilly grasped her hand tightly as the plane taxied down the runway and with a roar of the engines they were in the air. Tilly finally relaxed when the plane leveled out. "Thanks. You know how much I hate flying."

"Well, we have two hours until we land in Lexington. That's plenty of time to work out your Parker problem."

Tilly smiled, but sadly. "He's not a problem. He's a good guy. He saved my life."

"I know he's a good guy. His problem is he needs to see that you're perfect for him. So, there's only one thing you can do."

"What?" Tilly asked Willa.

"Seduce him."

Tilly giggled. "Yeah, because I did such a good job with Father Ben. Gosh, I can't believe I tried to flirt with a priest. As much as I hate to admit it, I think my chance with Parker is over."

"I don't think so. He wouldn't have worked so hard to avoid you unless he had feelings for you." Willa squeezed Tilly's hand to get her full attention. "They're worth the work, Tilly. I've never been happier and you know my relationship with Porter wasn't all sunshine and rainbows from the get go. He thought I could be a traitor and was forced to spy on me. Parker wouldn't have gone through all of this if he thought you were guilty. He could be fired for taking you to England. He may not be saying he has feelings for you, but what do his actions say?"

With that, Willa took off her seatbelt and walked the short distance to look into the cockpit, leaving Tilly to think. She'd been so wrapped up in the attack at the house, being arrested, and finding out her parents might be bad people that she hadn't really looked at everything Parker had done. He kept the others out of the room when she was naked and being arrested. He'd made sure she called Willa before she talked to him or his boss. He'd gone to bat for her with his superiors to secure her immunity. He'd never actually accused her of anything. Instead, he'd laid out the evidence they had and let her see why he had to do the things he was doing. He'd treated her with respect at her house. He'd never treated her like a criminal. Then he'd saved her life, taken care of Joel, and didn't even question her when she said they should go to England. Only now that Willa pointed it out did Tilly realize what Parker was putting on the line. His job. His reputation. His life. And he was doing all of that for her.

7

Parker and Tilly hugged Willa and Porter before they got off the plane in Lexington. "Tell Carter I'm taking a me day!" Reagan yelled out before putting her headset back on and ordering the plane refueled and filing her flight plans.

A car raced onto the private parking lot and a young woman and an older man leaped out. They flashed their ID badges at security and ran up the stairs to the plane seconds before they were rolled away.

"Sorry! We're here."

"Thanks for helping me co-pilot, Nadine," Reagan called out as Nadine ducked her head and entered the plane. Nadine looked to be about twenty-eight with bouncy curly hair and a big smile. Parker noticed Tilly instantly smiled back at her.

"Of course. Are you two also helping?" Nadine asked Parker and Tilly.

"What two? There're no two people here. Just you and me flying this plane and Mike here to help us take care of the horse during the flight," Reagan answered.

Parker had seen Mike around the farm some and gave

the man in his late forties a nod. "I don't see no one, Nadine. I'm going to sleep. Wake me when we're in England."

"But they're standing right there," Nadine said with big, round, brown eyes.

"I don't see anyone, Nadine, and neither do you. Got it?" Reagan said seriously.

Nadine reached out a finger and poked Parker in the chest. "He's real. They're right here."

Mike rolled his eyes. "Nadine, of course they're real. This is Reagan's brother, Parker. He's a US Marshal. I assume this whole thing has to do with his job. He's sneaking into the country so for all paperwork and if anyone asks, these two ain't here. Got it?"

"Ooh. Gotcha. My lips are sealed. I can keep a secret. Right, Reagan? I didn't tell everyone you started flying more and want to do so before you think about having baby number two. And I didn't tell everyone how I caught you and Carter having sex in the plane. Or when—"

"Thank you, Nadine. Let's get ready to go, okay?" Reagan looked ready to murder the young woman and gave Parker an eye roll but was nice enough to then give Nadine a smile. "You're doing really well with your takeoffs. You can fly this entire flight so you can log some more hours."

"Thanks, Reagan!"

"Oh, Reagan," Mike said, handing her a large shopping bag with something filling out the bottom of it. "Your grandma sent this."

Parker leaned forward and gave a sniff. "Why did Grandma send you one of her apple pies?"

"What?" Reagan asked as the engines suddenly roared to life. "I can't hear you," she said loudly as she tapped her headphones.

Parker shook his head. He had a bigger mystery to solve

than why his grandmother was giving Reagan an apple pie. For instance, why Tilly suddenly looked like she was about to pass out as the plane began to taxi toward the runway.

Parker took the small seat next to Tilly. They were pressed leg to leg, hip to hip, and since his shoulders were so wide, Tilly had to lean back against him as if they were snuggling on the couch. "Are you okay?"

Tilly took a deep breath and closed her eyes. "I don't like flying. Well, more specifically, I don't like taking off and landing."

"I'll protect you." Parker reached around and pulled her against his chest. Tilly's hand rested on his thigh while the other rested against his ribs. She didn't fight him when he began to gently stroke her arm. As the plane gained speed, rocketing down the runway, Parker pulled her tight against him as if he could absorb her fear. "It's okay. You're always safe with me. I'd never let anything hurt you."

"Unless you put me in jail."

Parker grinned and lowered his chin to rest on the top of Tilly's head. "I never wanted to put you in jail."

"You put me in handcuffs," Tilly said with anger as the plane began to take flight.

"But not the way I wanted to."

"What does that mean? There's only one way to put on handcuffs."

"Put on? Sure, but there are many reasons for putting them on. It could have been fun." Parker watched her eyes widen as she caught the sexual innuendo.

"You don't want to do that with me." Tilly sighed and ducked her head back to his chest.

"Are you serious?" Parker couldn't believe it. "I thought I was very clear when we met how sexy I found you."

Tilly leaned back so she could look back up at his face.

"Sure, when we met. But then you backed off as if I had leprosy."

"I did. But I didn't want to. I had to. It was a conflict of interest for me to pursue a relationship with you during an investigation," Parker admitted.

"You didn't want to?" Tilly asked as she wrinkled her forehead as if trying to make sense of it. "But you had to? So why are you telling me now? When we're really in the middle of an investigation now."

Parker sighed and frowned. "I know. I shouldn't have told you. I should have kept it professional. But when Campos had you, it made keeping my feelings a secret seem pretty stupid."

"So, you have feelings for me, huh?" Tilly smiled and Parker was lost. All those walls he'd built around his heart didn't just crack, they crumbled into nothingness.

"They won't prevent me from doing my job."

Tilly's smile widened. "I wouldn't expect them to." Then her smile slipped. "Parker, what does that mean for us? You know I like you. I have since I met you, but you're investigating my family and me."

Parker continued to rub Tilly's arm soothingly. Now that he had her in his arms he didn't want to let go. The frown on her face was contagious as he felt his lips turn down. "Tell me honestly, did you have any knowledge of any of this?"

Tilly punched him in the stomach. She winced, and he grinned. "Well, that didn't go as planned," Tilly said with a roll of her eyes. "I didn't know about any of this and I'll do everything I can to help uncover whatever this is."

"Will you be able to turn over evidence against your parents, your friends, and whoever else may be involved?"

He saw Tilly basically deflate. Tears formed in her eyes and Parker had to fight his reaction to tell her everything was going to be okay, but right now that wasn't a promise he could keep.

"I feel so guilty, Parker," Tilly said, resting her head back on his chest to hide the tears.

Parker ran his hand over her hair gently as his heart broke for her while anger at the people involved surged. "Why would you feel guilty?"

"They're my parents and I should always defend them. But, when I heard that my father laundered some money through my charity, which he knows means the world to me, I got angry with him. I'm so angry. And hurt. My heart actually hurts that he put me in this situation, but I still want to believe he is innocent. As for my mom, I have no idea if she had any role in this or not."

"I'll make you a promise, Tilly. I promise I will find the truth and I won't keep any of it from you."

"Except your feelings." Tilly sighed. "So stupid. I'm in the middle of my life falling apart. How you feel about me shouldn't matter. Our nonexistent relationship shouldn't matter. You shouldn't matter. But that's the trouble. You do matter. You matter very much to me."

"You matter to me, too, Tilly. That's why I made that promise. I want the truth. I need the truth. Only then can I be the man in your life I want to be," Parker admitted. He wanted to be *the* man in her life. He'd wanted it the second she'd stumbled all over herself and rambled embarrassingly when they met. He was used to buckle bunnies who chased rodeo stars as if they were stamps on their passports. Tilly was chasing, but it was the first time he wanted to be caught. She was adorable, crazy-smart, funny, and the kindest person he knew. He loved that she wore her heart on her sleeve since he never did. Today was the first time he'd taken the leap to talk about his feelings. He didn't like it, but he trusted Tilly with them. She wouldn't use them to manipulate him like others in his past would have.

Tilly nodded against his chest. He felt her ribs expand as she took a deep breath. "I need the truth, too. I know I'm not as experienced as I'm sure your past girlfriends have been. I'm awkward and I talk too much when I'm nervous. But as much as I want a relationship with you, I have to know the truth, too."

"So, we're in agreement? We find the truth, handle the fallout, and only then do we see if we still want to move forward together?" Parker asked. It was the reasonable, rational, and safe way to approach a relationship.

"Agreed." Tilly pulled back from him. "Then I better stop snuggling with you."

"Snuggling isn't a relationship." Parker pulled her back to him. A peace fell over him when he had her in his arms. She was so small compared to him and so precious to him that he could only relax when he knew she was safe in his arms. If he had to deny his other desires, holding Tilly would be the only thing to get him through this investigation.

Tilly listened to Parker's heartbeat as she closed her eyes. She was safe and warm in Parker's embrace. She felt the heat of his muscles, the way they moved with each breath, and the strength in them. It was a long flight to England, but she hoped she didn't move a muscle the entire time.

For as much as Tilly wanted to just sink into Parker and let him take care of everything for her, it wasn't in her nature to shirk what she felt was her responsibility. This was her family. Her charity. Her freedom and life are on the line.

Tilly tried to calm her mind so she could focus on the

issue. She'd learned about finance in business school, and every crime came down to one of three things: money, power, or passion. In some cases, all three.

Passion wasn't at play here. Money was, though, a lot of money. Power, too, probably. The key question was whose money and whose power? Her money was in banks and legitimate investments across the world, but her main trust was held in England. That was going to be the first step. She was going to do an inventory of all of her accounts and then her parents' accounts. Tilly was going to follow the money to find who was after the power. Only then could she think about a future not only with Parker, but with her freedom.

8

Parker had slept the rest of the flight. He was good at compartmentalizing and knew if he wanted a future with Tilly this case had to be wrapped up and handed over to the US attorney tied up in a pretty bow. To make that happen, he put the feeling of Tilly sleeping on his chest out of his mind and slept.

When he woke, he focused on the evidence and what he needed to find. Then Parker looked up the estate and how far it was from the private airfield they were landing in.

"We're almost there," Reagan whispered so as to not wake Tilly.

"Good. I need Mike to rent a car for me when we get there." Parker looked back at where Mike was emptying a large crate of hay.

"Got that all settled. We just need you two to get in the crate. We'll cover you and then unload you right into the back of a truck. It'll be how you get back on board, too."

"Settled? How did you do that?" Parker asked his sister. "Did you tell Dad what's going on?"

Reagan cringed. "No way. He'd totally come in and take

over. Thank goodness Greer is starting the President's Guard in Keeneston. It's given Dad something to do besides interfering with my life."

"Then—"

"Not now. Get in the crate." Reagan roused Tilly and smiled down at her. "Hey, princess. Rise and shine. Time to roll in the hay with my brother."

Tilly's eyes flew open in surprise and Parker punched his sister. Not hard, but enough to start a sibling back-and-forth punch party. "I'm telling Mom," Reagan snapped.

"I thought you were stronger than that. I guess you really are getting older," Parker teased back.

Reagan flipped him off and went back into the cockpit.

"Um, what's this about hay?" Tilly asked.

Parker and Tilly were sitting side by side with hay up to their chins as they felt the crate begin to move. Everything itched. When they heard the crate being lowered by a forklift, they ducked their heads. The top was cracked open and they heard talking and then it was closed again. They'd cleared customs.

Their crate was set down roughly in the back of a truck and then started moving. Within five minutes the truck stopped and the lid was pried off.

Parker instantly saw *military* written over the man's face, even as he was smiling. He reached for his gun, not wanting to fire on a soldier, but worried all the same.

"Hello, mate. I've heard a lot about you," the stranger said with both a smile and a crisp English accent.

"You have?" Parker asked, keeping his gun hidden in the hay.

"Sure have. My mate tells me everything about Keeneston."

"Who's your mate?" Parker asked as Tilly watched the interchange cautiously.

"Aiden Creed. I'm Byron Wickens, but call me Wick. Aiden and I served together. I was gutted I couldn't make the wedding. I'm also your driver to Derbyshire. A pleasure to meet you, ma'am."

"Thank you for helping us, Mr. Wick," Tilly said as she took his hand and was pulled from the crate of hay with ease.

Parker shoved his way out and then helped Wick put the top back on the hay box before moving to the cab of the pickup truck. He held the back door open for Tilly and then took the passenger's seat.

"So, you're a Bradford. Very cool. Here's a fun way to spend my day off," Wick said, turning back onto the road and heading for the main road to Derbyshire.

Tilly giggled as Wick described Aiden's reaction to a prank Wick and their team pulled on him. The team had mixed a stink bomb with chocolate pudding and filled Aiden's locker with it. The commander had come in asking whose shit was stinking up the whole place. That had been revenge for the time Aiden had loaded all their shampoo with temporary hot-pink hair dye the day before the family picnic, so in every family photo they had pink hair.

But then the laughter stopped. "Here," Tilly said, pointing to the small country road. "Turn here."

"This isn't the way to the village," Wick protested, but turned anyway.

"This is the back way to the estate. We won't have to go

through town and can sneak in relatively unseen. We can park in the back by the stables."

Tilly loved it here. The estate was massive, almost two thousand acres, and soon they pulled up to a back gate. "Enter one, six, seven, nine, then press the star button." The big iron gates swung open. Sheep looked at them disinterestedly and then slowly meandered off the compact dirt drive.

The estate had livestock, race and show horses, and crops to bring in income and help pay for the upkeep of the giant manor house. The house had been built in 1532. Wick asked questions about the estate while she noticed Parker was continually scanning the area for danger.

Finally, the stables came into view and with that the manor house. Parker cursed and Tilly frowned. Didn't he like it? It always reminded her of Pemberley from *Pride and Prejudice*. "You don't like it?"

Parker shook his head. "No, it's very stately, and I'm sure beautiful. But when you said manor house I thought more of a farmhouse. This is going to take forever to search. How many rooms does it have?"

"Two hundred, but don't worry," Tilly smiled as her home came into view. "I know exactly where to look."

"Bloody hell, I know this isn't polite to ask, but how do you pay for this?" Wick asked, staring up at the main manor after parking on the far side of the stables so the truck would be hidden from view.

"We make a fair amount on wool, plus our horses' stud fees. Then we also use the crops to make our own ale and horse feed."

"Wait, are you Derbyford Ale and Derbyford Feed?" Wick asked.

"That's us."

"You have to try their ale, mate. It's absolutely cracking," Wick said to Parker, but Parker was focused on the house.

"If we get what we need, I'll buy you a pint. Now, Tilly, where are we going?"

Parker was all business again and that meant she needed to be, too. "Fourth floor. The old servants' quarters. Wick, if any of the grounds crew stops you, just tell them you're with me."

"Ready?" Parker asked when she finished speaking. She nodded, but she didn't know if she'd ever actually be ready to face this. "Let's go. Stay behind me."

Tilly had her eyes glued to Parker's back. He was so much taller and wider than her that her body was completely hidden behind him as they used the back door into the kitchen. They had scared the house staff to death when she'd walked in with a man holding a gun.

"Is my father here?" Tilly asked Mrs. Barrow, the house manager. "Have you seen him since he went back to Florida four days ago?"

"No, lovey. Is everything all right?" Mrs. Barrow asked in her matronly way even as she gave Parker the side eye. Mrs. Barrow was close to sixty and had been looking after the house and had been in charge of the staff since Tilly was born.

"Has anyone been by asking to take a tour of the house or poking around?" Parker asked.

Mrs. Barrow looked pointedly at the gun and tapped her foot. Parker grimaced and tucked it into the waistband holster at the small of his back.

"No, they haven't. Should I warn the staff to be on the lookout for someone?" Mrs. Barrow asked.

"Please do." Tilly paused and then reached out and placed her hand on Mrs. Barrow's arm. "My friend is a US Marshal who had to arrest me the other day because it appears my father and possibly my mother are involved in something dangerous. That's all we know, which is why I came to look through Father's things."

Mrs. Barrow *tsked* and shook her head. "You checking the old valet's room?" Tilly nodded. "We should also check the old larder. Feels as if someone is walking over my grave in there, but I knew your father visited that room every now and then and then lied when I asked him about it."

Tilly saw interest spark in Parker's eyes for just a second. "Why don't we all go together? I'm guessing the old larder is nearby?"

"Right this way," Mrs. Barrow said before turning left out of the kitchen. "It's on the northeast side of the house to keep it as cool as possible and as far away from the kitchen as possible. It was all about keeping supplies cool and dry. Staff stopped using it when the kitchen was modernized in 1867 when they purchased an icebox and added onto the kitchen. While it's been enlarged and updated many times over since then, the general layout of the kitchen and great house are the same."

Tilly followed her past the wide staircase on the left that led up to the main floor of the house. Then Mrs. Barrow opened a door near the side of the stairs. "The old larder is under the stairs." There were eight or so steps under the main staircase that led down to another door. "Keeps things nice and cool to this day. Mr. Bradford uses it for overflow wine storage. He has his premier selection on display on the main floor in a temperature-controlled room, but this is used to store the everyday wine."

Mrs. Barrow turned on an ancient-looking light switch

and a bulb barely lit up the room, leaving most of it cast in shadows. Tilly understood why it creeped Mrs. Barrow out. It crept her out, too.

"I'm assuming since you manage this house so well that you came in after seeing Mr. Bradford in here a couple of times and found what he was doing." Parker grinned at Mrs. Barrow to show that he wasn't upset by her snooping.

"It's my job to know where everything in this house is. It was my professional responsibility to look." Mrs. Barrow drew herself up and met his eye with professional confidence.

Tilly had to purse her lips to stop from laughing as Mrs. Barrow crossed to the darkest part of the room and tapped a stone. "This one can be jimmied out."

Parker turned on his phone's flashlight, handed it to Mrs. Barrow, and looked closely at the stone. "The mortar is textured plastic, but looks real."

Tilly watched as Parker bent down and pulled a knife from his boot. He wedged it under the fake mortar and Tilly saw the rock move. "Is the rock also fake?"

"No, it's real, but it's not heavy," Parker said as he used his fingertips to pull the rock out from the wall. He turned it up and looked down at it. "It's been hollowed out. Hold out your hands."

Tilly held her hands out and Parker turned the rock so she could see that it was hollowed out. He lifted it over her hands and a small object fell out. "What is this?"

"It's a waterproof USB drive." Parker's fingertips gently brushed against the palm of her hand as he picked it up and shoved it into his pocket. "Now, let's see what else he has hidden in the other hundred and ninety-nine rooms."

. . .

Tilly climbed the back staircase to the fourth floor. Two centuries ago, there had been a warren of small rooms to house the army of domestic servants who lived at the manor. They'd been updated in the 1940s to what they are now, but beyond the basic upgrade of new electrical wiring, they remained the same and unused after the majority of live-in staff left during the war. Currently there were five live-in staff who now resided on the third floor. They each had their own apartments and several other apartments were put aside for when they needed more staff for an event.

"Every three months, the fourth floor is cleaned. You can tell it's almost been almost three months by the amount of dust," Mrs. Barrow explained.

"Why did you stop?" Tilly asked Parker when she almost collided with his back.

"Look at the dust. Footprints, but only one set coming and going," Parker pointed out.

Tilly looked down and in the dark with the light from the small window coming in, the dust seemed to hang in the air and the lack of it in places was evident.

"Your father was up here before he left," Mrs. Barrow confirmed from where she was stuck in the stairwell behind Tilly.

"This way," Tilly said, taking the lead. However, Parker quickly took the lead back as he scanned the area for hidden danger.

"Second room on the right. That's the valet's room," Mrs. Barrow called out.

Parker came to the door and opened it with his gun at the ready. Only after he scanned it did he tuck the gun away and allow Tilly and Mrs. Barrow in. Tilly walked around him and headed straight for the small fireplace. But the fireplace wasn't her goal. It was the wood panel next to it.

She looked up and lifted her hand to the sconce on the wall. Behind the bulb was a fleur-de-lis. She pressed it and the panel rolled up an old pulley system.

"This was originally a priest's hole. No one but the lord and lady of the manor, the valet, and the priest knew about it. The priest's room was next door. It was later turned into the butler's room. There's a hidden panel that connects the room. That way if someone came looking for Catholics, the priest could disappear or escape through the valet's room when his room was searched," Tilly explained as she dropped down to her hands and knees and crawled inside. "Flashlight?"

Parker handed her his phone with the flashlight on as she maneuvered herself in the small space to finally stand up.

"There is an old wood shelf up here where you could set a wine goblet and a Bible," Tilly explained as she brought the light up. Her breath caught as she saw a dark-shaped object sitting on the crude shelf. "I found something!"

Her heart raced as she noticed that while the shelf was filled with dust, the book was clean. It was small enough to be slipped into a pocket, but it was sturdy as she picked it up. It felt funny, and she ran her hand over it. "It's a waterproof notebook," she called out.

"Hand it over along with the flashlight," Parker said as his hand appeared near her knees.

Tilly handed them to Parker and then went through the awkwardness of backing out of the priest's hole. "What's in it?" she asked Parker as she crawled out on her hands and knees.

"I think it's an encryption similar to the notebook you found in Florida," Parker said as he held out his hand for Tilly to take. She clasped his hand and then he was pulling her up as if she weighed nothing. "Look, here're some of the symbols used in that notebook."

Tilly saw them, but the rest seemed like gibberish. "I don't know how to solve it."

"Maybe the key is on the flash drive," Parker said, slipping the notepad into the back pocket of his jeans. "Mrs. Barrow, are there any other hiding places we need to search?"

"Not that I know of, but I'll search the house from top to bottom. That I promise you." Tilly used Parker's broad frame to hide her smirk. Mrs. Barrow was about to uncover all the secrets of the Bradford family and love every moment of it. She reminded Tilly of a British Rose sister with her talent to ferret out gossip and secrets.

"Let's get going then. The sooner I can get this flash drive into a computer, the faster we can solve this mystery."

Parker headed out the door and Tilly followed directly behind him with Mrs. Barrow hot on their heels talking about where to start her search.

"Raise your hands!"

Tilly ran into Parker's back as he came to an abrupt halt. Mrs. Barrow crashed into her, yet Parker never wavered. He slowly raised his hands as Tilly peeked out under his raised arm to find a man aiming a gun at them.

"I found them. Fourth floor, east side," the man with the gun said into his communications device. "Miss Bradford, my boss would like a word with you."

"Have his people call my people and we'll set something up," Tilly said sweetly even as she felt her body tremble.

"Hands up!" he yelled at Parker who had begun to drop his arms.

"I'm unarmed. I couldn't shoot you even if I wanted to," Parker said calmly as he moved just a tiny bit to completely conceal Tilly. She wanted to roll her eyes as she took in his broad back. "Are you going to shoot Tilly?"

Tilly froze. Why was he asking the man that?

"Not at this moment, but I will shoot you if you don't hand her over," the man said, getting angry.

Tilly's eyes dropped to Parker's waistband out of fear. Then she saw that the grip of his gun was right at her hand level. That's when it hit her. Parker wasn't asking the man if he was going to shoot Tilly. Parker was asking Tilly if she was going to shoot him.

"Who is this boss you want me to meet?" Tilly asked, getting the man to talk as she reached for the gun. Parker didn't move as she pulled it from his waistband.

"None of your concern. Your father has something that he wants. You'll help us get it or we'll kill you."

Tilly swallowed hard as she felt the weight of the gun in her hand. She grew up using a shotgun for trap or hunting, but never a handgun. It had to be the same general mechanism as the shotguns she was used to firing, just more compact. Tilly felt for the safety and flipped it off. She wished she didn't pause, but she did. Could she do this? What if she missed? She'd never fired a handgun before but then came the sounds of boots on the stairs and the decision was taken from her.

Tilly put her finger on the trigger and tapped Parker's back. She took a deep breath, calming herself just like she did before she went over a large jump on her horse. Parker began questioning the armed man, drawing his attention from Tilly.

The sound of the boots grew louder, echoing up the narrow staircase. Tilly moved enough to leave the gun still concealed behind Parker's back. The man's eyes went to her, but then Parker drew his attention and the adrenaline kicked in. Tilly bit her bottom lip and moved. She pulled her arm out and fired.

"Ow!" the man grabbed the outside of his thigh as Parker simultaneously yanked the gun from her hand and shoved her back through the door.

Tilly stumbled into Mrs. Barrow and together they fell to the floor as Parker opened fire. Tilly rolled off Mrs. Barrow as Parker leaped into the room and slammed the door. "Is that secret passage to the butler's room still there?" Parker asked as Tilly scrambled to her feet.

"Yes, but I don't remember where it is," Tilly said, rushing to the shared wall.

"Move aside, lovey, I know exactly where it is." Mrs. Barrow pushed past her and began feeling along the wall. A moment later the panel swung open with a *creak* that was covered up by the sound of gunfire ripping through the door.

"Get over there and hide. Run if you have a chance," Parker ordered.

"What are you going to do?" Tilly asked as Mrs. Barrow slipped into the other room.

"I'm going to buy you time."

Tilly looked up at Parker as bullets flew through the door and into the room. He was sacrificing himself to protect her. Emotions overflowed and before Tilly thought about it, she yanked him down by the neck and kissed him. "Don't go dying on me before I have a chance to see you naked."

Then she did the hardest thing she'd ever done. She left him there.

9

Parker felt Tilly's lips touch his and then they were as gone as she was. He put a new magazine in his gun and prepared for battle. Growing up, he'd been more of a sniper, having exceptional range with his rifle, but he was still a good shot with a handgun although the main difference was how close you were when you used one versus a rifle.

Parker pressed himself against the wall by the door, which was the corner of the room farthest away from the secret panel Tilly had just slipped through. He felt the wall, feeling nothing but a thin layer of plaster and smiled. He had a plan.

While the last of the door was shredded by bullets, Parker kicked through the wall and fell to his stomach. Through the small hole in the wall, he could see the legs of two men. Scooting far enough back to be able to aim through the hole, he fired. The men howled, but Parker was already moving. He smashed through the plaster wall and stumbled out into the hall. With two quick pulls of the trigger, the two men who'd been shooting at the door were dead.

Parker heard more boots echoing up the stairs and moved toward them with his back pressed against the wall. He heard a door opening behind him and saw Tilly's head pop out when he turned to look. Right when he was about to tell her to run down the second set of stairs that led to the kitchens, a noise came from that end of the hall as well.

Parker motioned for her to get back into the room and she disappeared. With Tilly out of the line of fire, Parker listened to the boots racing up the stairs. He readied his weapon and had it pointed at whoever appeared.

An assault rifle muzzle appeared first and in that second Parker moved. He gripped the muzzle and yanked it out and down, sending the man attached to it by a strap stumbling into view. A shot to the head dropped him and Parker rounded the staircase to listen. He didn't hear anyone else coming, but he did hear others coming from the opposite end of the hall.

Parker used the stairwell as cover and waited to take down whoever was coming. He didn't have to wait long as four men raced down the hall. Parker fired. He took a man down before he was pushed back by a constant barrage of gunfire.

Parker had to draw them away from Tilly and Mrs. Barrow. He couldn't risk them capturing Tilly. "Run!" Parker yelled down the stairs as if Tilly were with him before reaching around the corner and firing off some shots at whoever these men were.

Parker heard shouts coming from outside and heard voices calling up from the first floor, but he didn't have time to answer them when the men began to kick in each door along the hallway.

Parker dropped to the ground and stretched around the corner of the hall and fired. One more man dropped, but before Parker could roll away, gunfire erupted. That wasn't new, but what was new was that the gunfire came from behind the men as the final two men fell to the floor.

"Bloody hell, you didn't tell me we were going to be in a shootout." Wick stood at the end of the hall with his gun at the ready.

Parker turned and aimed at the sound of voices coming up the stairs only to find someone dressed in riding gear and two men with pitchforks who had clearly been cleaning horse stalls.

"Oi, who are you?" the man in riding attire demanded.

"A friend of Tilly Bradford," Parker said, holding up his hands.

"Where is she?" he asked.

"Right up here with Mrs. Barrow." Parker turned back to the hallway to find Wick collecting the firearms and checking the bodies. "Tilly, Mrs. Barrow, it's safe!"

It took a moment, but the door opened down the hall and Mrs. Barrow stuck her head out. "Gracious me. It's safe, lovey. But you might want to close your eyes."

"Mrs. Barrow, Miss Bradford, are you hurt?" the man in riding attire yelled as he and the two stable hands began to jog up the rest of the stairs.

"I'm fine. This man kept us safe. Thank you for coming. It appears someone wants our girl."

Parker appreciated the fierce look on their faces at that news as Tilly finally emerged. Parker was there, using his body to block the sight of the dead. It was an automatic reaction he didn't even think about. He grabbed Tilly and pulled her to him. He tucked her head against his chest and just held her.

"Are you hurt?" he whispered.

"Not physically." He heard her struggling not to cry. "Parker, why are they after me? What has my father done?"

"That's what we are going to find out. You're not safe here, Tilly. We need to get you someplace secure."

Tilly wiped her eyes and looked at him. "Where? They've attacked me at both houses. If we go to the others, won't they just show up there too to try to take me?"

Parker nodded. "I think you're right, which is why we aren't going to one of your houses. We're going to one of mine. It's a small cabin in the woods outside of Keeneston. It was abandoned but when my brother and I were teenagers, we fixed it up with our cousins and friends. It's off the grid but it's comfortable. I bought the property a couple of years ago as a place to get away from it all and unplug. No one knows about it. You'll be safe there."

Tilly took a deep breath and color started to come back to her face. "I'd feel safe in Keeneston."

Parker turned to the group of staff now staring at Wick dragging the bodies toward the stairs. "There might be more people showing up. It might be a good idea to lie low."

"I can move the horses to the pastures near my house, then we can close up the estate," the trainer said.

"Not until I've searched every inch of this house," Mrs. Barrow said with determination. "Then maybe we'll take a week's holiday, if that's all right with you, miss."

"Of course, it is. You don't even need to search the house, just go. I wouldn't be able to handle it if anything happened to any of you just because you were helping my family." Tilly held out her hand. Mrs. Barrow took it and squeezed.

"Don't worry, lovey, we're made of stern stuff here. We'll be just fine." Mrs. Barrow hugged Tilly and Parker pulled out his card.

"Call me if you need anything," he said, handing it to her.

Parker worked with the men to move the bodies. These men were better trained and didn't have ID on them. Parker took photos and would give them to Kale to see if he could ID them. Since neither he nor Wick were supposed to be armed, and he wasn't even supposed to be in England, they decided the bodies would simply disappear instead of calling the authorities.

Parker knew where Tilly was at all times while he worked. It was as if they were connected by an invisible cord. Parker could feel when she stepped back into the house to help Mrs. Barrow and equally, he could feel when she was near again.

The talk they'd had on the plane weighed heavily on his mind and his heart. The more he threw himself into his job, the more trouble he had separating his desire for Tilly from being professional. It should have been the opposite, but throwing him into the job meant working closely with Tilly and damned if that didn't make him want her more. He wanted to protect her. He liked working with her. He respected her bravery and intelligence and wanted to talk out his ideas with her. He wanted her heart, her mind, and her body more and more with every passing minute.

Parker took a deep breath as they cleaned up and prepared to leave. He couldn't have any of that right now. He had to protect her, first and foremost, and that meant not only keeping her safe from the people after her, but also from him distracting her with his desires. He had to keep this professional. How hard could it be? He'd been doing so for the last couple of months just fine. What was another week?

. . .

The ride back to the airport was mostly filled with Wick talking about, well, everything. He filled the silence and tried to draw them into a conversation. Eventually Tilly began to join in and by the time they stopped outside the airport to get back into the hay cargo box, Parker was going to miss Wick's eternal peppiness.

"I always liked the smell of hay, but I don't think I'll ever look at it the same," Tilly muttered as she wedged herself back into the small hollowed out space in the middle of the giant box.

Parker folded himself up so that the two of them were pressed against each other as Wick worked to get the wooden lid in place. Before closing it all the way Wick stuck his face inside the box and smiled. "This has been a blast. No wonder Aiden loves Keeneston if this is the stuff you do. Oh, and Parker?"

"Yeah?"

"Thank your grandmother for that apple pie. It's the best I've ever had." He winked at Parker and closed the lid.

"What pie? Why is my grandmother sending you a pie?" Parker yelled, but Wick was already back in the truck.

"I didn't know your grandmother knew Wick," Tilly's soft voice said in the dark next to him.

"She doesn't." Parker frowned as they were on the move again. "Or at least I didn't think she did."

"Then why is she sending him a pie?"

"I'm beginning to think my father learned all about being a spy from my grandmother."

Tilly laughed, but Parker wasn't joking. His grandmother was up to something and she wanted it bad if she was baking that many pies.

10

Parker knew two things. One, having Tilly sleep against him during the flight home was cutting his resolve to be professional. She'd curled up against him and when she slept, she'd drooled on him. He knew he'd lost his heart when he thought it was the cutest thing ever. Two, no matter how badly he wanted it, he couldn't do anything about it until this case was solved.

"Where are you two going?" Reagan asked as they got off the plane deep into the night.

"I'm taking her somewhere safe. Thanks for all your help, sis." Parker hugged his sister. Some families went through fallouts, but not theirs. Even when he and Porter had tormented their older sisters on dates or when they exacted their revenge, they were always family, and family helped family.

"Let me know if you need any backup. We always have your back and you know Porter thinks he's some big spy now." Reagan rolled her eyes but smiled, showing her teasing was all out of love.

Reagan hugged Tilly and then headed for her car parked nearby.

"Now what?" Tilly asked. She looked tired, but she also looked determined.

"Now we go pay a fortune and get my car out of the long-term parking. No one will know where we are while we try to work out what we've found at your houses."

Tilly sighed, but fell into line behind him as they started the long walk from where the private flight landed to the lot that held long-term parking. Parker told himself not to do it, but it felt so natural to reach out and take her hand in his. Tilly looked up at him with surprise, but didn't pull away. Together they walked, hand in hand, to find his car.

Tilly had slept on the plane, but the sleep had not been restorative. It had been filled with memories of shooting a man, of strange men trying to kill her, and the feeling that she was constantly in danger. The only time she didn't feel as if she were in danger was when she was in Parker's arms.

Her heart wanted to open wide and accept him fully. However, there was too much pain in the past and too much fear of the future to open her heart freely to Parker. She understood now why he'd shut her off, but that didn't mean the rejection didn't hurt. And through it all, there was still the problem of her parents' possible criminal activity and the people who wanted to kidnap her.

Even as she tried to stay awake, her eyelids slid shut, unbeknownst to her.

"Tilly, sweetheart, we're here."

Parker's voice shocked her eyes open. She hadn't realized she'd fallen asleep and was now looking around trying to figure out where they were. They were deep in the woods.

She saw a well in front of a small cabin and she thought she heard running water nearby, too.

"Where are we?"

"We are in the woods outside of Keeneston. You know the big water tower? We're about a mile into the woods from there. To get here, I drive to the water tower and go through the field. There's what looks to be an ATV path, but that's what I drive down. If you ever need to escape, run for the water tower. It'll get you back to town."

Tilly shivered. When Parker put his arm around her, he probably thought it was from the damp air but it was from fear. The idea she might still have to run for her life was so beyond the scope of her normal life that it drew a physical reaction when she realized it.

Parker unlocked the handmade wooden door and let her into the dark cabin. She stood still as he went inside. She heard him moving around and saw his shadow before a match was struck and a second later the warm glow of a lamp filled the cabin.

A small bed was pressed against the far wall. A low chest was at the foot of the bed. Next to the door was a small table with two chairs and then what could be called a kitchen. It was basically a sink with some counter space and a couple of cabinets. Two rocking chairs sat on a small rug in front of the fireplace. When Parker had said the house was off the grid, he wasn't lying. No one would find them here.

"So, this is it. I'm sorry it's not fancy. There's a small bathroom right there," Parker said, pointing to the opposite side of the cabin from the fireplace. "I don't have running water, so you have to use the bucket of water to *flush* the toilet and there's also a small stall where you can take a shower with a bag of water acting as the showerhead. There's a hand pump attached to both the kitchen sink and bathroom sink. That water is from the well and is good to drink."

"And you do this for fun?" Tilly asked. Her idea of camping or roughing it was to be at a hotel without twenty-four-hour room service. Only right now she realized how bad that sounded. She would *not* be the helpless heiress.

"I do. I find it very relaxing out here. Sorry it's not what you're used to."

Tilly shook her head. "It's wonderful. I will be able to work on what we found without interruption."

"That's the plan. Now, would you like to sleep a little?"

Tilly looked at her phone and frowned. "No. It's almost five in the morning and that's what time I usually get up."

"Me too," Parker told her.

"I'm used to riding first thing in the mornings."

"I usually helped my brother feed the horses and do some farm chores before heading into work."

"Do you still own the farm with your brother?" Tilly asked.

Parker's lips tilted down. "Not technically, but I still like to help out as much as I can. The rodeo farm was Porter's dream."

"But you miss it?"

"Very much. More than I thought I would. However, I love what I'm doing now. So it's all good."

Parker lit another oil lamp and pulled out her father's notebook and set it on the table. "I'll have to run out and get us some food. I was so worried about getting you safe, I didn't think of food."

"There's a grocery store nearby?" Tilly asked, already thinking of things she might need to help her decode whatever her father left behind. She liked working with index cards and color-coded sticky notes.

"No. For right now I can go hunt something. Once I'm sure we're safe I can try to run into Lexington. I don't want anyone to know we are here, even in my own town. As much as I love them, they'll just want to get involved."

Tilly tried not to laugh because what Parker said was true as she remembered what she'd seen in the past. The town definitely got involved when Willa had needed help. "Why don't you want them to help?"

"I want to have a good handle on what's going on so I can answer questions and have a game plan. There's an expression about too many chefs in a kitchen, but in Keeneston's situation if there's not at least an outline of a plan, everyone and the PTA become generals."

Tilly smiled as she'd seen the town in action. There were a lot of generals, but they all worked well together—even PTA Pam who just liked to hit bad guys with her big truck.

"How do we run a computer to search things if we don't have internet?" Tilly asked as she moved to the small table and picked up the two notebooks that belonged to her father.

"I have a Wi-Fi hotspot if we need it," Parker said, pulling out a rectangular device from his bag. "I can see what's on it and if we need to charge any device. I do have a generator. Let's see if we can access the drive without the internet first."

Tilly leaned over so their shoulders were touching as Parker started up his laptop and slid the flash drive into place. A folder came up, but when Parker clicked on it, nothing happened.

"I don't have whatever program this is so it's not supported. I might have to ask for outside help on this. Let's see if we can make sense of the notebooks."

Tilly laid the books side by side. "Okay, in the Florida

book, I saw my nickname, Poppet, and what I think are code names and symbols." In the book from Derbyshire she saw those symbols and then a lot of random letters. "Do you think this book is the cipher for the Florida one?"

Parker shook his head. "No, I don't think so. I think they're encrypted somehow. See how the Derbyshire book is more to the point? It's all written together with only one of each symbol spread out in the lines of text. I think it's more likely a log of contacts related to the Florida book. Does your father like spy novels or is he a history buff?"

"History, yes. He's obsessed with our family history and our role in the British empire."

"Can you think of one person or one time period he talks about the most?" Parker asked. He hadn't pulled away from when they were scrunched next to each other looking at the computer, so now he was only inches from her face. She saw his hazel eyes drop to her lips. Suddenly the notebooks were no longer on her mind. "Tilly?"

Tilly couldn't tell if his whispered call of her name was to make her answer or a beg to kiss him. He liked her. She liked him. Why was kissing him a bad idea again? Tilly couldn't remember as she closed her eyes and leaned forward. Only her lips met with the floor and not his lips and Parker shoved her to the ground.

"Someone's coming. Lock the door and hide."

Parker had his weapon drawn and was out the door before she could process what had just happened. But then she heard it. The sound of an engine. They'd been found.

Parker closed the door and took off for the woods. He'd grabbed his rifle, and in less than twenty seconds was up a tree with a clear view of three sides of the cabin. It only took a few more seconds and then a truck came into view.

"Shit," Parker cursed as the truck came to a stop. "What's in your hands?" Parker yelled when the man got out of the truck.

"Groceries. Grandma Marcy said you probably didn't have anything to eat," his cousin Landon called out. "I also made a very nice breakfast quiche for you and Tilly."

Parker gracefully dropped from the tree. "It's safe, Tilly. It's just Landon." He heard the lock to the door turn and Tilly stuck her head out.

"Did I hear you say quiche?"

"You're not concerned that we've been here for less than an hour before someone found us?" Parker rolled his eyes and slung his rifle over his shoulder before helping his cousin with the groceries.

"Not if they come armed with breakfast instead of guns." Tilly bounded out the door and smiled at Landon. Landon turned and winked at Parker after Tilly kissed his cheek, grabbed the quiche, and ran back inside.

"Women love men who can cook." Landon smirked. "Good thing you two aren't together because, while some may think tequila makes clothes fall off, wait until you see what happens when she takes a bite of my cooking."

"Bite me," Parker snapped. He then glared at his cousin when Landon just laughed. "How did Grandma Marcy know we were here? Did Reagan tattle? Is that why she got a pie?"

"Whoa, wait up." Landon, bags of food in his hands, froze mid-step as he headed to the cabin. "Reagan got a pie? I didn't get a pie. Why did she get a pie?"

The moaning sounds and muffled *mmmpf, so good* coming from the cabin stopped Parker in his tracks. Visions of Tilly under him with her eyes closed in pleasure and making that sound had him frozen in place.

"Told ya," Landon said smugly as he walked by Parker and into the cabin.

Parker finally got his legs to move and hurried up the couple of steps and into the cabin behind Landon.

Tilly hadn't bothered with a plate. Parker watched as she used a fork to take a bite. Her lips closed around the food, her eyes closed, and then she slowly pulled the fork from her mouth. When the hell had eating become erotic? Tilly gave a throaty moan and his dick went hard. That's when.

"Wait until you try my dessert," Landon said, his voice dropping almost seductively, causing Tilly to moan again.

Parker shoved him. Landon laughed and Parker had never wanted to hit his cousin more. And no one ever got mad at Landon. In a family full of soldiers, law enforcement, and cousins who killed with a spoon, Landon was the quiet, calm one. The one who talked you down from the ledge, the one who made you take that deep breath so you could solve a problem, and the one who showed up with booze and food when you needed it most. He wasn't the one to steal the woman of your dreams out from under you. So, what was he doing right now by seducing Tilly with food and smirking at Parker while doing so?

"I take it everyone knows we are here?" Parker asked while reluctantly taking a slice of quiche Landon cut for him.

Landon shrugged. "I don't know. Grandma Marcy just called me and asked me to do this. I don't know if she's told anyone else. However, I also didn't know it was a secret since she knew. I thought you'd finally stop being a wimp and turned this into a romantic getaway."

Parker saw Tilly freeze next to him, but he tried to

ignore Landon's overshare. Instead of replying, Parker took a bite and had to clench his teeth together to keep from moaning. The quiche was amazing. "We're supposed to be in hiding, so I'd appreciate it if you didn't tell anyone else."

"Who would I tell?" Landon asked.

"Um, everyone?"

"Like I have time. I have two major food reviewers coming to my restaurant this week. You're on your own with whatever this is. Hopefully you know how to handle it or I can always come in and save the day with a nice smoked brisket."

"I love smoked brisket," Tilly said excitedly.

"She doesn't need your brisket. I make good brisket too and that's the only brisket she needs."

Tilly looked confused. Landon looked ready to roll on the floor with laughter. Parker looked ready to kill his cousin, even if he were the nice one.

"I guess I better be going then. Call me if you need me." Then Landon turned to Tilly and kissed her cheek. "And call me if you want my brisket."

If Parker didn't love Landon so much, he'd be dead right now. Freaking cousins and siblings. Gotta love 'em, can't kill 'em.

11

Parker had to admit the food hit the spot. So did the coffee he found in a thermos. With full stomachs and a caffeine fix, Parker and Tilly went to work researching the history of her family.

"My father was obsessed with his namesake, Theodore Edwin Bradford. He was awarded the title and estate in 1532 for services to the Crown," Tilly told him.

Parker searched the internet and began to read. "That time was taken up with the Protestant Reformation when Henry VIII left the Catholic Church in 1534. It lasted until Elizabeth I died in 1603. Your estate has a priest's hole, so I'm guessing Theodore was Catholic."

"He was. I remember my father telling me how Theodore had secretly worked to try to install Mary, Queen of Scots, to the throne instead of Elizabeth. Why is this important?" Tilly asked, but Parker was already searching for what he needed.

"Here. During that time, Vigenère ciphers were used to encrypt letters." Parker pointed to the screen and Tilly leaned over to look.

"What does this mean?" Tilly's nose scrunched just a little as if it made her mad she couldn't figure it out.

"These ciphers used letter substitutions based on a keyword. It's why it appears to be gibberish and why several lines are repeated. See, this line repeats this phrase, but this one is different. I think there are multiple keywords. I'm willing to bet each entry has a different key and algorithm. Also, to make things harder, you can substitute other alphabets," Parker explained. "If we solve the Derbyshire text, I think that will give us the names of the people in the Florida text."

"Do you think the cipher is on the flash drive?" Tilly asked.

"I don't know," Parker admitted.

"Can you break the code?"

Parker frowned. "It would take a long time if I did it by hand. The US Marshals and other government agencies have computer software programs that we could try."

"That's good, right? Why do you not sound happy about it?"

"Someone wants to either kill you or force your father to do something. Either way, you are in danger. I was told to keep you safe. Right now, I'm the only person in the government who knows where you are. If I enter the request and there's a mole or hacker looking for you, I would lead them straight to us."

Tilly frowned. "You think they can do that? My father isn't any kind of tech genius. He's in finance. Why would hackers be after us?"

"He might be just a money guy, but whoever is after you, and probably these books, could be anyone. Plus, this flash drive is encrypted with a pretty powerful program. He had to have gotten it from somewhere. I don't want to take the risk. My request and the evidence will also be reported to Patrick Arnold, the US attorney assigned to this case. And I sure as hell don't trust him."

Parker shouldn't have admitted that to Tilly, but Patrick didn't give a damn if Tilly was guilty. He just wanted another notch on his belt. People like that weren't above bending the rules to get that win.

"Where does that leave us?" Tilly asked, but Parker already knew. Just like he knew the car engine he heard wasn't someone out to kill them.

"I have an idea. Let's see who our new guest is first though." Parker stepped out onto the porch with his rifle aimed at the incoming noise. He used his scope to see better as the truck came into view. "It's my cousin Colton."

"The firefighter?" Parker's eyes narrowed at the way her voice rose slightly.

"Yes, the firefighter," Parker said between clenched teeth. What was it about women and firefighters? The guys at the Keeneston Fire Station had women chasing after them constantly. The Belles were even trying to get them to do a calendar where they were all half naked. Sure, it was for *charity* but by the way the single ladies in the Keeneston Belle charity group drooled over the firefighters, he was sure that wasn't the main reason.

The truck came to a stop and Colton bounded out. He walked first to the bed of his truck and reached in to get something. A second later he rounded the truck with an ax hanging from his hand. "Hey, guys. Grandma Marcy said your ax was broken and since the nights can be a little chilly you might need to cut some more wood."

"I can't believe Reagan sold me out to you all for a pie."

"Wait a sec. Reagan got a pie? I didn't get a pie."

"She did fly us to England," Tilly said, sticking up for Reagan, the traitor.

"Why were you in England?" Colton asked, leaning the ax against the side of the cabin. Parker gave him the brief rundown of events and Colton cursed.

"I know," Tilly said as she frowned. "It's scary."

Colton shook his head. "No, it's not that. Dammit, I put a bet on you two getting engaged tomorrow. I thought for sure this was a romantic getaway where you finally tell each other how crazy y'all are for each other."

Tilly's eyebrows flew up as she snuck a look at Parker from under her lashes. There was no ignoring this comment as he'd done with Landon's. However, before Parker could say anything, the sound of another engine sent birds flying.

"Now who?" Parker groaned.

The answer came soon enough as his brother's truck came into view with Willa in the passenger's seat. The second it came to a stop, Willa was out the door and running up the steps to wrap Tilly in a hug.

"I'm so glad you're safe. And I'm so happy for you!" Willa cried out before hugging Tilly again.

"You're happy my parents might be criminals and we had a shootout in England because someone wants to kidnap me?" Tilly asked against Willa's shoulder.

"Not that part. I'm so happy it finally brought you and Parker together and that you're getting married!"

Parker choked as his brother thumped his back at the news and offered his congratulations to a stunned, silent Tilly. "We are not engaged!" Parker finally managed to sputter.

Porter grinned and high-fived Willa. "Thank goodness. So, tomorrow night over a romantic dinner would be perfect."

Parker frowned and he had the urge to roll his eyes. "You placed a bet on us on the Blossom Café betting app, didn't you?"

"Hey, I picked tomorrow, too," Colton said, giving both Porter and Willa a high five. "Here's someone else."

Parker had already turned from his traitorous family to see who was coming down the lane now. "Are you serious?"

"Who is it?" Tilly asked as the old truck came to a stop and the man hopped out. "Oh God."

"Not God, just his messenger. But, why does everyone always say that when they see me?" Father Ben asked as he strode around the truck toward them.

Father Ben wasn't your average parish priest. For one thing, he was in his thirties. For another, he was built like he was a Special Forces soldier because he'd been one. He'd been a priest chaplain on the front lines and had been demoted for picking up guns on the battlefield to defend his brothers-in-arms. Keeneston's retiring priest, Father James, had heard of it and thought a town full of current and former soldiers and a town where a priest needed to know how to handle artillery might be a good match.

"What are you doing here?" Parker asked and then sniffed the air as Father Ben slapped him on the shoulder. "What is that smell?" Parker sniffed again. "My grandmother's apple pie!"

Father Ben's face formed an expression that could only be described as "at peace" with a slight smile and soft eyes that gave nothing away. "I hear congratulations are in order. About time too, if I may say. I brought all the paperwork for the wedding."

"Wedding?" Tilly finally found her voice as the word came out as a strangled whimper as she watched Father Ben stuff an envelope into Parker's back pocket.

"Just a day early, Father," Porter said as Tilly was trying to find her voice again.

"Yes, they're getting engaged tomorrow over a romantic dinner," Willa added.

"Right there by the firepit," Colton said as if he'd already planned it. "I even brought the ax so Parker could get it all ready."

Was Parker losing his mind? Was it already planned? Had he been on acid and run around the town spouting out a marriage plan and didn't remember it? Because the four people in front of him were acting like it was a done deal.

"We are not getting married!" Tilly finally got out. Parker frowned and turned to see her crossing her arms over her chest. "No way, no how, not ever."

Parker's frown deepened. He didn't like that surety in her voice when talking about a lack of future with him. Not that they had one, but he thought they could. They both liked each other and she made it sound like he wasn't good enough. "Why not? I would be a good husband."

Tilly's mouth dropped open in surprise before she slammed it shut again. Parker wanted to know why she thought they'd never be together. He'd finally wrapped his head around having feelings for her and the potential of a future once this case wrapped up. And now she was yanking it away. "I thought we'd reached an agreement. We'd give a relationship a try once you were cleared and all charges were dropped against you."

"We have to live in reality, Parker," Tilly said, dropping her voice as if trying to make the conversation private. As if she could do that. Everyone just leaned closer to hear better. "And the reality is we don't know the first thing about who is after me, and you know that attorney wants me in jail."

"And I know the reality is we wanted each other from

the first moment we met. There's no denying that." Parker stared back at her, challenging her to deny it.

"None of that matters if I'm in jail! Or dead."

"I won't let that happen." Parker's voice deepened as he tried to control his desire to reach over, grab Tilly's arms, and kiss her into the reality he was beginning to see. A reality where it wouldn't be so bad to settle down like his brother and have Tilly in his bed every night and in his heart every day.

"As if you can stop it? You can stop that attorney from prosecuting me? You can stop these people who are after me for who knows what?"

"Yes," Parker said simply. In his mind there was no question.

"So, we just solve whatever this problem is and then plan the wedding. Easy," Father Ben said calmly, pulling up the calendar on his phone. "I'll just pencil you in for next month. That should give everyone time to be arrested and for Parker to handle whatever this threat is."

"Now that's settled, you two," Porter said, cutting in, "just kiss and make up."

"Kiss, kiss, kiss," Willa and Colton quietly chanted and Parker and Tilly stared at each other.

Right now kissing her was on his mind, and so was tossing her over his shoulder, carrying her inside, and locking everyone out for at least thirty-six hours to prove he would be a worthy husband. Sure, he wasn't old money. Yeah, he was just a law enforcement agent and he rode rodeo instead of those flashy show horses. But he'd be a damned good husband. He was about to reach for her when another car approached. Geez, did everyone in Keeneston know he was here?

The sleek sports car pulled into the small clearing that

was now almost full and turned off. Kale Mueez, the youngest child of Rahmi super-soldier Ahmed and military dog trainer Bridget, stepped from the sleek car. His dark black hair was cut short for once and the slight smile he had on his face vanished as he saw Porter.

Kale leaped in front of his car with his arms outstretched. "Do you have the acid gun of death? I will not have my baby melted again."

"Not today, maybe next time though," Porter called out. Their cousin Sophie was a weapons developer and had developed acid grenades that simply melted anything it exploded on. Porter had a bad habit of shooting it off accidentally. One such time he melted Kale's sports car.

"Are you here for the wedding, too?" Tilly asked with a roll of her eyes. Apparently, she was over the pressure of it, but that made Parker frown again. Months ago, she'd been throwing herself at him. Well, he'd show her. He'd be the perfect man and she'd be begging him to get married.

Parker closed his eyes for a second and took a deep breath. What was he doing? He wasn't even dating Tilly. Why the hell was he thinking of marriage in the middle of a case?

"No, but congrats. About freaking time you two got together," Kale said, reaching into the car and pulling out a satchel. "I'm here because your grandma said you needed my help."

"I'm bugged and the cabin is bugged. Those are the only answers to how Grandma knows this." Parker started patting down his clothes and checking his phone for bugs.

Kale shrugged. "She could have borrowed one of my father's drones he used to use to follow Abby on her dates."

"Used to use?" Colton said with a snort. "Dylan shot one down last week."

Kale's father was slightly overprotective of his daughter, even though she was married to a former Delta Force soldier who was deadlier than he was. However, when she became pregnant, Ahmed had reverted to his daughter's teenage years levels of espionage and then some.

"If it makes you feel better, your grandma didn't know exactly what you'd need my help with, so you're probably not bugged." Kale stepped onto the porch and tapped his satchel. "Want to tell me what I'm working with?"

"You guys go ahead, I want a word with Tilly," Willa said, grabbing Tilly's hand and pulling her down the porch toward the Adirondack chairs by the firepit.

Parker sighed. Too many generals. He needed to take control and that meant putting business before pleasure. First he had to save Tilly's life. Then he could be a part of it.

12

Tilly grew madder with each step she took with Willa. She was mad at her parents. She was mad at herself. She was mad at it all. Willa practically shoved her into a chair before sitting down in the chair next to her with a sickeningly bright and happy smile on her face.

"I'm glad you're so happy my life is in danger," Tilly spat. Who was this person? Tilly was never this angry, but she couldn't control it any longer. Everything felt just so unfair.

Willa's smile immediately dropped. "Oh, Tilly. I'm not happy you're in danger. I was petrified when you called me and couldn't wait to get to you in Florida. And you know, that out of everyone, I know what you're going through. I lived through too many assassination attempts to count. I was thinking of what happened during that time, falling in love with Porter, and not how scared I was. I'm sorry for being so insensitive."

Tilly sighed and slumped back in the chair. "It's been a rough week. I shouldn't have snapped. Maybe I'll be lucky and have one of those nice Canadian assassins sent after me. How is Jared?" Tilly asked of the nicest assassin in history.

"He's walking now in physical therapy. Hoping to move to a cane soon."

Tilly giggled and shook her head. "I can't believe he didn't disappear with the rest of the hit men that just seemed to vanish after being caught."

"The Canadians promised to keep him in Canada. After that hit he took from Pam's Hummer, I didn't have the heart to see him in jail. I mean, he's suffered enough. Now we keep in touch via email. I think he has a crush on his physical therapist." They giggled and Tilly felt herself relaxing a little further. "Now, tell me everything."

So Tilly did. She told her about everything she and Parker had been through since Willa had left them in the plane.

"You shot someone? Sweet little Tilly Bradford shot someone?" Willa asked in disbelief.

Tilly nodded. "I did. I didn't like it. But I'd do it again."

"Can I ask about you and Parker or would you rather not discuss it?" Willa approached the subject gently and Tilly appreciated it.

Tilly took a deep breath and let it all out. "I'm mad, Willa. Mad that we could have already seen if we had something between us, but my parents took that away from us. I'm mad that the only reason he's here with me is because of this case. I'm mad that he didn't say to hell with the case and come get me before now. I'm mad that I forgive him because I understand the position he's in. And I'm mad at myself for never pressing the issue to find out what was going on before now. Instead, I just blamed myself. I'm mad that I thought I wasn't good enough or that I had done something to make him not like me. I'm mad that I still care so much about what he thinks of me. And I'm mad that I still love him."

Willa was quiet as Tilly recaptured her breath. It felt really good to purge that anger. "I'm glad you finally admit you love him. I knew the moment I saw you two together that he was the one for you. But, I'm mad you ever thought you weren't good enough. Tilly, criminal parents or not, you're the most amazing, smart, compassionate woman I know and you are good enough. He's the one not good enough for you."

Tilly felt the friendship and support from Willa and reached out to grab her hand. "Thank you, friend. But he is good enough. And you're right. I'm good enough, too. You fell for Porter while he was keeping you safe, right?"

"Yeah, so?" Willa asked.

Tilly smiled then. "So, Parker and I talked about exploring our feelings after the case, but I'm done waiting. I'm going to seduce him and show him just how perfect I am for him."

"I have an idea." Willa leaned closer and dropped her voice. "Text me when Parker is going to be gone."

"He's not going to leave me." Tilly shook her head. Parker would protect her with his life and never leave her side. It would make the seduction easy.

Willa grinned with a hint of mischief. "Leave that to me."

Tilly squeezed Willa's hand. "Thank you."

"What are friends for but getting you out of jail and helping you seduce the man you love?"

"What are you waiting for?" Porter punched him in the shoulder as Kale took up the small kitchen table with his computer. Parker had given Kale the photos of the attackers they encountered in England while he was working on the flash drive. "Why aren't you locked in this cabin alone having a good time?"

"All y'all are here, in case you hadn't noticed," Parker said dryly.

"He wasn't doing anything when I showed up either. I thought for sure I'd interrupt them, but nothing. Same with Landon," Colton tattled.

"Ah, I see the problem," Father Ben said and dropped his voice. "I can bless it, you know. It's worked for others. They say it's a miracle."

"That's nice of you, Ben, but we don't have a relationship to bless yet," Parker said, feeling ready to scream at everyone to leave. Well, everyone but Kale. Kale was the only one helping him right now.

"No, not your relationship. *It*." Father Ben dropped his gaze and Porter and Colton followed his gaze only to burst out laughing.

"You do not need to bless my dick." Okay, Parker was about to lose it.

"Maybe you need a miracle," Porter tried to say seriously but failed. "To raise it to its full potential."

Parker punched his brother's shoulder. Ben jumped out of the way. Colton laughed. Kale ignored the quick twin exchange of punches.

"Maybe Henry needs to come and give you some pointers. I'm sure he has some pick-up lines that would have Tilly throwing herself at you," Porter teased before dodging another punch.

"I don't need help getting laid. I need help solving this case so I don't have to worry about someone coming in while we're naked, killing me and kidnapping her."

"I managed both. I guess we know who the better

brother is now," Porter said before kicking Parker in the shin.

"I am," Kale said calmly. His voice cut through the teasing and silenced the room. "And I can tell you, your girl is in some deep shit."

Everyone was crammed into the small cabin. Tilly's back was against his chest as he looked over her shoulder and down at the computer Kale was showing everyone. Parker slipped a hand to her hip and leaned closer under the pretense of looking closer at the computer.

"It's a bunch of numbers," Tilly said sadly.

"Yes, but very important numbers," Kale told them. "These are detailed wire transfers using cryptocurrency. Money is taken from this legitimate account here," Kale explained. "Then it's converted to cryptocurrency, which is perfectly legal. However, then the money is transferred to a crypto wallet. That wallet is set up to be invisible so no one publicly or banking-wise knows what happens to it. Now, here's where it gets interesting."

Parker was pretty sure it was already interesting.

"Crypto wallets can be a physical device used to store your cryptocurrency. You use that device to send and receive transactions. It can also be a software program, which is less secure and more easily traced. In this case, he has both—some physical, some digital. I'm guessing Bradford has recorded in these books the logs of the transactions and the location of the wallets. I've managed to decipher that he has several wallets listed and named, but that the majority are still unknown," Kale further explained.

"How much do you want to bet there is a wallet for each of the names in the books?" Parker asked.

"I'm getting to that," Kale said. "But first, this is where the money gets interesting. So here are these wallets with all this money in them. They're all private. No one can access them without the key and the physical wallet. But here's the money that Bradford deposited, then the money is transferred out. Here's the wallet it's transferred to. Some are other physical wallets that are offline and others are software transfers. I've hacked a couple of those and will get to that in a minute. Then, here's cryptocurrency coming back in from the same person who emptied the account. But here's the catch. It's always twenty percent more than what went out."

Parker's mind was racing as he put it all together. "Bradford is a loan shark to criminals."

"Exactly," Kale said with a slap of his hand to the chair arm. "I've only been able to crack one of the wallets. It belongs to a drug trafficking organization out of Mexico. I was able to track several transfers from the cartel's wallet to several Hollywood actors and singers."

Parker felt Tilly stiffen under his hand. Her whole body was rigid and he thought she's stopped breathing until she sucked in a shuddering breath. "My father supported a cartel?"

Kale's smile at solving the puzzle faded. "I'm sorry, but it looks that way."

"Which cartel?" Parker asked.

"Tres Gatos out of Sinaloa."

"That's the gang Juan Campos belonged to. He attacked us in Florida."

Tilly rushed out the door. Parker wanted to go after her, but he had to solve the case, prove her innocence, and then he could chase her for the rest of their lives. Luckily, Willa and Father Ben were right behind her.

"But who are the rest of these people and how can we prove it?" Parker asked Kale.

"I had a hunch and ran one of the photos you sent me. It was from another black-market gang. I bet one of these wallets match up to them. We need to crack these books to get a list of all of the digital and physical wallets. But this cipher isn't a normal one that I can just run through a program. There are so many different levels of encryption that to solve who Scorpion, King, et cetera are, I have to solve several levels of ciphers. It's going to take time. I have to write a whole new program to try to solve it," Kale explained.

That wasn't the news Parker was hoping for. "I don't understand. By all accounts Bradford wasn't a tech guy. Why is this so hard?"

"Not a tech guy? This drive was one of the most heavily encrypted drives I've ever come across. If he doesn't know how to do it, he knows someone who does. I haven't seen this level of work since . . . shit."

"The Panther," Porter said into the silence. Parker had thought it, too, but thought the dark web hacker had been dealt with.

"This just changed everything," Parker said.

Tilly shoved out the door and raced down the stairs. Tears pressed against her lids, her chest heaved, and she couldn't decide if she wanted to cry or scream. In the end, she didn't decide, her emotions did.

Tilly's body shook with rage as she screamed with all her worth. She screamed in anger. She screamed as her heart broke. She screamed, knowing her life would never be the same again.

"Tilly!" Willa was there, trying to pull her into a hug, but a hug was the last thing she needed.

"Willa, let me," Father Ben's voice rumbled over her, but she was frantic with rage at the knowledge her father was a criminal who helped a drug lord who sent someone who threatened to kill her. "Here, Tilly."

Father Ben shoved the ax into her hand and pointed to the nearest tree. Tilly stepped forward and with tears streaming down her face swung the ax as if it were a baseball bat. It slammed into a small sapling, sending parts of it flying off into the woods as the power of the hit reverberated up her arms. But she didn't stop. Screaming in anger, she swung and swung and swung until the small tree lay chopped to pieces on the ground.

Father Ben's hands gently grasped her shoulders as he led her to the chair and sat her down. "Close your eyes," Father Ben instructed. "Now breathe in through your nose for three seconds and then exhale out your mouth for three seconds. Good. Now when your heart finally slows, open your eyes."

When Tilly opened them, she found Parker crouched in front of her with a worried look on his face. She'd wanted to seduce him. She'd wanted this picture-perfect future and now it was all gone. He was a US Marshal. He couldn't be with a crime lord's daughter. She'd been silly and naïve for thinking so.

"Are you okay? That was a big shock for you to hear about your father. What can I do to help?" Parker asked as he rested one large hand on her knee.

Tilly didn't want to talk when everyone was staring at her. She just wanted to be alone to process it all. As if he read her mind, Parker stood up and turned around, effectively blocking her from view. "We have some work to do here, so why don't we all catch up later?"

Tilly about cried with relief when Colton and Father Ben said their goodbyes and left. Willa was hovering, but Parker stepped between them and gave his sister-in-law a hug. "Thanks for visiting."

"Are you kicking me out?" Willa asked, incredulously.

"Yes. Tilly needs some time alone."

Willa was quiet, but stepped around him and kissed Tilly's cheek. "Call me."

"I will." Tilly promised, as if seduction was even on the table now. But right now, she'd promise anything to have a moment alone.

"Remember, family dinner on Friday," Porter called out. "Grandma won't care you're working. Just bring Tilly with you. You know she'll be safe with the family."

"I'm guessing everyone in town knows we are here, too?" Parker asked.

"Probably." Porter laughed and then it was just Kale left in the clearing.

"I'm sorry to be the bearer of bad news. If it helps, I don't think your father actually killed anyone," Kale said, trying to make her feel better.

"No, he just gives the killer the money to buy the weapons, right?" Tilly asked, even when she already knew the answer.

"That's a possibility. Right now, we only know about the drug cartel, but drugs and guns go together like Henry and bad pick-up lines." Kale patted the satchel he carried with his computer in it. "I have the notebooks and the drive. I'm going to try to decipher them and track down more of these wallets."

"Thanks, Kale." Parker was quiet until Kale's car was out

of sight and they were finally alone. "I'll be back in a moment."

For once, her eyes didn't follow him. Tilly was in her mind and her eyes became unfocused, blurring out the world, as she thought about everything her father had said to her over the years about his job and their money. Did her mother know? Did her mother help?

The sound of splintering wood brought the world back into focus. She turned her head and sucked in a breath. Parker's back was to her. His shirt was off as he chopped wood with the ax Colton brought and she'd just used to dismantle the sapling. His muscles rippled with each swing and seemed to glow in the golden hour of the setting sun. Well, maybe seducing him wasn't such a bad idea.

Parker reached over and picked up his shirt and slid it back on over his head. Tilly frowned as if a commercial interrupted her favorite show. Turning back to the empty firepit, she closed her eyes. What was she to do now?

She opened her eyes when Parker dumped the firewood on the ground nearby. He was putting logs in the firepit, and as the sun began to dip beneath the trees, a chill entered the air. They didn't talk as Parker lit the kindling and the fire began to slowly flick along the logs. A trickle of warmth began to creep toward her when Parker headed into the cabin, but by the time he came back out with a blanket the fire was roaring.

"Stand up," Parker told her quietly. Tilly didn't question him. A longing for Parker was almost overwhelming even when she knew she couldn't have him. For tonight, everything had changed. She was the daughter of a criminal and it was his job to arrest criminals.

13

Parker handed Tilly the blanket, but before she could sit back down, he placed his hand on her waist and slid into the chair while pulling her onto his lap. He didn't talk when he drew the blanket from her grasp to spread it out over her legs before wrapping his arms around her as if he could protect her from all the pain that the future held.

Hearing her scream with the pain of her parents' deception had broken his heart. His sweet, innocent, see-the-best-in-everyone Tilly had had her blinders ripped away and all he wished was that he could give them back to her. However, once you saw the truth, it was hard to unsee it.

"I'm not going to break," Tilly whispered as they stared at the fire.

"I know you're not," Parker said, his lips brushing the side of her cheek as he rested his head against hers. "But you're going to hurt and I want to help."

"This changes everything between us, doesn't it?" Tilly then sighed as she gave her head a small shake. "I can't believe I'm thinking of myself at a time like this. I should be thinking of how to break those codes. I should be thinking of where my father is hiding. I should be calling my mother to find out her level of involvement. I should be doing . . . something. Anything."

"It changes nothing between us, Tilly. And you are doing something. You found the books. You led us to the drive. You are the reason we know as much as we do. I'm only sorry it's caused you pain." Parker bent his head and placed a soft kiss on the slope of her neck. "It's been a long couple of days. Let's take tonight to just be Parker and Tilly."

He felt Tilly wiggle closer to him. He also felt the moment she realized what that wiggling was causing. "I guess it's a good thing you declared snuggling isn't a relationship."

Parker smiled at her sarcasm. Right now, he wanted to say to hell with the deal they made not to pursue a relationship until the case was over. So, he did what he'd been doing since he was a little boy. He pushed the boundaries. That's how he was a junior rodeo champion by fifteen. That's how he became a top pro rider, a hell of a rifle shot, and how his mother claimed she got some of the gray in her hair.

"Hmm," he murmured noncommittally into her ear as he slid his hand under the blanket to her thigh.

Tilly's head fell back against his shoulder as he gave her thigh a squeeze before moving his hand slowly upward. His fingers skimmed the inside of her thigh before squeezing again at the same time he kissed her neck. The sexy little moan from Tilly had him throwing the case out the window, if only for one night. He was tired of being professional. He was tired of denying his feelings for the only woman he'd wanted like this. Tonight, he was going to give in to temptation.

Only instead of reaching for Tilly, he reached for his gun as the sound of another engine echoed in the evening air.

"Get down," Parker ordered to Tilly as he set her on the ground behind the stone firepit. He knelt behind her and aimed at the incoming car. "You have got to be kidding me."

The car came to a stop and the door opened. Poppy, the waitress at the Blossom Café, got out. "I can't believe this place is out here. It took me forever to find it. How cute is this?"

Tilly's head popped up and Parker didn't fight it when she stood up. "Hi, Poppy. What are you doing here?"

"I brought y'all dinner. I got your favorites. How romantic is this? I heard tomorrow is the big day, but are you sure there isn't news to report for tonight?" Poppy winked at him and handed him a monogrammed thermal carrying case filled with food.

"I guess everyone in town is up to date on the case?" Parker asked as he took the carrying case.

"Pam's already putting that big grill back on her Hummer. She's hoping to punt someone even higher than that nice Canadian assassin that was after Willa." Poppy giggled at the memory of the epitome of a PTA mom in slacks, loafers, and a polo shirt hitting the assassin with her Hummer. Poppy's phone pinged with an email or text alert and she glanced down at it. Suddenly her grin fell. Parker had never seen Poppy so frightened, and she'd been held hostage before.

"What is it?" Parker asked, instantly back in marshal mode.

Poppy shoved her phone into her pocket and gave him the fakest smile he'd ever seen. "Nothing. I'm just needed back at the café for the dinner rush. Call me if you need anything tomorrow!"

"That was not *nothing*," Tilly said as they watched Poppy drive away.

"No. It wasn't. I'll talk to Lucas. Have him keep an eye on her." Parker pulled out his phone and sent a message to the polar bear-obsessed FBI Hostage Rescue Team member who had a crush on Poppy. "Done. Want to have dinner by the fireside?"

"That would be romantic." Tilly placed the blanket she'd been using on the ground for them to sit on, and gave it a little pat. "I thought you'd be more freaked out by all this marriage talk."

Parker shrugged as he handed out their dinner. "I'm used to the town always being involved in everyone's love life."

"Who you take to prom or who was caught trying to sneak out of your house the morning after a date is a little different to a priest showing up and setting our wedding date."

Parker laughed. "Yeah, that was a first. I'm actually surprised my parents haven't shown up. Or my sister Riley."

"It's still early."

And what a prophetic statement that was as a stream of traffic arrived over the next three hours that would rival the Thanksgiving parade. All his friends, every cousin, his sisters and their husbands, and then Lucas wanted to know more about Poppy. Parker looked over to where the firepit was surrounded by people to find Tilly hiding a yawn as they made s'mores.

"How come Reagan got a pie? I didn't get a pie," Riley complained.

"You can't fly a plane, sweetheart," Matt pointed out as Reagan stuck out her tongue, taunting her sister.

"Mere technicalities. It's not fair to give one of us a pie and not the other."

"But you get s'mores. She doesn't." Matt placated his wife by giving her the s'more he'd just made.

Parker talked to his friends and cousins with military and law enforcement training. As he'd expected, everyone in town already knew all the details of the case and his assignment. Henry had then called Isabelle and filled her in. The attorney was going to fly to Keeneston if and when she was needed, but had passed along a message that she'd work her current and past clients for information on Bradford and his deals in the criminal world.

"You should talk to Holt and Knox Everett," his cousin Dylan told him. "I heard Kale traced some entries to celebrities. Holt has music industry connections and as a pro quarterback, Knox is connected to a lot of Hollywood. Obviously, his mother is, too."

Holt and Knox's mother, Taylor, had been America's Sweetheart. "For that matter, I could also call Skye Jessamine." She was the current sweetheart of the silver screen and married to their cousin Trent Faulkner in Shadows Landing.

"Good idea," Dylan agreed. "Holt and Knox will be here tomorrow, though. Want me to go with you to talk to them?"

"Sure, but I can't leave Tilly here alone."

"Parker," Tilly said as she joined them. "Did I hear you're going someplace tomorrow?"

"To talk to the Everetts about the Hollywood connections Kale found." Parker slid his arm around her and pulled her against his side. He loved the way her head fit perfectly against his shoulder and the cute way she always seemed to rub her cheek against his chest as if finding the perfect place to rest it.

"Willa has offered to bring some friends over so I could have some girl time and just relax. That way I'm not alone, but I can also take a breather from all this."

"Only if Porter is there, too," Parker told her.

"Nonsense," Dylan's very pregnant wife, Abby, said with a wave of her hand. "I'll come. You know my father will be monitoring the situation with his drone." Abby pointed skyward, causing Parker and everyone else to look up. Sure enough, there was a drone. Parker waved.

"Okay. Thanks, Abby." Abby might be pregnant, but that didn't stop her from being incredibly deadly. Parker also had no doubt that the drone was armed.

"Excuse me!" Parker's cousin Wyatt called out from the firepit. "Since everyone is here, we thought this was as good a time as any." His wife, Camila, was holding his hand and smiling in such a way Parker already knew what it was. He'd seen that look on each of his sisters' faces. "We're going to have a baby!" Wyatt said and then let out a whoop of celebration.

As quickly as the noise rose, it fell as Zinnia stepped forward with her sister, Poppy. They'd arrived thirty minutes earlier after closing the café for the night. "The winner of the bet on the Wyatt/Camila baby announcement is . . ." Zinnia said, enjoying holding everyone in suspense. "Evie!"

Evie squealed and jumped onto her husband, Jackson. "That's the second-best thing I've heard today!"

"What's the first? That Camila is pregnant?" Greer teased her sister-in-law.

Evie rolled her eyes at Jackson's sister. "I guess it's the third-best thing then, since Camila and Wyatt's happy news is the second-best thing. The first best is they aren't the only ones who are going to have a baby. I'm safely past my first trimester today."

Everyone was quiet as they looked back and forth between Evie and Jackson. There was that smile again.

Cheers erupted again only to quiet and turn to Poppy and Zinnia for the winner of the bet. "The winner is . . . Greer!" Zinnia announced and Greer looked smug as everyone else groaned.

"That's not fair. She had insider information," Landon called out.

"She didn't know. No one except Jace, and he's the one person in this town who can keep a secret. How did you know?" Jackson asked her.

"Easy. I counted twelve weeks forward from when you came back from the mission with me to rescue Sebastian. I know what it's like getting back from a dangerous mission and figured it was only a matter of time," Greer said smugly.

"Hmm," Jackson said, looking at Greer and her husband, Sebastian, who seemed out of place wearing a three-piece suit around a campfire, but that was the billionaire businessman for you. "You came back from a mission about six weeks ago . . ."

Betting erupted. People were shoving money at Poppy and phones placing bets on the app were brighter than the fire. Parker placed his bet after seeing Greer roll her eyes. Sebastian's face never gave anything away, but when he whispered into his wife's ear and Greer blushed, Parker placed a bet farther away. They were still in that honeymoon phase of their relationship. While they'd start a family sooner rather than later, it wouldn't be right now.

Parker placed his bet and then put his arm back around Tilly. "Are you doing okay?"

Tilly nodded against his chest. "Just tired."

"Dyl," Parker said to his cousin. "Help wrap this thing up, will ya?"

"Sure thing." Dylan scooped his wife up into his arms and machine gun fire erupted from the drone, sending people scattering.

"Put my daughter down at once. You could trip and drop her, sending her into labor. You will not put my grandchild at risk!" Ahmed's voice rang out from the drone.

"I owe you one," Parker said to Dylan as he placed Abby carefully back on the ground.

Everyone clambered up from where they'd taken cover and began to say their goodbyes. In true Southern fashion, that lasted another thirty minutes, but finally Parker had Tilly to himself.

"I believe we were interrupted by the firepit," Parker said, pulling her back against him and wrapping his arms around her as they watched the last car leave.

"Let's see, what was I doing? Oh, that's right." Tilly pressed her bottom against him and he groaned. "Go ahead and get inside while I douse the fire. I'll be right in."

Tonight, everything had changed. He'd seen his cousins and siblings happily married before tonight, but seeing them moving on to having children and how their love was only growing had made up his mind. Screw this case. He had love within his grasp and he was going to take it.

Parker put out the fire and strode up the stairs to the cabin, ready to put his heart on the line. He opened the door and the soft glow of the lantern lit the room enough for him to see Tilly. She was sound asleep in the sexiest bra and panty set he'd ever seen. Sheer pink cups with a black lace overlay covered her breasts as the same material made up the panties, except they were held in place by two strips of black fabric that ran along her hip.

Parker silently closed the door and turned off the lamp. He made his way to the end of the bed and looked down at the woman who had taken up residence in his heart. She looked so small and delicate, but she had the heart of a warrior. He took off his cowboy boots and yanked his shirt over his head. He stepped out of his jeans and silently climbed into bed behind her. He reached down and pulled up the covers before wrapping her in his arms and drifting to sleep with her body pressed against his.

14

Tilly knew the sun was up. Its rays were causing the darkness behind her eyelids to fade to the point she knew it was time to wake. However, in her half-awake dreamlike state, she was too content to open her eyes. She'd never felt so warm and safe. And she didn't want to wake from the dream she'd been having of Parker. He'd been chopping wood again, but this time when he turned around, she got more than an eyeful.

He stalked her like prey and she was only too happy to be caught. In her dream, Parker had grabbed her and kissed her—hard. He hadn't treated her like a delicate heiress who was fragile or like a cold business merger. They'd gone at each other like animals and she'd never been so turned on.

He spun her so her back was pressed against his chest. His lips were on her neck. His hands on her breasts. If Tilly moved her hips, she could swear she felt his erection from where he held her tight against him.

"You're killing me, Tilly," Parker groaned against her neck. "But what a way to go."

Tilly's eyes flew open. This wasn't a dream. Well, it had

been, but now it was very much real life. She was spooning with Parker, his hand was on her breast, his lips were on her neck, but it was her grinding against him and it was even better than in her dream.

"I fell asleep last night, didn't I?" Tilly wanted to smack herself for that if this was what she missed.

"You were so tired I couldn't wake you. You needed your rest." Parker's hot breath seemed to caress her skin as he talked. "Should we stop?"

Parker put the ball in her court. He was asking permission to move forward, but only if she consented. "No, Parker. I'm done stopping."

"Thank God. I have to tell you something, Til."

Parker moved his hand down to her hip, his fingers plucked at the two thin strips of elastic that held her panties on.

"What?" Tilly's breath was already faltering at his touch.

"I love"—he paused as if he wanted to say more, but instead he kissed her again—"the way you feel against me." His finger dipped below the waistband at her hip and then began to skate across her belly. Tilly's breath caught as his hand stopped moving. "Are you sure you want me to go on?"

"Parker Davies, don't you dare stop!" Tilly's breath was coming fast, her heart pounding and dear Lord, what this man was doing to her insides was enough to have her melting into his touch. She'd known from the first day she met him that he was the man for her and she was done with waiting. She wanted to love him openly, with no more secrets, with no more pretending, and with all the benefits that loving Parker Davies would have.

His lips were back on her neck, he'd maneuvered her so his other hand was across her chest, pinning her to him and giving him complete access to her body. She wiggled against his erection to hurry him up. She needed his hand on her more than she needed her next breath. His finger dipped below her panties and then the sound of an engine filled the air as someone drove up to the cabin.

"Ugh!" Tilly leaped from bed, grabbed the rifle leaning against the wall, and flung the door open aiming it at the new arrivals. "Who does a girl have to kill to get laid around here?"

Dylan's eyes dropped to the ground, Abby tried not to laugh, and the drone hovering in the air did a one-eighty to look away.

A blanket was thrown over her and suddenly she was in Parker's arms, being dragged back inside. "I'll just be a minute, Dylan," Parker called out.

The second the door closed, the rifle was pulled from her hands. She expected Parker to be mad, but instead his lips were on hers as he backed her up to the door. "That was the hottest thing I've ever seen. I want you so bad right now."

His lips came back to hers. Hard, demanding, and a million times better than her dream. "But, when I finally get to be with you, it won't be with my cousin on the other side of the door. Ahmed probably has heat vision on that drone, too. But, I'm glad to know how much you want me."

"Yeah, how much do you want me?" Tilly challenged. Parker made her feel secure in herself and she reveled in her newfound self-confidence. She wasn't stumbling over her words or worrying about how to act. She was just being herself and the freedom of that sent her confidence soaring.

"Enough that the heat vision on Ahmed's drone doesn't seem like a big deal." Parker's hands were on her and he was kissing her again. His tongue surged into her mouth in time with his hips pressing against her.

"Um, Parker," Dylan called out. "The Everetts are expecting us."

"Willa just pulled up, too," Abby called out a few seconds later.

Parker and Tilly pulled apart, both breathing heavily. "I'm going to wrap this case up, then I'm coming back to you, Tilly. Nothing will stop me, I swear."

"And I know you never break your promise. I'll be waiting."

Parker stepped back and, with a muttered curse, got dressed. Tilly pulled on a pair of sweats and a T-shirt from a show jumping event and followed Parker out the door.

"I'll be back after I meet with everyone. Call me if you need anything." Parker dropped a sweet kiss on her lips in front of everyone and Tilly knew their relationship had just changed forever. He wasn't hiding it. He wasn't holding back anymore. He was all in.

"I take it things have progressed." Willa winked at her as she and Abby joined Tilly on the chairs on the porch.

"Tilly welcomed us, wearing a sexy bra set and a rifle threatening to shoot us so she could get laid. I don't think we need to worry about seducing Parker into realizing his feelings anymore." Abby smirked.

"Men cannot be seduced. We're too focused and strong to fall for that when we have a mission," Ahmed's voice said, coming from the drone now sitting near the porch on the wood chopping block.

"Dad!" Abby yelled.

"Ahmed, stop playing with your drone right this second!"

"Yes, dear," Ahmed said in response to his wife's voice.

Abby rolled her eyes. "We'll have a little bit of privacy

now, but it won't last long. We'll have to go inside when the others get here."

"Others?" Tilly asked, just as the sound of another car could be heard.

"Here they are," Willa said, standing to greet the new arrivals.

The door opened and Aniyah stepped out from behind the driver's seat. Aniyah was a force of nature with dangerous curves, sass, and the biggest heart, all packaged into a five-foot frame. Her hair was natural today with soft coils clipped to the side by a giant sequined barrette that somehow looked sweet and fierce at the same time. Then the passenger door opened and a man stepped out, looking impeccable in navy slacks and a lavender button-up shirt. His brown loafers were polished to the point the morning sun reflected off them and made him appear to be walking on sunshine.

"Oh dear," the man said, sliding the sunglasses down his nose to take a look at her. "You called right in time. Don't worry, Evan is here now. I'll take care of everything."

"Don't let the T-shirt and sweats fool you," Abby smirked. "She has sexy lingerie on under there."

"Thank goodness. Sexy lingerie is the literal foundation of fashion success."

"So true," Aniyah said as she reached into the back and pulled out a large tote bag.

"Are those handcuffs?" Tilly asked.

Aniyah reached into the bag and pulled out a pair of fuzzy handcuffs. "Evan has the fashion covered. I have the seduction covered. Besides, I heard Parker handcuffed you. I figure turnabout is fair play."

Tilly's lips turned up into a grin. "I think we're on the same page, Aniyah. What else do you have in there?"

"Oh, sugar, just wait and see." Aniyah sauntered up the steps and into the cabin.

"But first, Evan will transform you," Evan said, pulling out a large garment bag. "You have the sweet girl look down, honey."

Tilly's smile dropped. "I know. I'm always the cute one or the sweet one."

Evan smiled as he tossed the garment bag over his shoulder. "I know, which is why I went in the other direction. The point of a seduction is to open the eyes to all the possibilities, not only the ones you know. Trust me, I know how to make a man beg." He smiled at Tilly, "Just ask my husband."

Parker and Dylan sat in Trey and Taylor Everett's living room, waiting. Not more than fifteen minutes after leaving Tilly, he was already itching to get back to her.

"Dude, calm down," Dylan whispered as he pointedly stared at Parker's bouncing knee.

"You said dude." Parker looked at him in shock.

"Crap," Dylan cursed. "I've been around Alex too much. It's freaking contagious." Alex was a computer hacker with Dylan and Abby's black ops group. Parker wasn't sure if Alex knew any other words besides "dude," but it was as versatile as "bless your heart" for Southerners.

Parker stopped bouncing his knee when Taylor and Trey joined them, carrying drinks. Holt saw his parents coming and hurried to end a phone call right as his brother, Knox, rushed inside.

"Sorry," Knox said as he dropped a duffle bag on the ground. Knox was the quarterback for the Lexington Thoroughbreds. His father, Trey, was the head coach and several people from Keeneston, including Will Ashton and Prince Mo, owned the team. "My workout ran late. What's going on? Aren't you getting engaged tonight?"

"Yeah, I placed twenty bucks on tonight. Don't let me down," Holt said, sliding his cell phone into his pocket.

"I'm not getting engaged. We're not even together," Parker told them as Trey and Taylor sat down.

"That's not what I heard," Trey said with a smirk. Parker looked at the head coach questioningly. "Oh, there's drone footage of this morning."

"Freaking Ahmed," Parker cursed.

"Tell me about it. His drone follows us everywhere." Dylan had a point. He had it much worse, and at least Parker felt comfortable leaving Tilly knowing Ahmed, and his armed drone, were watching over them.

"Thank goodness you all don't do that," Holt said to his parents.

His mother smiled. "We don't need to use a drone. I have insiders all over Nashville telling me about your antics. And well, Knox, you work with your father and so do your friends. There's nothing that goes on that I don't know about. *Nothing.* Like who goes into your hotel rooms after concerts or who leaves the stadium with you after a game. But what I don't get is what Tilly Bradford has to do with us."

Parker tried not to laugh when both Holt and Knox both gulped. He gave them a break and told them about Tilly's father, the accounts he found linking him to Tres Gatos, and then the celebrities linked to Tres Gatos.

"I know Barrett Tracy," Holt said, leaning forward, placing his elbows on his knees. "He's a popular new-ish country singer in Nashville. Word on the street is he has a drug and gambling habit."

"I know Spence Habberstone," Knox said, looking at the list Parker produced. "He's a rapper, but he hangs with a lot of pro athletes. I didn't think he did drugs though. He's friends with Jaylen Cox. Comes to some of the games every year."

"How does he know the team's star running back?" Parker asked.

"They went to college together," Trey answered. "I've talked with Spence. He's smart. Super smart. He's built his career from singing in the college choir to one of the top selling rappers of all time. Now he's moving into producing, where he claims the real money is."

"And I know Alicia Wicks," Taylor said. "She's younger than I am, but she played my daughter in the last movie adaptation to your mom's book. I can see her using drugs, but I don't think she'd do it to get high. I think she did it to lose weight. Her agent was on set, berating her for being too fat. The girl can't weigh more than a hundred and ten pounds. It was so disturbing I kicked him off the set, since I was also directing. I talked to Alicia who just said I wouldn't understand the pressure she was under." Taylor rolled her eyes. "Younger kids always think they're the first. As if I didn't have the very same issues."

"Do you think you can talk to them and find out if they've ever heard of Bradford or see who and what their connection is to Tres Gatos?" Parker asked. "I know it's a long shot, but right now it's the only lead we have."

"I'll ask Jaylen to make the call," Trey said, standing, but Knox stopped him.

"Let me do it. It will be less pressure on him if it's coming from me instead of the head coach." Trey nodded and Knox headed out the front door.

"I'll be right back, too. I don't know if I can get Barrett on the phone, but his assistant has been trying to get me to go out with her so I know she'll talk." Holt pulled his phone out and walked out the back door to make the call in private.

"I'll call Alicia. I'll see what I can find out." Taylor headed for an office and closed the door.

"Well, I feel kinda useless right now," Trey joked.

It didn't take long for Knox to walk back inside. "Jaylen is calling Spence right now, but he did ask for something in return."

"What?" Parker asked. "Immunity?"

Knox shook his head. "When he found out it was for you, he asked for your grandma's apple pie."

Parker rolled his eyes but gave him a nod. "Done."

Taylor came into the room looking pale. Trey leaped up and rushed to her side. "Honey, what is it?"

"Alicia is dead." Taylor dropped to the couch and stared off into space. "Her agent answered and told me everything. It will hit the news cycle tonight."

"What happened?" Parker asked.

"She was vying for a part in a huge blockbuster series. She'd be the lead for a three-movie deal. Her agent said Alicia got the audition on her own. She told him she had 'a new contact' that could make things happen. He warned her against contacts that could promise her the moon and weren't industry professionals. She told him, 'But he is known. He's a huge financier.' Then she went to a party with the guy to schmooze some Hollywood insiders. She told her agent that directors and all the A-list actors and big financiers would be there. It would be an informal audition. If they liked her, she was in."

Taylor took a deep breath to steady herself before going on. "Alicia had been starving herself and taking drugs to lose weight for this party. There were drugs there, too. One of the actors told her they had to have chemistry if she wanted the lead. He had her snort a line of cocaine and then filmed them having sex. Alicia thought she had the role. She went home and told her agent she had it. Alicia overdosed two hours later. Her agent found her. The last message on her phone was from the actor with a clip of the sex tape thanking her for her audition, but telling her they went with someone else that he had more chemistry with."

"What about the actor?" Parker asked.

Taylor shook her head. "He claims the sex was consensual and that he's devastated to hear about Alicia's death."

"Who was the Financier who got her to the party?" Parker asked next.

Taylor shook her head. "Alicia never said. Just that he was big."

Knox's phone rang and he answered it. "Jaylen, the pie is yours if you have any news." Knox put the phone on speaker. "You're on with Parker and Dylan."

"Hey, fam. What kind of crazy shit do you have me looking into?" Jaylen asked.

"What did you find?"

"Spence said there's this guy who people call The Financier. He makes dreams come true. Spence got his number from another singer. He makes things happen. For Spence, it wasn't drugs he got from Tres Gatos, but guns. He said he had to front to make it appear he was bigger than he was. He started a beef with a rival rapper and used the guns in his videos and had his team carry. All illegal, of course, but it was all about the image. For a large fee, this guy got him in touch with Tres Gatos. After Spence was solidified as a top artist, he contacted The Financier again to give him a business line of credit. He had the money to start the production company himself. But to make the kind of splash he wanted, he needed more. So he asked The Financier for help. The man got him the cash, but it had a thirty percent interest rate."

"That's more than the twenty percent Bradford charged. Someone was acting as a middleman. I wonder if Bradford knew that?" Parker asked Dylan.

"I think the better question is who is The Financier? What did Spence say?" Dylan asked Jaylen.

"He wouldn't say anymore except it was a deal with the devil. He couldn't talk or he'd lose everything. There was evidence against him. I didn't have time to ask more. Spence told me to never mention this again if I wanted to stay friends with him. But if he ended up dead, it was this guy."

Parker couldn't ask more because Holt walked in with a frown. "Thanks, Jaylen." Knox said, hanging up and turning to his brother.

"Like I thought," Holt told them. "Barrett wouldn't talk to me, but his assistant did. She said there's a man who visits Barrett on tour when he's in New York and sometimes L.A., Barrett told her he's The Financier. He knows everyone and gets anything Barrett wants—for a price."

"Is there a name?" Parker asked.

"No." Holt handed over a piece of paper. "But I got a phone number."

"Thanks for your help." Parker stood up and took the piece of paper.

"Let us know what you find. In the meantime, I have the career of a certain actor to destroy." Taylor stood and Parker gave her a hug.

"Let me know if I can help."

"I won't need your help. Your Aunt Morgan and I can handle this, but thank you." Parker's Aunt Morgan was an owner of a well-known and prestigious PR firm. She did all of Parker's mom's book PR and all of the PR for basically everyone who was anyone. She'd semi-retired and now only handled family and friends, which still kept her busy. Something else about Aunt Morgan: she went for the kill. That actor's career would be over by dinnertime.

"Thank you all for your help. Let me know if you find out anything else." Parker and Dylan left with their one lead. "Let's drop this off with Kale and see what he's found," Parker said as he got into Dylan's SUV. He had a lead and he wanted to shake the branch hard to see what fell out.

15

Tilly looked at the items laid out on the bed. Some she recognized. Others she didn't. Evan was busy putting together a wardrobe for seduction. Willa was helping him match clothes to lingerie. Abby was sitting on the kitchen chair with her feet up staring at all the objects on the bed along with her. Aniyah was acting like she was a presenter on one of those cable TV shows where a 1-800 number was flashing on the bottom of the screen as she picked up item after item from the bed.

"It gives you a tingle of warmth to enhance the experience," Aniyah told them, holding up a bottle of massage oil. "Trust me. You'll love it."

"What do I do with it? I mean, do I handcuff him to the bed and then give him a back massage?" Tilly took the bottle and looked it over.

"Oh, honey. You don't rub a man's back with that." Evan came over holding a flimsy wisp of material. "You wear this, handcuff him to the bed, and then put some oil on your hands and, well, you know." The hand gesture Evan made filled in the missing piece for her.

"Oh! Gotcha. And you think the handcuffs are the way to go? Parker doesn't seem to be the kind of guy to submit to a woman handcuffing him."

"Trust me. He'll love it." Aniyah handed her the key. "Now, put that someplace safe."

"I have everything laid out for the next couple of days. Makeup is here, along with a list of which color to use for which outfit. The outfits are numbered here. Then the nighttime wear is hidden here. It goes from sweet to porn star, depending on the mood. Now, tonight I want you to wear this." Evan handed her a really pretty set of lingerie before handing her an outfit to wear over it.

"I'm going to be a little cold, don't you think?" Tilly looked at the micro mini sundress with a skater skirt that would flip up at the barest suggestion of a breeze.

"I do. Why do you think the bra isn't lined and why I put you in cheeky panties? There is an art to seduction, honey. Trust me, he won't be able to keep his hands off you."

"That's when you slap the cuffs on." Aniyah jumped in holding up the fuzzy cuffs. "It's the best kind of payback for him putting you in cuffs."

"Shouldn't I just talk to him about how I feel?" Tilly asked as she took the outfit from Evan.

Evan rolled his eyes. Abby groaned. Willa snickered. Aniyah shook her head. "Girl," Aniyah said seriously. "There's a time for talk and then there's a time for action. These Davies men are men of action, so all we're doing is helping you show him you're ready for that action."

"Now, go get changed while we set up the finishing touches," Evan ordered.

Tilly headed for the small bathroom to change into the outfit Evan had handed her. That afternoon had been fun, but as the hours ticked by, she was ready to see Parker. She wanted to somehow know about the progress of the case while simultaneously forgetting about it and focusing all her attention on Parker.

Tonight was a long time coming. She'd always been a dreamer, but to actually experience love at first sight wasn't the fairy tale it had always sounded like in books. She'd fallen in love with Parker the instant she saw him quirk his lips in amusement. He was confident, sexy as sin, smart, funny, and one look from those hazel eyes had her panties melting off. But it was more than that. He had been kind to her and Willa well before she became a case to him. He was kind to the horses, and even if he rolled his eyes, he was kind to his over-involved family and town. There was something very sexy about a man who could seduce you with a look and still say "thank you, ma'am" to one of the elderly Rose sisters when they patted him on the cheek as if he were still six years old.

Tilly slid on the lingerie, and with a quick glance in the mirror, realized Evan's genius. Tilly could be called "cute" most of the time. Wearing this outfit, she was not cute. She was *sexy*. Even when she put on the dress, it was clear its purpose was to highlight her sex appeal while still keeping the innocent factor. The sexiness was in her face. It was the subtle hints of curves, feminism, and sex while somehow making her not cute, but still sweet.

"Wow, Evan. You're amazing," Tilly said as she opened the door of the small bathroom.

"I know, honey. I'm glad I can help and look at you!"

"You are hot!" Aniyah made a sizzling sound and then set down the final candle. "These candles are filled with sex pheromones. You light them before he gets home and he'll walk in here and his mind will go straight to sex. Now, about tonight. Would it be possible for you to seduce him before dinner so he can still propose by midnight? I have twenty bucks on tonight."

"Girl, we all have twenty bucks on tonight." Evan rolled his eyes as he began to clean up.

Tilly looked to everyone in the room. They were all nodding. Well, no pressure then. If she didn't seduce an engagement out of Parker, the whole town would be upset with her.

"Call me if you need anything, sugar." Aniyah kissed her cheek and gave her a wink before helping Evan carry his many bags of supplies out to her car.

Then it was just Willa and Abby as they settled down to wait. Tilly loved being a good friend but as Willa and Abby talked about babies and marriage, Tilly's mind went to Parker. Could she *really* seduce him? Would she need to? He seemed ready to throw the case out the window already.

Tap. Tap.

The drone tapped the window and suddenly Tilly was on edge. Abby removed a gun from her bra and with a heave got herself out of the chair and waddled to the door.

"Who is it?" she asked the drone.

"Dylan and Parker," Ahmed answered through the drone.

"Dad, why do you have a missile ready to launch?" Abby asked as she slipped the gun back into her bra.

"What missile?" Ahmed asked innocently as if a missile hadn't just lowered from the drone.

"Come on, Abby. Let's leave Tilly to seduce her man. Ahmed, don't you dare shoot him. We all have money riding on a proposal tonight," Willa called out before kissing Tilly's cheek. "Have fun."

"It's been fun. I'll help you kill him if he messes this up. I'm ready to kill anything at this point. My hormones are all

over the place." Abby gave her a wink and then she and
Willa headed down the steps as Dylan's car came into view.

Well, here goes nothing. Tilly smiled and hoped for a
breeze. The cheekies were too cute not to show off.

Kale hit a wall with his programming. What Parker had
thought would be a simple code to decipher turned out to
be anything but. However, the lead to The Financier was
more promising. Kale had told them he'd hope to have an
identity in twenty-four hours.

"What about Sebastian?" Dylan asked as he drove
through town.

"What about him?" Parker's mind was still on the case
and Dylan's comment seemed out of left field.

"The Financier obviously runs in circles we do not, but
Sebastian might know enough of those types."

Parker pulled up the billionaire's phone number and
sent him a quick text. Now that he was married to Parker's
cousin Greer, Sebastian was spending more time in
Keeneston. Parker hoped this was one of the times.

*I'll be back for family dinner tomorrow. Will see what I can
find.*

Parker read the text from Sebastian and nodded. Great.
More waiting. Parker looked up from his phone as Dylan
parked in the clearing. Parker first saw Willa getting into her
car and then saw Abby and the drone approaching. Parker
scanned the area until his eyes locked with Tilly's.

He audibly exhaled when he saw her standing on the
small porch. Her hair was shining in the setting sun. Her
eyes were bright but had a hint of worry in them. Her lips
seemed to shine and were so kissable he almost missed the
outfit. The dress was a pale blue with small daisies on it. It

seemed so thin it was almost see-through. Even from here he saw the way her nipples were tight and the way the tiny skirt fluttered in the breeze. He'd never wished for a gust of wind as much as he wished for it now. The little skirt seemed to be playing with him. It would flutter, giving him a flash of pale pink panties, but only for a second. So short of time he actually couldn't tell if he'd seen anything or if it was just his imagination.

"Thanks for the assist today, Dyl," Parker said absently as he got out of the car. His eyes never left Tilly. Abby might have said something, but he didn't hear it. Instead, he followed the invisible pull between him and Tilly until he had his hands on her hips and his lips covering hers.

"I've missed you." Parker brushed his lips against Tilly's neck and felt her tremble under him.

"Then come inside. I have a surprise for you."

Tilly spun around and Parker got a flash of her bottom in cheeky panties. Parker's mouth went dry and his hands went straight to Tilly as he followed her inside. The second the door closed, he had her pressed against the door with his knee between her legs and his hands buried in her hair.

"I've been thinking of this all day. Did you mean it? That you were ready? I can wait. I should wait. But I'll do whatever you want me to, even if it's backing away and not touching you until the case is over."

"Is that what you want? To wait?" Tilly's voice was breathless as she pressed her hips against his thigh.

"No. But I'll do whatever it is that makes you happy. You're worth the wait."

"I told you," Tilly said, looking him in the eyes. "I'm done waiting."

Tilly reached down and yanked his shirt from his pants and over his head. Thank goodness. He'd stop if she said to, but he was so happy she didn't. His lips crashed down on hers as they finally gave into months of anticipation. His tongue surged into her mouth. His hands ran up her sides and cupped her breasts. Handcuffs were slapped on. Wait, what?

Parker pulled back and looked down at a pair of pink cheetah-print fuzzy handcuffs. "What the hell?"

"Payback." Tilly grinned, but it wasn't in humor. It practically dripped sex. She pushed him back until the back of his legs were pressed against the bed. "I know how you like handcuffs."

"You'd be very sexy in these and nothing else." Parker tested them out and sure enough they were locked.

"Poor Parker. No longer in control. Can he handle it?" Tilly asked as she trailed kisses down his chest.

"Hell yes, I can handle it," Parker said when Tilly unzipped his jeans and shoved them down. He helped kick them off and when he was off balance, Tilly pushed him back onto the bed.

Parker had never been so turned on before. Tilly turned so her back was toward him and slowly pulled the dress up and over her body. The cheeks of her ass begged to be grabbed, but when he tried, she turned around and wagged her finger at him. "Not yet. Lie back in bed, Parker."

Parker scooted until he was in the middle of the bed and about cried with joy when she straddled him. Tilly leaned forward, her barely-there bra shoved her breasts up and out. They brushed against his face and then when she sat back he realized she'd hooked the handcuffs over and down a broken spindle on the wire bed frame.

"Are you going to have your wicked way with me?"

"You bet. I told you, nothing will stop me." Tilly leaned down and kissed him as she pressed her hips suggestively down. Parker would hand over control in the bedroom anytime she wanted. "Unless, you want me to stop?"

Tilly pulled the straps down on her bra so they hung against her arms. A deep breath would have her breasts tumbling free.

"Never. I'm yours."

Tilly bent forward and placed her lips on his. This time it was slow and sexy as she kissed him.

"Parker!"

"Yes, Tilly?" Parker asked.

"That wasn't me." Tilly sat frozen on him.

"Parker, honey?" the voice called out.

"Mom?" Parker didn't know if he wanted to curse or cry in frustration at this point.

"Cy, they're inside," his mother called out.

Tilly squeaked and leaped off him. She was pulling her dress on as he was struggling to get the handcuffs up and over the spindle when the doorknob began to turn.

"Tilly!" Parker hissed.

She spun, her eyes were wide as she yanked the dress down and took in the sight of him naked in the middle of the bed. There was no time to free him so she grabbed the extra blanket and threw it over him so that only his head poked out.

The door opened and Parker wanted to die.

"Finally," his mother, Gemma, said as she walked in with his father, Cy, behind her. "You've been here for how long and not even a phone call? You could be dead for all we knew." Right now he wished he were.

"Why are you in bed?" his father asked, looking around the room. "And what's that smell?"

Tilly cleared her throat. "Candles. You know, since we

don't have power out here. And Parker just got back from a long day and wanted to take a little nap."

Parker yawned. His father narrowed his eyes, but his mother just walked over and sat down on the bed. "You've been working so hard."

"You have no idea," Parker muttered in agony as he tried to shift away from his mom.

"Well, I wanted to make sure you haven't forgotten about family dinner tomorrow."

"Of course not, Mom."

His mother beamed and turned her smile to Tilly. "And of course, you must come."

Tilly's fake smile slipped. "We're not dating."

"That's not what we hear," Cy mumbled again. "And you know what else we don't hear? We don't hear you asking for help. I'm a freaking spy and you're getting help from the Everetts and not me?"

"Dad, are you pouting?"

His mother shook her head. "He's been pouting since you got home and didn't ask for help. Now, come on and get up. You and your father can have a little talk about the case while Tilly and I have a little girl talk."

"No!" Tilly and Parker both shouted at the same time.

"Um, he's really tired. Why don't you and I go outside to chat and he can stay here and rest while he talks to his dad." Bless her. He'd never loved Tilly more than he did right now.

His mom shrugged and stood up from the bed as Tilly rushed over to the door. "Don't you want a blanket?"

His mom reached for the blanket covering Parker and Tilly reached out and grabbed his mom. "No need. I'm plenty warm."

Parker let out a breath as they finally left and his dad

took a seat at the small table. One down. Now he just had to get away with lying to his father, a.k.a. the human lie detector.

"You're naked under there, aren't you?"

Parker thought about trying to lie, but it would be futile now. Instead, he told the truth. "Yup. Thanks for interrupting."

"That's what you get for not asking me to help. My own son."

Oh my gosh. His father, the CIA spy badass, crossed his arms over his chest and pouted. "Are you seriously guilt-tripping me right now?"

"Is it working?"

Parker rolled his eyes at his father. "No."

"Okay, then." His father dropped the pout and instead his face turned to stone as he smirked. "I'm not leaving until you give me something to do. I'll cockblock you until the day I die. You want to know how long I can stay here in a cabin with you and Tilly? Remember, I'm older, I'm wiser, and I'm very patient."

"Two can play this game, you know," Parker threatened, not bothering to ask how his dad knew he was naked. Freaking spies. "I feel like moving back home. Mom does love to look after us. You know, she bakes me my favorite cookies and wants to watch movies with me all the time."

Parker narrowed his eyes when his father glared at him. Silently they stared at each other, each evaluating the other's threat. His father glared at him. Parker couldn't cross his arms since he was handcuffed to the bed so he glared right back.

"Or I'll just take off your blanket and leave. I'm sure your mom would love to see you handcuffed to the bed."

Parker's jaw tightened. "How did you know?" he hissed.

His father looked smug. "I'm a good spy. I notice everything, including the fact that Tilly's dress is on inside out." His father paused and tilted his head. "I hear them coming back in now. What's it going to be? Help you or suggest to your mother we spend the night to keep you all company?"

His father stood up and grabbed the blanket at the foot of the bed. Parker heard his mom and Tilly talking on the porch. Dammit. "Fine. Kale has a code he can't break. See what you can do with it."

"See, that wasn't so hard." His father spun on his heel and opened the door. "Come on, honey. We need to go. Parker needs my help looking into something."

Parker closed his eyes and counted to ten before opening them to find Tilly standing at the foot of bed looked shell-shocked, but then she burst out laughing. "Your dad totally played you, didn't he?"

Parker didn't want to talk about it. There were other things he'd rather be doing. Namely, Tilly. "You have me at your mercy, cuffed to the bed. Do you really want to be talking about my dad?"

Tilly's lips tilted into a sassy smirk. She reached down and yanked the blanket off. "Talking is overrated."

Parker's breath caught as she stripped the dress from her body. "Wedge the chair under the doorknob and come take everything you want from me because I am all yours."

Parker only spoke the truth. He'd been hers since the first time they met. He was tired of fighting it. He wanted Tilly more than he wanted anything, including his job.

"Oh, I intend to take it all."

16

Tilly was feeling bold and beautiful. She felt like a seductress as she straddled Parker's body. She felt his immediate reaction and gloried in it. She was doing that to him. Because of his reaction and the heat in his eyes, she felt no fear or embarrassment as she reached behind her and unclasped her bra.

Tilly dropped her arms as the scrap of fabric fell off, freeing her breasts. She loved the way Parker's eyes darkened with desire at the sight. Feeling emboldened, she rose up and hooked her fingers into the waistband of her panties. Parker's eyes dropped from her breasts and were glued to every inch she exposed as she slowly lowered her panties.

"You're so beautiful, Tilly." Parker's raspy words drove her wild. She felt them in her core and it only made her love him more.

Tilly reached over to the small drawer and opened it. She pulled out a bottle of oil and squirted it on her hands. She rubbed them together and then rubbed the oil on

Parker's chest before teasing him by running her hands slowly down his abs.

"Your turn," Parker said, gesturing to her chest.

Tilly smiled as seductively as possible and rubbed her oiled-up hands on her breasts. She loved the way Parker's breath caught. His eyes went wide as he watched her hand trail down between her breasts, over her stomach, and between her legs.

Sweat broke out on Parker's forehead as she grabbed hold of him and stroked. "So . . . hot." Parker was gasping now.

Tilly thought she must really be working Parker because she began to sweat. Only it wasn't her forehead that was sweating. It was her boobs. The sweat mixed with the oil and rolled down and plunked onto Parker's chest.

"So hot," Tilly said, taking a deep breath. "Holy crap, my boobs are on fire!"

That wasn't the worst of it. Tilly felt a warmth begin to spread from between her legs. It started off pleasant enough, but then . . . "Hoo-ha! Hoo-ha!" she half yelled and half panted.

"Now is not the time to practice Lamaze," Parker said between clenched teeth.

"No, my hoo-ha is burning!" Tilly rolled off Parker and began to jump up and down.

Parker roared. "Hot! Hot! So fucking hot!" Parker yanked his arms so hard the metal spindle on the bed broke as he leaped up. "What did you put on us?" Parker was hopping from one foot to the other trying to fan his dick while Tilly was blowing on her boobs.

"I don't know. Aniyah gave it to me!"

"No! You *never* take the oils from Aniyah! All the guys know this. Follow me!"

Parker shoved by her, kicked the chair out from under the door handle, flung the door open and ran handcuffed and completely naked outside.

Tilly didn't think twice about following him. They ran as if they were on hot lava. Only their privates were on fire, not the ground. Tilly ran past the firepit, through a small tree line, and then she saw it. A creek. Parker practically jumped the last six feet into the creek. It wasn't deep, maybe two feet at most, but it was enough to lie down in. The water hit Tilly's feet and then she belly-flopped down, letting the cold water wash over her as she lay flat on the bottom of the creek with her legs spread wide.

"This feels so good," she groaned as the heat finally dulled. "But I'm starting to think we're cursed. Every time we get close something happens. Is the universe telling us we shouldn't be together?"

Parker sat up in the creek and reached for her. Tilly let him pull her onto his lap so that she was facing him. "I think the universe is telling us to never use anything Aniyah gives us."

Tilly felt Parker's erection press against her. "Or maybe the universe just wanted us to be one with nature."

"I've always loved nature." Parker placed his handcuffed hands over her head so his arms encircled her body, then pulled her close to him. "And I love you. You are a force of nature. You could have broken under the pressure of this case. Instead, you've risen above it. You're strong, brave, and determined to find the truth. All the while being kind and gracious in the eye of this storm."

Tilly's breath caught. Parker's eyes never left hers as if he were willing her to feel the truth of every word he said. "Oh, Parker. You're such an honorable man and I'm so sorry my family put us in the position where you had to choose between your feelings and your job."

Parker shook his head. "Right now, I don't want to think of either of our families. I want to talk about us. Did I blow it, Tilly? Did I miss our chance by not telling you how I felt months ago?"

Tilly leaned her forehead against his. She breathed him in, felt him against her, and felt the way he filled her heart. "No. We didn't miss our chance. We're just fashionably late. I love you, Parker. I have since the first day we met."

"Then take these cuffs off me and let me love you." Parker tilted his head and slowly kissed his way down her neck.

"Ummm, about that."

"About me loving you?"

"No, about the handcuffs."

Parker stopped kissing her. "You do know where the key is, don't you?"

Tilly gave him a mischievous grin. "I do, but what will you do to get it?"

Tilly didn't have time to react. Parker bent down and before she knew it, she'd been tossed over his shoulder as he strode from the creek. "I feel the answer to this question is better shown than said."

Tilly's breath caught when he set her down onto the small bed in the cabin and stared down at her. She watched as he reached for a small paring knife on the counter and in a second had the cuffs falling to the floor.

"I guess you didn't need the key."

Parker smirked as he dropped to his knees. "Nothing can keep me from you. Even handcuffs."

Then he stopped talking.

Tilly's mind stopped spinning as months of fantasies came to life. And boy, she'd thought she'd had some hot fantasies, but when Parker slid into her and began to move as if their whole world was narrowed to where they were joined, she realized her fantasies were nothing compared to real life.

Tilly woke to the sound of her phone ringing. It was early in the morning, and after a night of putting her fantasies to shame, she felt . . . delicious.

"Phone," Parker muttered, but didn't release his hold on her for her to get it.

Tilly had to wiggle free of his grip and laughed when it made him groan. "Get back to bed. You can't move like that and leave."

"I'm coming, give me one minute. It's Mrs. Barrow." Tilly noticed her battery was nearly dead as she answered her phone. They'd need to charge it with the generator. "Good morning, Mrs. Barrow."

"Oh, lovey!" Mrs. Barrow cried and the warm fuzzy feeling of waking up in Parker's arms turned to ice. Tilly put the phone on speaker and turned to see Parker already sitting up with a frown on his lips. He'd heard the distress in Mrs. Barrow's voice.

"What happened?" Tilly asked.

"These men broke into the manor. They dragged me from my bed and . . . and . . . and they beat me. I'm so sorry, lovey, but I told them where you were and who you were with." Mrs. Barrow managed to get her message out and then burst into tears.

Tilly's legs went out and Parker caught her. He helped

her to the bed before taking her phone from her. "Mrs. Barrow, it's Parker Davies. Are you hurt?"

"They broke my arm, lad. I'm in the hospital now, but I'll be right as rain in no time."

"Do you know who they were?"

"No, lad. They only asked about the files and where they were. I held out and tried to pretend I didn't know, but then they broke my arm and were threatening to break my other one. I told them everything. I'm so sorry."

Parker's jaw tightened when he heard Mrs. Barrow begin to cry harder. "It's okay, Mrs. Barrow. I'm just glad you're safe now. Don't worry about a thing."

"Lad, get me some payback."

"I will, Mrs. Barrow. I swear I'll make them pay."

The phone died and Parker tossed it on the bed. He didn't say a word as he grabbed his jeans. "What are you going to do?"

"I'm developing a plan, and to execute it I'll need the town's help." Parker attached the gun holster to the small of his back before pulling on a T-shirt.

"What do you want me to do?"

Parker turned and stared down at her. "Are you ready to fight or do you want to stay safe here? There's no wrong answer. Either way I'll keep you safe."

"I'm ready to fight. Mrs. Barrow is a second mother to me. In many ways, she's more of a mother to me than my own mom. No one hurts the people I love and gets away with it."

"Good. Get dressed. We're going to the Blossom Café."

∼

Aniyah sat in the small room at Dr. Jace's office and tried not to think about how slowly time was ticking by. Her husband sat next to her, staring at a medical poster. Why was this happening to them? Hopefully Jace would have some answers.

The door opened and DeAndre took her hand in his. Her love, her support, her protector—he couldn't do anything to help her now but he still tried.

"You were right, Aniyah. You're not pregnant," Jace told her as he closed his file and took a seat on the stool.

Her whole world seemed to crash down around her. She felt as if her heart had been ripped from her chest. Again. The emptiness was almost too much to stand. No one knew what she and DeAndre were going through. Everyone always thought she was happy, that she was the life of the party. But no one knew the silent torment she and DeAndre were going through at home.

"It's been almost a year. Why can't I get pregnant? It's so easy for everyone else, but it's not easy for me? Why not? Why don't I deserve a baby?" Aniyah had to look away so Jace wouldn't see her cry.

"Baby," DeAndre said softly, pulling her to him so that she could cry into his shirt. "Maybe Doc has an answer for us. Do you?"

"I do," Jace answered, his voice full of sympathy, but also hope.

Aniyah's head popped up as she looked at Jace. He'd been her friend before he became the town doctor. Sometimes the line blurred between the two, but when it came to her fertility struggles, he was the only one she wanted to see. After trying to get pregnant for almost a year, she'd finally come in and told Jace of her problems the other day. Now he held the answer to whether she'd ever be a mother.

"What's wrong with me?" Aniyah asked, hoping it was something they could fix.

Jace smiled at her with compassion. "One in seven couples suffer infertility, but of those who do, around fifty percent of the time it's an issue with the man. As it is in this case. DeAndre, your sperm quality and quantity were very low."

Aniyah felt as if her head was spinning. She had thought her body turned against her, refusing to give her the one thing she wanted more than life. A baby.

"Me? What's wrong, Doc?" DeAndre asked with worry in his voice.

"I'd like to do an ultrasound if you don't mind. I can do it now if you have the time."

Aniyah moved her hand from DeAndre's grip and placed it on top of his hand. It was her turn to be strong—to be his support. For the last ten months he'd been holding her hand as she waited for each negative pregnancy test. He'd been the one telling her not to worry, next time it would be positive. It was DeAndre who had held her when she cried, cursing her body for turning against her. It was DeAndre who had never complained about her demands for sex when she was ovulating, and it was DeAndre who told her he'd love her no matter what. Now it was her turn to show him the same strength and support.

"What do I need to do?" DeAndre asked.

Aniyah held her husband's hand as Jace performed an exam and then an ultrasound. He made noises to himself and looked closely at the screen. Finally, he sat back and waited for DeAndre to get dressed. Aniyah was having trouble waiting. She wanted to demand to see what he saw. She needed to know now.

"DeAndre, you have varicocele. It's when the veins within the scrotum are enlarged. When that happens, blood doesn't circulate efficiently and leads to low sperm protection and quality," Jace explained.

"So, it means I can't father children?" Her sugar bear sounded so defeated that Aniyah's heart broke.

"Not at all. I'm sending you to a surgeon in Lexington. You'll be sore for a couple of days, but it's treatable in most cases. We'll give it a couple of months and then retest your sperm. If it's good, you can try naturally and if that fails, then there are plenty of options that involve a little more medical intervention."

"There's a chance then?" Aniyah asked.

Jace nodded. "A very good one."

DeAndre's arms were around her and it wasn't just her crying. For the first time in almost a year, she had hope.

17

Parker stared at the café from his car. This was a safe place. It was filled with friends and family . . . and questions, interrogations, and gossip. The lunch crowd wasn't as large as the dinner crowd, but since Parker had sent out the text asking for help, the place would be packed.

Now he was looking at the café as a hostile location. "They're going to ask you a lot of questions," Parker warned Tilly.

Tilly rolled her eyes. "Duh. I've been here before. I know the drill."

"No, I mean they'll make that little bit of questioning in Miami look pleasant."

"I know," Tilly said again. "Look, I'm determined and we need their help, right? So, let's go."

Tilly shoved open the door and strode into the café as Parker scrambled to catch up. A broom slammed down in front of them and Tilly stopped in her tracks.

"You think you can hide in town and not ask us for help?" Miss Lily asked as her sister, Miss Daisy, tapped a wooden spoon against the palm of her hand. Their other sister, Miss Violet, was menacingly swinging a crepe pan. Pretty intimidating, too, for someone who was north of ancient and prehistoric ages. "Now you come in here needing our help? We won't do it without you paying a price."

Tilly turned slowly and looked up at him. "You're right. I was wrong. I'll be in the car."

"Not so fast, missy," Miss Lily called out, stopping Tilly in her tracks. "No one leaves without answering our questions."

"Help," Tilly mouthed at Parker.

"What can I answer, Miss Lily?" Parker asked, taking pity on Tilly.

"The most important question is," Miss Lily started to say as everyone in the café went quiet and leaned forward to hear, "if you're engaged yet."

Tilly spun back around. "*That's* the most important question? Not if my parents are guilty of being involved in a criminal enterprise? Not if I'm guilty, too? Not that there's someone after the drive and books we have that could name all my dad's clients?"

Miss Daisy rolled her eyes. "Oh, dear, we already know the answers to all of that. Yes, your father is guilty. Odds are running fifty-fifty on your mother's guilt. You're not guilty and we love when new people come to town. Pam has the welcome sign on the front of her Hummer. Matt and the rest of the sheriff's department are already doing patrols."

"I polished my crepe pan," Miss Violet said with an eager smile as she held up her new lightweight crepe pan.

"Wow, Miss Violet. I can see my reflection," Parker said, giving her a compliment on the crepe pan that shone so brightly it could blind someone.

"This isn't our first rodeo, dear," Miss Lily said.

"Terrorists, assassins, murderers, oh my! But we have money riding on this engagement. So, are you or aren't you engaged?"

Tilly's mouth was hanging open in silent stupefaction so Parker answered for her. "We're not."

"Ugh." Groans filled the room as forks were dropped loudly onto tabletops and curses were flung.

"Father Ben!" Tilly gasped.

"What? The church needs a new air conditioner," Father Ben said before turning to the retired Father James. "We didn't win the bet," he said, raising his voice.

"Fear not, my son. I placed one for next week to hedge our bets."

"Thank God."

"People want to kidnap me!" Tilly shouted.

"Eh, it's not murder. No biggie," Kenna Ashton said with a shrug. She was still in her judge's robe as she picked up a to-go order.

"Kale just sent us the books to see if any of us could crack it," Uncle Pierce said before going back to his lunch. "One of us will get it."

"But people know where I am and they know we have the drive and books," Tilly sputtered.

Nikki shrugged one shoulder and Parker thought the artificially enhanced bachelor-hunter looked at them but her fake eyelashes were so long and thick that they weighed down her eyelids, so he wasn't sure. "Stop being so dramatic. A little attempted kidnapping never hurt anyone. Now, if you call in more US Marshals, I would be here every second to help you. Or better yet, call in that sexy Crew from Dylan's team. That man is fine."

"Okay, I'm only going to say this once," Tandy Rawlings said as she stood up. Tandy was the new town prosecutor.

She and Nikki were archrivals in the Keeneston Belles charity group. Nikki wanted to focus on husband hunting while Tandy wanted to focus on charity. "I agree with Nikki. Crew is one sexy man and US Marshals are totally badass."

Nikki turned her head in what might have been a "see, told you so" look, but her face was frozen from too many injections for Parker to be sure.

"I disagree," Colton said, standing up from his table filled with firefighters who also stood up. "Firefighters are not only badass, but we're damn sexy. You don't see any US Marshals on calendars, now do you?"

"Well, now that you mention it," Tandy looked to Nikki and grinned. She gave a little nod and Nikki's over-injected lips might have tilted up into a smile.

"I'd love to slide down your pole," Nikki purred.

"For charity!" Tandy quickly added.

"I'd do you for Keeneston." Nikki placed a hand over her heart, but in her case, it was one very enlarged boob.

"To help our charitable endeavors," Tandy clarified as Parker swore he felt hell freezing below his feet. Tandy and Nikki agreeing on something? It was so bizarre apparently no one in the café could process it since they all just stared in wonder.

"You want us to do one of those half-naked calendars for the Belles?" Colton asked, finally figuring out why the two women were working together.

"You don't have to limit yourself to just half naked," Nikki said with what might have been a wink of her eye, or faulty lash glue, it was hard to tell.

"I'm in," Flint said, raking his eyes over Tandy. Tandy's face blushed a cute shade of pink in response.

"Besides the firemen's calendar, which I think we'll all buy," Poppy said before turning her attention to Parker and

Tilly, "what do you need us to do? I take it you came here with a plan?"

"Yes. You all can work on the codes, but also one of the main players is called The Financier. He's known in the sports and entertainment industries for funding people to make their deepest desires come true. But no one is telling us his true identity. If anyone can find out who that is, it'll be a help."

"Oh!" his cousin Sydney gasped. "I've heard of him."

Sydney had been a famous model before starting her own brand and now was a top designer and had products from haute couture to housewares.

"What have you heard?" Parker asked.

"I'm trying to remember. He always was looking for up-and-coming models to act as servers at exclusive parties he threw. Some went on to become household names, but most just disappeared. Let me ask around and see what I can find out."

"I've got ten dollars on Sydney finding his identity by the end of the day!" Landon shouted and then the bets began flying. Some were placed on DeAndre, some on John Wolf, and others on Sebastian. But the consensus was someone was going to find the information out and soon.

"What do we do now?" Tilly asked Parker.

"We wait. We let the Keeneston grapevine do its thing."

"What you should be doing is preparing for battle," Willa whispered as soon as she and Porter joined them.

"I thought that's what we were doing?" Tilly looked confused and so did Parker. Sure, someone was bound to come after them, but he doubted it would be like the countless assassins who came after Willa.

"Not for the case, for family dinner! I heard you were coming tonight. Get your food to go. We don't have a moment to lose." Willa practically dragged Tilly to the counter to place a to-go order.

"Family dinner for girlfriends isn't so bad, right?" Parker asked his brother. "The women took it over so we're kinda out of it now. Cassidy needs to find a boyfriend. I miss our group interrogations."

"Oh, bless your poor dumb heart. You might as well kiss your relationship goodbye if you haven't prepped her." Porter was shaking his head.

"It can't be anything compared to what we put Sebastian through," Parker thought about how much fun they'd had welcoming Sebastian to the family until Greer interrupted them.

"Axes, spoons, shooting, and I'm pretty sure Greer's leading hand-to-hand combat," Willa told him. "All the while getting peppered with personal questions."

"Oh shit," Parker muttered as the reality of family dinner came crashing down on him. "I'm so sorry. I failed you. I protected you from kidnappers and attempted murder, but not from my family."

"We have six hours," Willa said, grabbing a large to-go order from Poppy. "And we're not wasting one minute."

"Here goes nothing," Parker muttered as he got out of his truck and walked around to open the door for Tilly. His grandparents' house looked warm and inviting. Wonderful smells floated out of the cracked windows and open front door. But now he knew the terror that lived inside.

"It's okay, Parker. I've got this." Tilly smiled at him as if she didn't have a care in the world.

"Tilly, if they put you through what we guys put the boyfriends through . . ."

Tilly rolled her eyes. "If you're that worried about it, why do you all put the boyfriends through it?"

"It's fun. We bond."

"See, no problem. It's just a little bonding time for the women."

"This isn't a tea party, Tilly."

"You've obviously never been to a society tea. There's more backstabbing and subterfuge there than you could ever imagine. And it's all done in pearls, heels, and always with a smile."

Parker stood staring as Tilly sailed right into the house, leaving him behind.

"Hello, everyone!" he heard her call out.

Parker scrambled to get up the stairs, but a figure moved to block the door.

"I have shockingly little information for you."

Parker was torn between talking to Sebastian and rescuing Tilly, but in the end Sebastian won out. "You couldn't find anything?"

"I didn't say that. I just said I have very little." Sebastian was never flustered. Even when they bonded over family dinner, he kept his cool.

"What did you find out?"

"The Financier is out and about. Public. People know who he is, but they're not saying. Apparently, when you go to him it's like making a deal with the devil. The *good deeds* are never good. He has blackmail on everyone he funds, which is why no one is talking. There's also a shocking number of people gone missing or dying of overdoses, mostly acquaintances of his, that has the others keeping their mouths closed."

"And that's why no one will turn on him since their secrets would get out. We have to find another way to identify him." Parker thought about the books and the wire transfers. "It's all in those books. We just have to find it."

Parker ran his hand through his hair and glanced into the house where Tilly was laughing, surrounded by his cousins. She was like a lamb led to the slaughter and didn't even realize it.

"I've talked to the gang. Kale is trying to figure out the code while Alex and Roxie hunt for rumors on Bradford. Kale followed that phone number, but it's a burner that was disconnected a year ago. Kale's guess is he uses a new one every few weeks."

"What Kale, Alex, and Roxie have found shows that Bradford is bankrolling criminals. Nothing has been found out about his wife's involvement. After a look at the financials we were able to dig up, they have lots of old money. They used to have a lot more but the family fortune has dwindled since he married her thirty-three years ago," Sebastian explained.

"There was a lot of spending, and while they have old money investments, after twenty-eight years they were at a turning point, and needed to dip into them. Instead of cutting back on personal spending, Bradford took out a chunk of his family's money and started loaning it to criminals. We found some of the old transfers. They were sloppy and obvious, but he managed to cover them up as investments. But something happened three years ago and his system went from childish to unbreakable."

"Do you think it could be Panther who helped get him set up?" Parker asked.

"Kale, Alex, and Roxie believe so, but we have no hard evidence of it. They said it just feels like Panther's work."

"I thought Panther would sell Bradford's secrets to the highest bidder?"

Sebastian shrugged his expensive-suit-covered shoulder. "All I can say is they're looking into it. The level of frustration they are encountering makes them think it's Panther."

"Did you learn anything else?" Parker tried to look inside, but Landon was now filling up the door, blocking any view inside.

"Nope." But Sebastian didn't make a move. He stood there, then looked at his watch. "Okay, we can go in now."

Landon moved out of the way and Parker hurried inside to get to Tilly. Only when he got inside she wasn't there. In fact, his serenely smiling grandmother was the only woman present.

18

"We've got this," Willa whispered to Tilly as the cousins and aunts ushered her out the back door before Willa ran off in a different direction from the group.

Parker had been far too serious about tonight. Even Willa had been serious to the point that it scared her, but Tilly wasn't the least bit nervous as she was led outside. She'd listened to Willa and Parker instruct and advise her all afternoon, but tonight was all Tilly. Luckily, Willa was a great friend and did exactly what she'd been asked.

The questions started to fly the second they were away from the house. *How old was she? What was her dating history? What was her ideal relationship like? Could she walk away from her family if they were guilty? Did she want children? What was her favorite thing to do and how would Parker fit into her life?*

Tilly answered them all. She didn't tell them that her favorite thing to do was Parker himself, but Abby guessed it and hid a snort when Tilly had hesitated in her answer.

"So," Gemma said, taking control of the interrogation as was her right, being Parker's mother. "This is how it's going to go. First up is spoons with Layne. Then archery with Cassidy. Rifle marksmanship with Greer followed by hand-to-hand with Riley and Reagan. Twins, what can I say? They do everything together." Gemma blinked as if two on one weren't a big deal.

"Okay," Tilly said with a bright smile which surprised them all. "Except we're going to do all this my way."

"Your way?" Gemma asked, uncertain of what Tilly meant by that.

Tilly nodded. "I thought we'd up the challenge a little bit. You all are obviously very talented in ways to kill people. But you're also Keenestonites, right?"

"Right," Riley said slowly, trying to understand where Tilly was going.

"And I'm sure you're all excellent riders growing up on the best horse farms around," Tilly said, leading them right into her trap.

"Of course we are," Reagan said, sounding insulted.

"Good. Then we'll do all your challenges . . . on horseback." Tilly nodded and Willa came back into view, leading a group of horses, all saddled and ready to go.

"I love it, but I'm out. Jackson would kill me if I rode in this condition," Evie said, placing a protective hand over her abdomen.

"Well, this bloody sucks," Camila, the horse trainer from Ireland, muttered. "Finally, an event I could kick ass in, but Wyatt would freak if he found out."

"I'm so in, and you already have my vote of approval just for coming up with this idea," Reagan said, taking her horse from Willa. Before dinner, Porter and Willa had gotten everyone's horse or at least for the ones who could ride. They had transported them over to the farm and got them ready.

"I'm in, too," Riley grinned.

"I haven't ridden in far too long, but I'm totally in," Cassidy said.

"Me too," Layne agreed.

"I can shoot from a rooftop. I can shoot from a shop. I can shoot nonstop. And, of course, I can shoot from a horse." Greer smirked as she grabbed her rifle and mounted as everyone laughed.

"I knew this was going to be fun," Tilly told them as she mounted one of Willa's horses that she used for hunter-jumper and cross-country events.

Tilly had listened to all the worry her friends had about dinner. However, one thing they all seemed to forget: the Davies family had welcomed all the prospective in-laws with open arms and hearts. If they wanted her and Parker to get married so badly that they'd sent a priest, a little dinner wasn't going to change their minds about her. With the realization that they had already approved of her, Tilly relaxed and decided to have some fun tonight. She'd heard of smash rooms before where people broke things to let out their frustrations. So why not turn the family dinner challenge into a girls' night smash room?

"So, what do I do with this?" Tilly asked as a soup spoon was handed to her.

"You kill the dummy with it. You get one chance, and it has to be a kill shot," Layne explained. "My father, Miles, taught us all the versatility of a spoon as a weapon. In fact, Porter used a spoon to kill a man when he was protecting Willa."

Tilly's lips tilted down as if she smelled something bad. She remembered Willa telling her about Porter taking down an assassin by shoving a spoon in his neck.

"Don't know how you're going to do it on a horse, but

those were your rules." Layne shrugged and pointed to a straw dummy hanging from a tree.

"No problem." Tilly squeezed her thighs and sent the horse charging forward. She slid her feet free from the stirrups as she approached the dummy. As the horse charged by, Tilly leaped off and onto the dummy. The dummy was ripped from the rope and cushioned her fall to the ground where Tilly moved to straddle it. She gripped the spoon with two hands, raised it over her head, and slammed it through the front of the dummy's neck.

"Does that work?" Tilly asked as she looked down at the spoon sticking out of the hay.

Everyone was silent and then Willa let out a whoop and began to clap.

"That was totally badass!" Abby said, joining in with applause.

"Amazing! I loved it. You're in. I don't care if you bomb everything else. I want someone as my cousin-in-law who can leap from a horse and stab a person in the throat," Layne said before hugging her.

Willa brought the horse back and handed her the reins. "I can't believe you did that! That was awesome. And you actually look like you're having fun."

"I told you, it's all about your mindset. See, we're just a group of girls bonding."

"Ladies!" Gemma called out. "Look! I got it on slow-motion video. Your father-in-law is going to be so proud of you."

"Mom, I would remind you that they're not engaged yet," Reagan said. "But after seeing that, you now have to be my sister. I won't take no for an answer. If Parker doesn't ask you, I'll totally dump Carter and marry you myself."

Tilly laughed as they all chatted and walked their horses to the next event. The entire atmosphere changed from tense to upbeat. Everyone was talking, telling stories, and forgetting to interrogate Tilly anymore. Instead, it was like a party.

"Okay, you can leap from a horse, but how will you do shooting an arrow from one?" Cassidy asked as she handed a bow and arrow to Tilly.

"Considering I've never shot one before, I'd duck and cover if I were you."

The group laughed, but she wasn't kidding.

Then they were off. Cassidy was racing toward a target on the left and Tilly to the right. Considering she'd never even notched an arrow before, she considered it a win that she did just that. Only when Tilly pulled back on the bow, the tip of the arrow angled up and before she could correct it, the string of the bow twanged free from her fingertips. The arrow shot up into the night sky.

"Whoops."

"Whoops what?" Cassidy called out from where she shot a perfect bullseye. "Where's your arrow?"

"Um, up?"

"Up?" Cassidy looked over and Tilly pointed up in the air. "Take cover!"

Cassidy kicked her horse hard and took off. Tilly followed suit. They raced to the edge of the range and stopped as the other women screamed and dove for safety.

When they spun around, the arrow was still gone. "Where is it?" Cassidy shouted to the group of women on the other side of the range.

They slowly stuck their heads out and looked around. "I don't see it!" Gemma called out.

"It can't just disappear," Cassidy called back to them.

There was a giggle and then another and another. "Found it," Sienna called between fits of laughter.

Tilly looked for her and found Sienna, Sydney, and Sophie standing way behind everyone else.

"That's not possible," Cassidy muttered as the growing group of women gathered around.

Cassidy and Tilly trotted back to the starting area and then further back twenty more feet. There in the ground was her arrow. It had somehow shot backward.

"Well, let's not tell Cy about this one," Gemma said, deleting the video. "Next!"

Five minutes later, Tilly was thundering down another shooting range with a rifle to her shoulder. This she could handle. She grew up in the English countryside, hunting on horseback was nothing new to her.

The rifle was different from her regular shotgun, but Tilly didn't have trouble acclimating. She charged down the range that had three targets and Tilly hit them all. They weren't perfect, but they were respectable. Gone was the negative, hyper-competitiveness she'd heard was the usual atmosphere in these "bonding experiences" with the family. Instead, Greer high-fived her as they came to a stop.

"Nice shooting!"

"Thanks." Tilly was smiling. "This is so much fun!"

Greer laughed as they trotted toward a now-growing group of people. "We don't hear that often about family dinner. Oh, look!"

Out in front was Parker. She could see him smiling from down the length of the range and it did very funny things to her insides in the best possible way.

"If you liked this, you'll love the fight against Riley and

Reagan," Greer told her as they approached the larger group of men and women.

"I'm looking forward to it because we're going to do it my way—a horse race. If you're placing bets at the café, you might want to place it on me."

"Oh, someone's cocky. I like it," Greer said with a wink. "Hey, Uncle Cy, I bet you ten dollars Tilly beats your daughters at the race."

"What race? Why are you on horses and not punching each other?" Cy called out.

Greer rolled her eyes. "You do things your way. We do things our way. If you have a problem with that, we can settle it on the range. You want to take me on, old man?"

Tilly heard Greer's husband, Sebastian, chuckle and saw several men trying to hide smiles even as they took a giant step away from Cy in fear.

"I'll shoot you for it. I win and we men take over your poor excuse of an interrogation," Cy said, pointing to the men. "You win and you do this little horse race thing."

Greer's father, Cole, burst out laughing. "I don't think that's a good bet, old man."

"Cole, you do realize I'm younger than you, right?" Cy said along with the click of the safety being turned off.

"I do, but I also know something you don't," Cole said, still laughing.

"What?"

"Greer takes after her mother, not me. She could outshoot you blindfolded."

"I'd like to raise the stakes," Tilly said softly. Everyone fell quiet and turned to her in surprise. "Greer wins and the men have to race against the women."

"You are so in. Welcome to the family," Riley said as she rode her own horse up to join Tilly.

"Come on, super spy. Let's see what you've got," Greer called out as she handed the rifle Tilly had been using to Cy.

It took less than a minute to crown a winner. Tilly had to give Greer credit, she didn't say a word when she won with three shots that entered the same hole right in the middle of the farthest target.

"Honey, I have your horse." Gemma wasn't even trying to hide the very amused smile on her face.

"My father is an incredibly skilled rider," Parker whispered to Tilly. "And my brother is riding, too. You know Porter's an excellent rider."

"Oh, I know. But we aren't wrangling cows or riding broncs." Tilly gave him a wink and then faced the group of riders who had grown to include Parker's Uncle Cade and cousin Wyatt. "Willa was nice enough to lay out a race course for us. It's through the pasture, into the woods following the ATV path, and then out the pasture by the house. First one to the porch wins."

"The course is marked with neon yellow flags with lanterns, but if you get a move on you won't need them. The sun won't set for another thirty minutes or so. Good luck!" Willa called out.

"Tilly's going to need it," Porter said with all the cockiness of a rodeo champion.

Willa looked at him with pity. "Oh, honey, I wasn't wishing Tilly luck. I was wishing you boys luck."

"Wait a sec," Abby said, stopping everyone at the starting line. She looked up and around and when she didn't see what she was looking for she ran in place for a moment. A humming sound could suddenly be heard and then a drone appeared.

"What are you doing? Your heart rate went up," Ahmed's voice came through the drone's speaker.

"Trying to get your attention. Does that thing have a record option?" Abby asked.

"Of course it does. What are you all doing? Why are you on horses? Dylan, you'd better not let her on a horse."

"I promise I won't let my wife get on a horse. This is Tilly's interrogation. She's challenged the guys to a race," Dylan said as if it were completely normal to be speaking to a hovering drone.

Tilly thought she might have heard a snicker, but she wasn't sure. Suddenly phones pinged with incoming text messages. "I sent you a live link. I'm guessing my daughter summoned me to record the race."

"You got it, Dad! Thanks!"

"Okay, is everyone ready now?" Gemma asked.

Tilly settled the reins in her hands and then let out a breath. She kept her focus on the course ahead of her and as soon as Gemma yelled, "Go!" she squeezed her thighs tight as she kicked her heels back. Her horse shot forward and the race was on.

19

"Why did you let her do this?" Parker hissed at Willa as he watched Tilly trapped between his father on one side and his brother on the other.

"It was her idea, Parker. Have a little faith. She knows how to play to her strengths. Honestly, Parker, you've seen her ride before."

"Let's get to the finish line!" his mother called out.

It didn't take long to pile into the trucks the guys had brought with them and drive across the fields to the front of the house. His grandparents were already on the front porch, watching their phones.

"Abigail," Grandma Marcy said as they all clambered onto the porch and found seats on the stairs. "Your father is very talented with his drone camera. My, I feel as if I'm in the middle of the race!"

Parker agreed. He could feel every beat of the hooves, every bump his father gave Tilly, every corner Porter and Wyatt cut Tilly off on. He could also see the grins on Reagan and Riley's faces as they charged forward, playing just as dirty.

Matt snorted when his wife, Riley, cut off Uncle Cade to take first place right before they entered the woods. Reagan was right behind Cade, giving him hell as she tried to overtake him.

"Your son is just toying with the poor girl. I thought I raised him better than that," Grandpa Jake said to Marcy about the way Cy was taunting Tilly.

Slowly and steadily, Tilly made her way forward through the field of horses. She passed Wyatt first. Then, side by side, she and Cy shot into the woods.

Parker's breath caught. The trail was only wide enough for two horses at a time. Reagan's horse slowed when it crossed the creek, but Tilly and his dad charged forward, passing her. The drone picked up the creative cursing Reagan let out at that move before she cut off Porter.

"That's my girl," Carter said, leaning forward to get a better view of the race.

"Hey," Parker said, suddenly frowning. He knew that path. "Isn't there a tree down across the path?"

Willa just smiled and Parker thought his heart might leap out of his chest.

Sure enough, up ahead a downed tree covered most of the path. It wasn't a big tree, but he didn't know if Tilly knew it was there. But she was about to find out.

"There's something I know that you don't," Cy said, taunting Tilly.

"I'm sure there is. I don't know anything about C-4 except it looks like sad silly putty."

"I'm about to win. Right here."

"I'd bet you're not."

"What's the bet?" Cy asked as he took the trap she laid.

"If I win, you don't get to interfere with my relationship with Parker. No *when are you going to get married?* No *when are you going to have babies?* Nothing. Is it a bet?"

"And if I win, I get to teach your children spy things."

"I guess that means you approve of me?" Tilly grinned as she realized he talked about the future.

Cy only grumbled.

"Deal," Tilly said. "Provided you teach me the spy things, too."

"Deal," Cy said. "Now, get ready to lose."

Riley and Cade veered sharply off the trail and were forced into a single row. Cy cut her off and followed right on Cade's tail. Tilly grinned and urged her horse to an even faster pace.

"Slow down!" Cy yelled but Tilly ignored him.

She rose up and forward into her two-point stance, tightened her hand in the horse's mane, and squeezed with her knees. The horse didn't slow as he leaped into the air. It was only three or so feet so the horse didn't think anything of it. They were flying and then the front hooves came down and Tilly's form was show-worthy and tight so she wouldn't fly over the horse's head. By jumping the downed tree, she'd passed both Cy and Cade.

"See ya, Pops!" Tilly called over her shoulder as she and Riley battled neck and neck through the woods with Cy and Cade right behind them and then Porter, Reagan, and Wyatt bringing up the rear.

"I'm so happy my brothers met you and Willa," Riley called out. "But I'm still going to beat you."

"We'll see about that," Tilly said with a wink.

The opening to the pasture was getting closer. They broke through the tree line and into a full-out sprint to the finish. Tilly's heart was racing, but she couldn't stop the confident smile spreading across her face. She lowered herself practically to her horse's neck and pushed the final quarter mile. Up ahead, there were two fences with two open gates. The thing was the gates were positioned a bit further down the fence-line, away from the finish line at the porch. Riley began to angle her horse toward the front gate with Cy pushing forward to pass Tilly and race Riley to the gate.

"Let's get that apple pie I promised you," Tilly whispered to her horse before heading straight for the fence.

Parker looked up from the video feed to see them race out of the woods and into the pasture in front of them.

"Why isn't Tilly heading for the gates?" Carter asked as Reagan battled Porter and Cade for fourth place.

"Oh my gosh, no," his mother gasped. She reached out and grabbed Parker's arm. "She can't jump them. They're almost five feet tall."

Parker couldn't even respond. He stared in horror as Tilly leaned forward so that she was practically lying across the horse. He could see her smile and then the horse jumped.

Parker didn't breathe. Time and space slowed to a near freezing pace as they sailed over the fence. When all four hooves were on the ground and they were racing forward, Parker finally dragged in a breath.

His mother did not. She only clutched his arm tighter as Tilly rode straight for the second fence that was no more than a hundred feet from them. The big, beautiful, confident smile never left Tilly's face as she approached the fence. With powerful elegance, she and the horse sailed over the fence. Parker was sure his mother drew blood as she dug her nails into his arm, but he didn't care. His eyes never left Tilly's body as she lay flat against the horse's neck, seeming to become part of him as they flew through the air. A lifetime passed in that split second it took for her to land. Then she was sitting up and reining her horse in. She was patting his neck as she trotted him right up to the base of the stairs.

"So, did I pass?"

Parker didn't know if he wanted to haul her down and kiss her or spank her for those stunts. In the end, he didn't need to do anything. His mother stormed forward.

"Young lady, no daughter of mine is putting herself in that much danger again. You will never do that again. Do you hear me?"

"Oh, Mrs. Davies! I'm so sorry I scared you. The fences are almost a foot shorter than I normally jump so it was easy for me, especially riding this good boy. He's Willa's eventing horse. He's used to doing cross-country and jumping events well over five feet high. I should have let you know but I wanted to teach your husband a lesson."

His mother sputtered, but Parker realized what Tilly said was true. The jumps she and Willa regularly made were above five feet and the cross-country event was usually four miles of high and wide obstacles for horse and rider. Parker suddenly let out a bark of laughter.

"You played them. You brought in an expert and rigged the course."

Tilly acted insulted. "I'd never do something like that. I just picked the right horse at the right time."

The others raced through the gate as Cy and Riley finished neck and neck followed by Porter and Reagan, Cade, and then Wyatt. Parker put his arm around Tilly when he saw his father storm toward her.

"Dad . . ." he warned, but Cy was in a towering rage.

"That's cheating!"

Tilly blinked innocently at him. "What is?"

"You can't just jump fences like that! How did you jump those? It doesn't matter. You lose because you went off course and took a shortcut."

"She was on the course the whole time." Willa got everyone's attention with that. "If you'll notice, the flags were right on the top board where Tilly jumped. Actually, the rest of you detoured off the course to pass through the gate. You also went off the trail through the woods. Therefore, you're all disqualified and Tilly's the only one who completed the course."

"Babe, that's not fair," Porter complained. "You and Tilly are the only ones who could make those jumps."

Willa and Tilly shrugged as if it weren't their problem. "And Greer's the only one who can shoot a target like she does. And Cassidy is the only one who can shoot a bow and arrow. And—"

"Okay, I get your point," Porter said, holding up his hands.

"You men were so sure you'd beat us that you never asked for any specifics. Guess you should have asked if it was a cross-country course, which it obviously was, and then you'd know you'd have to make some jumps," Tilly told the grumbling men.

Grandma Marcy chuckled as the men pouted. "I think it's time for dinner and to the victor goes the spoils. I have an apple pie just for you, Tilly."

20

Parker couldn't believe it. Dinner had been fun, actual *fun*. Tilly and Willa amused everyone with stories of the horse world while Sydney and her mother, Katelyn, jumped in with stories from the model world. Then Sophie and Piper had them all cracking up with stories about being women in the male-dominated fields of weapon development and virology. Not to be outdone, Parker and Porter had them all laughing with stories from the rodeo circuit. Then Landon jumped in with crazy diner stories and Colton with funny fire response calls.

In the car, they held hands as they drove to their hideaway. Parker thought about Tilly in his life and it was no longer scary. He knew he had a job to do and he'd do it well. But when it was over, Tilly would be his forever.

Love. He couldn't believe it. Parker Davies was madly in love with a woman he'd never imagine as being "the one." He tended to be a little mischievous, a little quiet, a little serious, and a lot alpha. Tilly was sweet, funny, big-hearted, and radiated joy and kindness. She didn't care about his family's standing in the world. She didn't care what his job was. She loved him for him.

Parker was turning into the field where the water tower was when his phone lit up with a text message. He came to a stop in the field and picked up his phone.

"What is it?" Tilly asked when she saw him frown.

"It's from Miss Lily. They saw several cars that didn't belong in town drive by the café ten minutes ago. They took pictures of the license plates and Cody, the deputy sheriff, ran them. They belong to some company and Cody can't find out who owns it."

Another text came through.

"Miss Daisy and Miss Violet are with Pam following them. They're here." Right then, headlights turned into the field and Parker floored the gas. "Hold on!"

The truck bounced along the uneven earth as they flew through the field.

"Where are we going?" Tilly asked, holding on for dear life as he pushed the truck faster than he should.

"Halfway into the woods. Then you're going to jump from the car and hide in the woods. I'll make my way to the cabin and draw their fire while you wait for Pam. Flag her down and have her take you to my parents' house. There's no one I trust more to keep you safe than my dad." Parker reached up and turned off the automatic dome light so no one would see the door open.

"I'm not leaving you!" Tilly's voice rose in fear. As much as Parker wanted to comfort her, he didn't have the time. He needed to keep her alive.

Parker reached across and unfastened her seatbelt. "You have to listen to me right now, Tilly. Get ready. I'm going to slow, then I need you to jump. I can't do my job without knowing you're safe. Now jump!"

Parker slammed on the brakes and Tilly—thankfully—listened. Even with tears running down her face, she opened the door and jumped seconds before the truck speeded back up again. Parker didn't wait to see where she hid. He kept driving.

He made it to the cabin. As he unlocked the door, he heard the SUVs racing down the trail as he grabbed his weapons and ammunition. He shoved ammo in his pockets and slung the rifle over his shoulder. He stepped out onto the small porch and reached up for the overhang. He stepped up on the railing and then pulled himself up onto the roof. The thick stone chimney would be his only protection. He just had to keep them at bay until help arrived. He was sure Miss Lily had already called it in.

Parker saw them enter the clearing. The SUVs spread out. It was a smart move. They could cover more ground that way. Their doors opened and men slid out and into the darkness. Parker wanted to curse when he saw the night-vision goggles. He pressed himself against the chimney and tried to make himself part of the shadows. These men weren't untrained gang members. By the way they moved, the weapons they carried, and the way they positioned themselves, it was clear they were most likely private mercenaries.

Pam's Hummer hadn't flown into the clearing so that had to mean Tilly was safe, and right now that was all that mattered.

"Marshal Davies, we don't want to hurt you. Just turn the girl over and we'll leave," one of the men called out from behind the hood of the front SUV. His accent was barely discernable but it was there. They could be former military from anywhere, but since he didn't speak a lot, Parker couldn't figure out their nationality.

Parker didn't answer. He didn't want to give away his location.

"I'll give you three seconds."

Parker counted them off in his head and at three, every man there opened fire at the cabin. Glass shattered, wood splintered, and Parker used the opportunity to lean around the chimney and fire.

Aim. Breathe. Pull. One.

Aim. Breathe. Pull. Two.

Aim. Breathe. Pull. Three.

But that was all Parker was able to kill before the gunfire was aimed at him. Roof shingles exploded around him. Bullets ricocheted off the chimney and Parker slid off the back of the roof.

Parker softened his knees to absorb the impact as he landed on his feet and took off for the woods. It would be easy to take him down since they had night vision, but it was the risk Parker would have to take. He knew these woods and they didn't. That, at least, gave him a small advantage as he ran between the trees.

Parker heard shouting as he made his way toward the water tower. He heard them saying there was only one person. "Find her!" someone yelled and then Parker heard the SUVs take off.

Parker ran, even as he heard the shots from behind him. Bullets ripped into the trees around him. Bark was sent flying. Leaves rained down on him and small branches were shot off trees. Parker didn't bother slowing down to return fire. He was outnumbered and he had a plan. Instead of his gun, he reached for his phone.

"Call Ryan," Parker ordered his phone.

"Hey, cuz. What's going on?" Ryan's voice came over the phone. "Are those gunshots?"

"Coming in hot through the woods. Three men on my tail. Heavily armed with night vision." Parker was breathing hard. He was almost to Ryan's and needed backup.

"Got it."

Ryan's house was on the other side of the woods. It was over a mile away from the cabin, but Parker had the benefit of knowing this area. He'd grown up running through the woods all over Keeneston. And it wasn't exactly the first time he ran while being shot at.

Finally, he saw the break in the trees. Beyond that was Ryan and Sienna's house. Ryan had probably sent Sienna and their son, Ash, to safety at his parents' house. And if he knew Ryan, the rest of the cousins would be on their way here.

Parker burst forward and into their yard even as bullets slammed into the ground by his feet and ripped through the air by his head.

Woof.

Hooch, Sienna's massive, ugly beast of a dog, was the size of a donkey, had more rolls of wrinkles than you could count, and his large, slobbery jowls flapped in the wind exposing an impressive row of teeth. His feet were the size of horses' hooves. His long tail was thicker than tree limbs and the earth shook with the deep bass of his bark and his thundering gait.

A bulletproof vest emblazoned with *FBI* covered Hooch's chest, back, and sides. The dog thundered past him as Parker leaped over a woodpile and took cover. He pulled the rifle from his back and saw Ryan taking cover behind his FBI cruiser in the driveway. Sienna's car was missing, but their cousin Layne and her husband Walker's, SUV was also in the driveway. Walker, a former Navy Seal, was always helpful in a shootout.

Parker didn't have time to find Walker in the dark when the first man screamed, "*Dios Mio!*" as Hooch's growl echoed off the trees. There was a high-pitched scream that was abruptly cut off, followed by an eerie silence.

Parker scanned the woods for any movement he could see in the dark, but found none. He was about to move toward Ryan when the quiet of the night was thrown off by something. Just a breath, but it was out of place.

Parker scanned with his rifle, and right when it registered with his brain that he'd seen something, a shot rang out. The wood in front of him exploded and Parker felt something strike his eye. As he dropped to the ground, he heard the sound of running feet. He clutched his eye and pulled his service pistol. His left eye had dirt and pieces of bark in it and he couldn't open it without stinging and tears. He was a sitting duck.

Shots erupted around him as he blinked furiously to try to clear his vision. A shadow appeared by him and Parker had only a split second to decide what to do. He didn't have time to ask who it was. Because of that, he didn't want to shoot if it were a cousin. So Parker sprang forward and tackled whoever was near him.

There was a surprised grunt and no laughter, so it definitely wasn't a cousin. Parker closed both eyes and relied on instinct and years of training. His father had always played hide and seek with the kids. However, it was always done in the dark and he'd moved the furniture around so no one knew where anything was. Then paintball became a thing when they were teens and his father was also into that. After making a corn maze course and playing in the pitch dark where he took Parker and his siblings one at a time,

Parker's mom made their father stop playing with them. Instead, he was in charge of creating the courses and determining the winners. Apparently, his father and his spy games had actually taught them something after all because the fear of not having his sight wasn't overwhelming Parker as he threw a punch and jabbed his knee.

The man he was fighting grunted and rolled away. Parker sprang to his feet, hearing the man's heavy breathing. He heard a knife being pulled from its sheath, but the sound of the attack was lost when Ryan's gun fired. A man Parker didn't realize had been behind him fell. That single moment of pause gave the man Parker was fighting a chance to attack. Parker felt the sharp blade slice through his upper arm, but even blind, he knew something had altered the stab.

Grrrr. Grrrr.

What was that? It wasn't loud and it wasn't big, but it was close.

"What the hell, man? Get it off! Get it off!" a man with a slight Spanish accent yelled.

Suddenly water was pouring down onto Parker's face. "Hold still," Ryan ordered. "We got them. Let me clean up your face."

Grrrr. Grrrr.

There was that sound again, but the water felt so good that Parker didn't care what it was even when he heard the laughter among the cursing.

"Your papa will be so proud of you. Yes, he will," Parker heard Walker coo.

Parker wiped his hand over his face and blinked his eyes open. At first the image seemed fuzzy, but he could see a couple of splotches of white that seemed to glow in the low moonlight. But every second the white would disappear and then reappear. Parker blinked his eyes some more and the image became clearer.

A very large man in black fatigues was spinning around and around shoving at his crotch. The man faced him again during his spin and Parker saw why he was shoving at his crotch.

"Get it off! Get it off!" he screamed as he tried to shove Fluffy Puppy off him.

Fluffy Puppy was Layne's little Maltese. He was no more than eight pounds of super-soft, super-long white hair. Long white hair was blowing in the breeze, as if he were a male romance cover model, from being spun around and around. Fluffy Puppy held on to the guy's crotch and growled as if he were playing tug-of-war, completely unaffected by the fact that the only thing under his four fluffy paws was air.

"Man, you got to stop spinning for me to get him off," Walker said, even as he was recording it with his phone. "Your mommy is going to give you a steak. Yes, she is," he baby-talked to the little white ball of fluff swinging from the man's crotch.

Grrr. Grrr.

"FP, leave it," Walker commanded once he got his hands around the little dog.

Grrr. Grrr.

Fluffy Puppy did not release. Instead, he shook his head violently as if he were trying to kill his prey. The man screamed and flailed his arms in distress.

"*I'll do anything, just get him off my dick!*"

"FP," Walker began to say, but Parker stopped him by holding up his hand.

"Who sent you and what are you trying to get?" Parker asked.

"Bradford sent us to rescue his daughter. He said she's in

danger and you were too busy trying to put him in jail to keep his daughter safe."

"Where's Bradford?" Parker demanded.

"I don't know. Once we got his daughter, we were to send an encrypted email and then he'd tell us where to take her. I swear." The man gave a strangled breath when Fluffy Puppy shook his head again. "Please," he whispered, "save my dick."

"Give me your phone and tell me who The Financier is and I'll get the dog off," Parker promised.

The man handed over his phone, but the movement made Fluff think he was still playing Tug so he bit down hard and shook his head.

"He's biting my dick off!" The man's voice hit High C.

"Man, he has like four teeth left," Walker said with a roll of his eyes. "He's only gumming you. You're lucky. Your buddy over there got Hooch."

"Does he still have his dick?"

"Dick, yes," Ryan called out from the tree line. "His throat, not so much."

"I should have asked for more money."

Parker nodded to Walker who had to pry Fluff's mouth from the man's crotch. Parker made sure to video that part. While he was doing that, Ryan pulled Hooch's giant jaws from the other man's throat. The man came to his feet shakily, his face white and neck awash in drool. Two shallow puncture marks on each side of his neck made him look like the middle of a vampire sandwich.

He was muttering in Spanish about *el perro del diablo* as Ryan walked him to the back of his cruiser. Hooch followed happily, trotting along in his FBI vest. Fluffy Puppy had hold of the man's pant leg as Walker marched him toward the cruiser. Fluff just wasn't going to let that man go without a fight.

It was then that Parker could read the tiny bulletproof vest Fluff was wearing.

On one side it read: *My daddy is a . . .*

On the other side of the vest was a cartoon picture of a scary neon green frog sitting on top of the Navy Seals emblem.

"Why does Fluff have a vest?" Parker asked as the little dog renewed his effort to eat the man's ankle.

"Miles gave it to him for Christmas," Walker grumbled.

"Still calling you a froggie, huh?" Parker laughed as he sent a text to his father, letting him know what happened and that several men were still looking for Tilly.

"Well, I gave his dog a shirt that had a cartoon picture of a soldier with loopy eyes and a dopey grin that just *happened* to look like my father-in-law with a caption that said: *Delta Farce*. Hey, did you know you're bleeding?"

"I'll take care of it after we find the other guys."

"Found them!" Ryan called as he looked down at his phone.

21

Tilly didn't think she took a breath until she got into Cy's house and was in Gemma's arms. Not because of the men who were after her, but because of Pam's driving. Dear Lord, that woman would scare the devil.

"Shh, it's okay," Gemma said, holding her as her body shook. "Be thankful it wasn't Kale driving."

"We hit a cow and sent it flying twenty yards when she cut through a field," Tilly whispered. Even with her eyes open she heard the *thunk!* Followed by a *mooooooo*. And then another *thunk* as it landed. "It landed on its feet. I thought only cats did that? Then I swear it flipped us off. I know cows don't have fingers but he raised a hoof and shook it at us."

"Dear, you're going to need a tougher stomach than that if hitting a little cow gets you so upset," Miss Daisy *tsk*-ed.

"One? If only. She hit three more after that. How did you not see that? I don't know how they're alive, but they are. And let's not count the entire section of fencing she took out, some car she shoved out of the way because he was driving too slow, and I'm pretty sure she hit a kid on a bike when she jumped the curb to pass another slow-moving car."

"Bike, yes, but the kid saw her coming and ran for cover. We teach our kids to be proactive about personal safety here. And that person she gently nudged out of the way was driving very slowly. I should know, my husband drives slow." Miss Violet paused. "Come to think of it, that car did look familiar."

The sound of a shotgun being loaded and snapped closed drew Tilly's attention. "Here. Gemma said you were familiar with them. Shoot anyone you don't know that comes through that door." Cy shoved a shotgun at her and handed a bag of shells to Miss Violet. "Well, since you're new here, you may want the ladies to tell you if you should shoot or not."

"I hope you like the shotgun, Tilly," Gemma said with a huge smile as she locked and loaded a rifle. "It's one of my favorites."

"Um, thank you?"

"Pam's in the Hummer, patrolling the road in front of the farm. I'm going to take my position. Don't go near any windows," Cy ordered before looking at Miss Daisy and Miss Violet. "Are you two armed?"

"Of course," Miss Daisy said, looking offended at being asked. She reached up her long sleeve and pulled out a wooden spoon. "I never leave home without it."

"I got it somewhere," Miss Violet muttered as she looked into the deep pit that was her purse. "I can't carry the crepe pan. It's too clunky on the go. Ah, here we go." Miss Violet pulled out a spatula and grinned.

"Good. If you need it, there's a crepe pan in the kitchen." Then Cy was gone. He seemed to just vanish. Tilly blinked and then he wasn't there. It was like magic.

"You think those moves are good, you should see what he can do in the bedroom," Gemma said with a contented sigh.

"Oh, I think it must run in the family. See that silly little grin on her face," Miss Daisy said, pointing the wooden spoon at Tilly.

Tilly didn't speak as the women chatted about recipes, complained about their husbands, and gossiped. Suddenly, they heard the sound of an engine gunning and tires squealing. The women did the exact opposite of what they'd been instructed. Instead of hiding in the house, they raced out the front door and stood out on the porch.

Tilly gasped as Pam's Hummer rammed full speed into the side of a black SUV with its lights off as it was in the process of turning into Cy and Gemma's driveway. Pam's massive grill hit the side of the SUV, sending it rolling backward.

"One, two, three, four," Miss Daisy counted as the car rolled down the street. "Six. Oh, that's a new record for Pam. We'll need to give her a congratulatory piece of bread pudding at the café."

A second SUV came from behind Pam and rammed into the back of her Hummer.

Miss Violet *tsk*-ed. "I always told her she'd take one from behind."

Gemma covered her laugh with a cough, but rapid gunfire covered up Tilly's reaction. She heard bullets hitting the SUV and suddenly the gas tank exploded, sending the SUV's back end over the hood. Pam floored her Hummer and the flaming SUV missed her by inches.

All their phones sounded, but it was Gemma who got to hers first. "A third SUV was captured. Apparently, they thought to cut through a back gate of Desert Sun Farm and the Rahmi soldiers apprehended them. I'll tell them we have two of them here."

It took only a minute but then another text sounded and Tilly saw Gemma's jaw tighten. "Walker is making Parker meet Jace at his office. He says he has a scratch that needs to be cleaned."

"What does that mean?" Tilly asked.

"It means he was stabbed, dear," Miss Daisy said, reading the now flood of incoming texts on the Keeneston tree. "Also, the men said they were sent by your father to take you to him. So far no one knows where they were supposed to take you."

"Give me fifteen seconds and I'll let you know," Cy said, as he strode past them, his rifle at the ready.

"Step back, sonny. I've got this." Miss Violet tapped her spatula against her hand and followed along.

"Like heck. It's my turn to interrogate!" Miss Daisy yelled as she shuffled after them.

Tilly stared after them as her heart stopped. She had too many questions going through her mind at once to be able to say anything. Was Parker alive? Was he badly injured? The men were sent by her father? How did he know where she was? Why were they armed? What would happen to them? What would happen to her? Where was her father?

"You'll get used to it," Gemma said with a fond smile as she looked after the Rose sisters. "So, do you think you'd like a shotgun like this for a shower gift? We could make it the wedding theme—a shotgun wedding! Of course, we aren't forcing Parker down the aisle. He'll happily marry you."

"He's been stabbed? Shouldn't you be freaking out instead of planning a wedding when we're not even engaged yet?"

Gemma's smile widened. "*Yet*, not never. And you

showing concern over a little stabbing tells me just how much you love my son. Okay then, let's get going. You can see for yourself that he's patched up right."

Gemma tugged Tilly's arm toward the back of the house. They entered the garage and Gemma ushered her into an SUV. Because of the number of townsfolk out on the street giving Pam high fives, the fire department putting out the fire, and the community interrogation of the captured mercenaries, Gemma took the back way out of the farm. It didn't take long, but it felt like an eternity to Tilly who tried not to think the worst.

Parker sat on the edge of the examination table as Jace stuck the numbing medicine into his arm. His dad had said Tilly was safe and sound at home and the men had been rounded up and were being interrogated.

"I have to go to Desert Sun when I'm done with you," Jace was saying. "Apparently Pam punted an SUV. There're some broken bones. However, I'm not sure if they were a result of the punt or your father's interrogation."

"Could be either," Parker said, making sure he didn't move his arm as Jace began to clean it. "How bad is it?"

"It's just a scratch like you said. Lots of blood that made it look worse than it is, but it'll heal well." Jace began to hum as he stitched up the wound.

Even from the exam room, Parker heard the front door being thrown open. Jace didn't pay attention as he finished the last stitches. But Parker had his gun drawn and aimed at the door.

Parker heard the first exam room door open and then the doorknob turned in his exam room. Jace continued to hum as he cut the sutures and looked at his work. "Just remember that Stella will kill you if you let someone shoot me," Jace whispered as he went to grab more gauze to clean the blood off the rest of Parker's arm.

The door was flung open and Parker lowered the gun. "Tilly? Are you okay?" Her face was so pale he was worried she'd pass out.

"Parker!" she half gasped and half sobbed. Her hand covered her mouth as she took in his bloody arm, the row of neat stitches, and the pile of blood-covered gauze. "Are you dying? Do you need blood? I'm a universal donor. Jace, take my blood to save him."

Parker blinked as words poured out of her mouth without so much as a pause.

"He's not dying," Jace said kindly, but Tilly paled further.

"He's dying! No!" Tears poured down her face as she ran toward him. "You can't die, Parker. I love you. I love you so much. Please, do whatever it takes to save him."

"Sweetheart," Parker said gently, using his good arm to reach out and cup her cheek. "Look at me, Tilly. Jace said I am *not* dying. It's just a scratch. I'm fine. I promise you. I told you nothing would keep me from you, and I meant it."

Tilly hiccupped. "I thought you just meant keep from having sex with me."

Parker grinned. "Well, that too."

Tilly hiccupped again as tears rolled down her face. "You swear you're not dying?"

"I'll give you two a moment," Jace said, grabbing the pile of bloody gauze and tossing it in the trash away before sneaking out the door and closing it behind him.

"It'll take more than a couple of hired mercenaries to take me out. So, you love me that much, huh?" Parker had never smiled more broadly than he was right now. Earning Tilly's love made him feel like a superhero.

"You know I do! I've loved you from the first time we talked. Oh Parker, tell me the truth, are you badly hurt?" Tilly wrung her hands as if trying not to touch him.

Parker reached out and took her hands in his. He felt the slight tug of the stitches but it wasn't painful. "I'll tell you the truth if you're up to hearing it."

Tilly nodded and then took a deep breath. "Okay. I'm listening."

"I was stabbed. It hurt, but not badly. I'll have a scar, but I have lots, so what's one more? Right now, the only thing I care about is that you love me because, Tilly," Parker paused and waited for her eyes to move from his wound to his face. "I love you, too. More than anything in this world and I'm never letting you walk away from me again. It was torture these past months seeing you, but not being with you. If it means my job, so be it. I can buy back into my brother's farm and work with him. What matters is that you're my heart and I'll never be separated from you again."

Tilly sniffed, but smiled sweetly before swatting his good arm. "Then stop getting stabbed!"

"I can't promise that, but I can promise a kiss will make it all better."

"Is that so?" Tilly leaned forward as Parker raised his lips to hers.

Tilly kissed like the person she was—with pure happiness, love, a little mischievousness, and complete devotion.

"I love you, Tilly," Parker said against her lips as he pulled her between his legs and moved to deepen the kiss.

"Knock, knock!" his mother called out as she opened the door.

"We need a place with lots of locks," Parker whispered with a groan.

"Just wanted to see how you're doing, dear. And to let you know Father Ben is here if you need him." Gemma smiled, but he could tell his mom was upset when she saw the blood and stitches. She did a good job of hiding it, but he saw her hand flex and her jaw tighten before pasting her smile on again. "Are you okay, dear?"

"It was just a little scratch. Nothing too bad. Tilly's taking good care of me." Parker winked up at Tilly who rolled her eyes.

"Good. I'll send Father Ben in, just in case."

His mom gave him a smile, but he stopped her before she left. "Hey, Mom. Thanks for looking out for Tilly. Also, can you tell Dad we'll be staying at my house now? I don't want him charging in after I set off some unknown alarm I'm sure he has rigged somewhere."

"I'll let your father know." His mom stepped forward and Tilly slid to his side as his mother kissed his cheek. "I'm glad you're not hurt. Love you, sweetheart."

"Love you too."

"I hear you've been saying those words a lot." His mother winked at him and spun around to the door. "Father Ben, they're ready for you."

Tilly laughed and Parker shook his head, but that was his mother for you.

After a quick prayer of healing, no wedding date set, and one last exam by Jace, they were on their way to his house on the back of the farm. "It's nothing special, but I like it. It's quiet and has a great view of the rolling Kentucky hills."

Tilly looked up at the house that was a fraction of the size of the houses she grew up in or owned. "I love it. That porch swing has my name written all over it." Parker breathed a sigh of relief. He knew she wouldn't care that it was small, but he wanted to give her the world. "And

Willa's just on the other end of the farm, right?" Tilly asked.

Parker nodded as they walked up to the porch. "About a mile and a half that way," he said, pointing to the dirt road that led straight to Porter's house.

"Willa showed me the plans for her new training arena and house. Where is that in relation to here?"

"Right on the other side of that ridge. Porter and I have cleared a path so you can drive there now."

"I'm so happy for her. She has everything planned out for her future, from her horses to her husband to their children."

"Porter has become insufferably happy since marrying her," Parker joked as he opened the door to his house and turned on the lights. He watched as she took in his living room and open kitchen. It was clean with neutral tones. Paintings by his cousin Tinsley from Shadows Landing hung on the walls.

"Is this you?" Tilly asked as she pointed to a painting of a man on the back of a bronc with his head down and free hand flung up in the air.

"Yes. My cousin Tinsley painted it. It was my last professional ride."

The loss of the rush of adrenaline from riding bulls and broncos didn't hit as hard anymore, but he still felt it.

"It's stunning, Parker."

Tilly turned and looked at him with something new in her eyes. It was as if there'd been a subtle shift since they told each other they were in love. Parker didn't know how to explain it, but it was as if all the barriers he'd put up had crumbled down while knowing Tilly was just as vulnerable. However, in their mutual vulnerability, they found strength. Not the weakness Parker had expected.

Parker reached for Tilly. He had to touch her. He had to feel her. He had to kiss her. She was his heart, his life, his every breath, and job be damned. He'd never give her up. He'd never walk away. Instead, she'd be by his side through thick and thin. Through crimes and kidnappings, through pushy priests and Blossom Café betting. With one look into Tilly's eyes, he saw his future and it was here, with her.

22

When they made love that night it was different. Parker had thought their first time together had been unbeatable. But when he looked down at Tilly and told her again that he loved her a moment before making love to her, it eclipsed their first time together. It was as if the more they shared their feelings, the deeper the physical connection they had during sex.

There had been no holding back and Parker felt as if they'd opened a secret level of sex he'd never known before. He also now fully understood his brother's annoying happiness. As Parker lay in bed that night, holding Tilly as she slept, he was sure there wasn't anything better in the world than this.

His phone buzzed and Parker reached out to see who was calling him this late. Parker slowly eased himself from the bed when he saw the number was Kale's. Naked, he hurried from the bedroom and closed the door behind him. He answered the phone in a whisper as he headed for the living room.

"Yes?"

"Hey, we got something," Kale said without preamble. Straight to the point and Parker appreciated that. "We found out the guys who said they were there to bring Tilly to Bradford were not in fact who they said they were."

"A criminal lying? I'm shocked," Parker deadpanned.

"Yeah, well from their devices we gathered they came from Miami."

"How do you know Bradford didn't send them?" Parker asked

Kale blew out a long-suffering breath. "Your father and my father decided to see if they still had it. They each took a guy to interrogate and somebody set a timer. The good news is they broke them and both got the same information. These men were hired by someone they call The Financier. When pushed, they said he's not famous, but all his friends are."

"The bad news?" Parker asked.

"They don't know or won't give a name."

Tilly woke when she felt Parker slide from bed. She stretched and smiled. Now she knew why it was making love and not just sex. Wow. Her body was still tingling with pleasure.

Tilly's burner phone lit up and she reached for it. Only Parker and Willa had the number, but when she looked at the caller ID it read "Unknown."

The happiness Tilly had felt faded as dread sat like a stone on her stomach. "Hello?"

"Miss Bradford. I'm sorry we didn't get a chance to meet tonight. I was so looking forward to it." The voice was deep and it rubbed her the wrong way. She knew why. This was a person who expected to get exactly what he wanted every time he spoke.

"Who is this?" Tilly asked.

"Someone who wants something from you."

Tilly's mind raced. He could be anyone in any of her father's notes or any rival, but she seemed to know who it was. "You're the Financier." His voice also sounded faintly familiar but she couldn't seem to pinpoint it.

The man chuckled. "That's right. I have your mother. If you want her alive, you will do exactly what I tell you."

"I don't believe you have my mother." Tilly was shaking. Her whole body shook with fear as she looked for a way to warn Parker.

"Here you go." Her phone buzzed with an incoming text message. Tilly's hands trembled as she opened the attachment. It was a picture of her mother tied to a chair with a gag in her mouth. Her eyes were large and tear-stained. Mascara ran down her face making her look wild.

"Tell me what you want me to do."

"Listen closely and start moving before your boyfriend gets back or he'll be killed. I have a sniper in the woods behind the house. Make a wrong move and I'll have him killed. You will sneak out of the house right now and head straight into the woods. My man will pick you up and bring you to me."

"Why? I don't know anything."

"Neither does your mother, but I have the two things that matter most to your father. It's called checkmate. He'll hand over his empire for your return. You have three minutes to get to the woods or my man starts shooting. See you soon."

The line went dead and Tilly pulled up a text message and typed as fast as she could before tossing the phone on the bed. She grabbed her clothes and dressed so fast she didn't care if her shirt was inside out or even if she had her shoes on the correct feet. This was her only option. She had to save her mother, as it was now clear she was not involved in whatever her father was doing. Plus, she had to save Parker. She couldn't let this madman kill him. With a final look around the room, Tilly slipped through the French doors that led to a back patio and into the night.

Parker and Kale went over the information they'd received so far and set up a plan to meet the next afternoon to try a test run of Kale's decoding program. Parker turned off the lights and quietly slipped back into the bedroom so he wouldn't wake Tilly.

He froze as soon as he closed the door. Something wasn't right. Something was missing. Parker flipped the light on and thought his life ended in that split second. Tilly was gone. Her clothes weren't on the chair. Her shoes weren't on the floor. The light to the bathroom wasn't on either, but he turned on the light anyway. All her personal items were still there. Parker pushed down the panic and called her phone.

He heard the vibrating and followed it to the bed. Her phone was lying face down on the bed. Parker picked it up as he ended the call. On the screen was an unsent text message to him.

Financier has my mom. She's innocent. Will kill her and you if I don't come. I'm sorry. I had to go. He's trading us for my father's criminal empire. I'll come back to you. I love you.

Parker was already on his phone. "They have her. Meet me at the security building."

His brother would call everyone. They'd find Tilly. They'd have to or his life was over.

. . .

"Where. Is. He?" Parker slammed his fist into the man's kidney with each word. Anger unlike any he'd ever experienced coursed through him. His mother hadn't been able to stop him. His father hadn't tried. His brother was standing next to him.

"Nowhere you'll find him."

Parker turned his back to the man. He knew something. Parker had gone through every man throughout the night. They knew nothing. But this one . . . this one knew and Parker wouldn't stop until he discovered what it was.

"Parker," Porter said softly. "Let Ahmed at him."

"No. He already had his chance. Is Aunt Annie here?"

"Yes. Everyone is here."

"Watch him."

Parker walked from the room and found everyone watching the interrogation on the big screen. He didn't pay attention to anyone in the room except for his aunt who had been an undercover agent with the DEA and he was pretty sure she still freelanced with them.

"I've heard stories about your interrogations."

Annie's red hair was up in a ponytail. She, like everyone there, had thrown on jeans and a T-shirt and raced over to the farm as soon as word was out that Tilly was gone. "I have my things in the car. I'll be right back."

"Babe, have you been interrogating people without telling me again?" Uncle Cade asked his wife.

"How was your guys' trip last month?" Annie asked instead of answering.

"Um, good talk. Get to it then."

"How is the decoding going?" Parker asked Kale.

"Partial at best. Here's what I got so far." Kale turned

toward the printer and Grandma Marcy stood, holding out the papers.

"It's not much, dear."

"Thanks, Mrs. Davies."

"I'm sure you'll get it. You're such a smart young man." Grandma Marcy patted his cheek before taking a seat next to Kale's desk.

"Here's what I got so far. But like your grandma said, it's not much." Kale looked as if he hadn't slept in days. Knowing how his friend got when on a project, he probably hadn't.

"I brought knives and food." Landon walked in carrying a basket of food in one hand and a leather-bound knife set in the other. "Which do you want first?"

"Knives!" Annie called out. "Let's see how good you are with those." Annie took Landon's arm and nodded at Parker. "Come on. Let's have a little chat with this guy."

Marcy Davies might look serene on the outside, but on the inside she was madder than the proverbial wet hen. No one, absolutely *no one*, could come into her town and mess up a wedding and potential great-grandbabies and live to tell about it.

Everything had been going according to plan. Everything. The sheer number of apple pies that went into this task still had her hands hurting. Then there were the favors, the digging, and making sure the right people were in the right places at the right time and this little asshole went and messed it up. Well, there was still one pie left and she'd use it.

Marcy glanced around and saw Kale disappear down the

hallway after his father and made her move. She'd taken computer lessons from a teen who was forced to have volunteer hours at the senior citizens center in Lexington for just this reason. Marcy took a seat at Kale's computer and got to work.

Still chasing after me I see? The dark web message from Panther said when it popped up.

Marcy: *I need a favor.*

Panther: *The mighty hacker needs a favor? I'm dying with anticipation.*

Marcy: *I'm not the person you think I am.*

Panther: *Well, this is certainly interesting. Did you kill him?*

Marcy: *No. I'm borrowing his computer. We have a crisis here and you're the only person who can help.*

Panther: *Why should I help you?*

Marcy: *How was the apple pie?*

Panther: *Look, I don't know who you are or how you found me and because you did, I've had to move again. But that apple pie was worth it. What do you need? I'm not promising anything and I'll only hear you out once, so it better be worth it.*

Marcy: *Someone named Financier has kidnapped someone important to me and I want her back.*

Panther: *Tilly Bradford?*

Marcy: *Yes. Can you help?*

Marcy waited. The Panther wasn't writing back. Marcy glanced at the door, but so far Kale wasn't heading back into the room. She gave Lily, Daisy, and Violet a look and they nodded in return. They'd delay Kale if he came back too soon.

. . .

Panther: *I owe Bradford. I'll help you find his daughter and you let him know we're even. Besides, The Financier is a business rival, or at least he thinks he is. His name is Guy Fausto. I have to know. How did you find me?*

Marcy: *Thank you for your help. If you ever decide to stop your criminal activities, let me know. There'll be an apple pie in it for you.*

Panther: *Wait. Who are you?*

Miss Lily dropped her broom in warning and Marcy closed the chat. She shoved away from the desk and slowly ambled away as Kale came into the room. In the back of the room, Knox and Holt Everett were talking to Cassidy. The desire to get that situation sorted out was pushed aside by the current situation.

Instead, Marcy turned to Trey and Taylor Everett. "Oh, isn't this situation horrible?"

"It sure it, Mrs. Davies," Taylor said, her voice full of worry. "I wish there was something more I could do. I know the guy has to be in my circle of acquaintances, but no one is talking."

Marcy made the appropriate noises and nodded her head. "You know, I was thinking about that. He has to be very popular to be known in movies, music, and sports. There can't be that many people who crossover into all three worlds. And with an ego like that, I'm sure he's in all the event photos like that one well-dressed *Guy*. Well, it's been a long night. I need to sit down."

It wouldn't take them long to connect the dots and for Tilly to be rescued. Damn Guy. She's produced all the evidence, all the clues, and all the documents and put them together so that Tilly was cleared of any of her father's mess when Guy went and messed it all up.

"You have that look, Marcy. What are you going to do?" Miss Lily asked.

Marcy narrowed her eyes. "No one messes with my future great-grandchild and prevents me from dying happy and gets away with it."

23

Tilly had been handcuffed the second she'd walked past the first tree in the woods. A hood had been tossed over her head and she'd been pulled down a rough path. She'd then been hauled into a vehicle before being put on a helicopter, followed by a plane.

Then she'd been put back on a helicopter before being stuffed into a large piece of luggage and carried to where she was now. She'd been stoic through it all. Tilly refused to show fear, refused to cry, and refused to beg. If this was what she had to do to protect Parker and her mother, she'd do it.

Tilly refused to think about the consequences for her father. Right now, she was still too emotionally conflicted to process the decades of love with the decade of criminal deceit. She was only focused on saving Parker and her mother.

The trunk she was being carried in was dropped unceremoniously, unlocked, and the lid opened. Tilly blinked up at the face of the man pointing a gun at her, but it was the room that drew her attention. She knew exactly where she was. She was in a room that held very bad memories for her. She was in a mansion on a small private island on the south shore of Long Island, right by the ritzy Hamptons.

Six years ago, she'd been invited to a party here along with Willa, Callum, Marguerite, and more socialites, actors, sports figures, and models than you could count. It was a charity event, ostensibly hosted by a relatively unknown young actor named Mason Hemming. He had just won the title role in an action movie series and then got a DUI. He became the new face of this charity strictly for PR purposes and was using the fundraiser to show that he was really a good guy who'd made one teeny mistake so the studio wouldn't dump him.

Tilly and Willa had gone together to Guy Fausto's mansion for that charity event. Guy had been in his late forties at the time. He was handsome, outgoing, and well known for helping struggling professionals get their big breaks. He had spoken about how great Mason was and how important his work was and that's why Guy had offered to host the fundraiser at his famous island home. Mason's face was all over the news but not for the DUI.

Guy's home was unforgettable. It was modeled after the Newport mansions of the Gilded Age, but with a modern twist. The best of the best and latest technologies hid among the antiques. Guy was known for his exclusive parties and everyone who was anyone attended them.

At one point during the party Tilly attended there, Guy had interrupted Willa and Tilly's conversation. He told her a friend of Tilly's father wanted to speak with her. Guy had led her into this very room where a man far older than her father waited for her. She'd never met him before, but Guy told her that he was a special friend of his and a very important potential business partner to her father. Guy told her that if she wanted this big deal to go through, then she needed to impress this man.

Tilly smiled with the practiced poise of a debutante and hadn't noticed that Guy locked her in the room alone with the man. They had talked pleasantly for a couple of minutes before Tilly got the creepy crawlies. There hadn't been anything specific that he'd done or said that had triggered that reaction women got when they realized something just wasn't right. Tilly smiled politely when he'd reached out and touched her arm, but she'd taken a step back to pretend to look at a painting. The man advanced. She retreated. Because of years of having proper manners drilled into her, Tilly never once said to leave her alone. Ladies were always polite. Ladies always smiled. Ladies always made other people feel at ease. Well, Tilly had not been at ease. Every instinct had screamed at her to *run*.

"Oh goodness," Tilly had said, pulling her phone out of her purse and sending a secret SOS to Willa. "I just have to see who painted this. Are you a collector?"

He'd stalked her around the room. The pretense was gone. He was bigger, and he thought because he had a dick he could take anything he wanted. Tilly rebuffed him politely. She'd struggled to find the words to get him to back off. She'd darted around the silk couch as he told her what he was going to do to her on it. She'd grabbed a silver candlestick to defend herself as he'd laughed and said it turned him on when they fought. The hunt made the kill worth it. Tilly had been frozen with fear as he prowled around her, teasing her, playing with her as if she were already dead but didn't know it.

He had maneuvered her into a corner when there was a knock on the door and the doorknob rattled. "Tilly!" Willa called out. "We have to go. Your mom is in the hospital. They called me when you didn't answer your phone."

The man's face grew tight with anger as he glanced between Tilly and the door. Willa was doing a good job of making him believe it was an emergency. "Tilly, why is the door locked. Where's the key?"

"Yes, it's stuck. We've been trapped in here," the man had answered smoothly as if he hadn't just threatened her for the past ten minutes.

"Guy! The door is stuck and people are trapped inside!" Tilly could hear Willa's voice rise above the music and the conversation.

"I'll save her!" Mason Hemming shouted a moment before he put his shoulder to the door and busted it open.

Willa had taken one look at Tilly's ashen face and rushed her from the room. That was the last time Tilly had seen Guy or this room. She'd declined all subsequent invitations as politely as possible until they just dried up. Apparently Guy was now demanding her presence. Well, she wasn't a shy young woman unsure of her place in the world anymore. She had purpose. She had friends. She had love. She had support and she'd killed a dummy with a spoon, darn it. She was woman and by God, she was ready to roar.

"We know who it is!" Holt Everett called out as he and his family rushed into the interrogation room.

"Are you sure?" Annie asked. "We're about to get to the fun part."

"We're sure," Knox said.

Parker, Landon, and Annie followed them out into the

hall where the Everett family was practically bouncing. "It's Guy Fausto," Taylor said the second the door was closed. "He's the only one who crosses all entertainment fields and has the wealth, power, and ego to make dreams come true, for the right price."

"Who's Guy Fausto?" Landon asked.

"Technically he's a financial consultant, but that's just a fancy term for con artist," Kale said, joining them. "He inherited some money after his parents died and invested it. He started calling himself an investment banker. Using a couple of rich friends of his parents as a way to get into the elite clubs in New York and Los Angeles, he began offering to invest celebrity money. There have been some lawsuits that were sealed, but it looked like those investments were Ponzi schemes and he used the money gathered to invest in real estate and movies, thus getting closer to even more rich and famous people. But I'm at a loss on his dealings with Bradford. There's pictures of Guy with Bradford and hundreds of rich and famous people, but I can't find a business connection yet."

"Well, let's go ask him. Where is he?"

"He owns a private island right outside the Hamptons," Kale replied. "Also, I found Bradford's satellite phone number. It took a lot of hacking, but I got it." Kale handed Parker a piece of paper with the digits written on it.

"Did you say Guy Fausto?" Willa asked as she ran toward them. "Parker, there's something you need to know about him."

Parker listened to a story about a party at his house where he locked Tilly in a room with a man who was making very aggressive, very unwanted advances on her. After he found Tilly, he'd take care of whoever that asshole was.

Taylor nodded her head. "Several of my young actresses have mentioned similar things happening, but it wasn't Guy's name they said. It was directors or producers or big celebrities who approached them at the parties Guy hosted. Guy was never blamed for it."

The crowd was growing and Sydney was nibbling on her lip. "Give me a minute." Sydney made a call and then turned back to them. "Skye Jessamine said the same thing. He promised to introduce her to all the right people. And he did. However, one of them did the typical asshole casting-couch thing. Skye didn't connect it to Guy, but the introduction was made by Guy and the implication was that this director could make or break her. What the director didn't know was she'd already landed another role and was going to the audition solely as a courtesy."

"Take my plane," Sebastian said. "I know Guy. I'm ashamed I didn't think of him in the first place. He's a big supporter of the arts. Most people sing his praises. There have been some grumblings about inappropriate behavior, but like you all said, it wasn't him but his connections who were inappropriate. The nickname, though, I should have put it together. He loves being the one to pull someone from the masses and make them famous. He gets off having Hollywood's top actors thanking him at award shows. And it's not just actors. It's musicians, models, sports stars, politicians . . . anyone who is a public figure."

"Thank you," Parker said to Sebastian. The man was more upset than he'd seen him since Greer had been hurt. It was clear that while Sebastian liked to be tough, he cared about people underneath it all.

"Let's go," Willa said, grabbing a gun from the armory.

"I'll call you when I have her," Parker promised.

"Like hell. She's my best friend. There's no way you're going without me."

"Porter," Parker began to say when Willa narrowed her eyes at him.

"He doesn't have a say in this. I'm going. With or without you."

"You can't—" Parker began to say.

"Gemma, I think I'll have my tubes tied," Willa said sweetly.

There was the sound of a shotgun being taken off the rack and Parker turned to see his mother and father armed. "We're all going."

"I don't think I can fit the entire town on my plane," Sebastian said slowly.

Parker shook his head but felt the support. He loved his family and his town. "Let me do this my way. Please. I have a plan."

He was surprised when his family backed down. He told them his plan, got the weapons he needed, and then they were gone. He didn't have a minute to waste. It had been fifty-one minutes since Tilly had been taken and he needed to move.

24

Tilly had been kept waiting for what she thought was at least an hour if not more. She was still handcuffed but was now sitting on the silk couch she'd once been told she'd be raped on. Across from her was the same gunman who simply stared at her. He didn't speak and neither did she. Instead, she sat with her ankles crossed, her handcuffed hands resting on her knees and looking off at the priceless art with a carefully blank expression on her face.

Finally, the door opened and a smiling Guy Fausto strode in as if he were welcoming her to a friendly visit. "Matilda Bradford. It's such a pleasure to see you again. You've been very busy these past years. Too busy to come to any of my parties. You've been missed."

Tilly pasted on the perfect socialite smile as Guy bent and kissed each of her cheeks. "Guy, still hospitable as ever. I'm sorry that it was such a blow to your ego to realize that I don't give a shit who you are or who your friends are and wouldn't bother coming to any more of your horrible parties. But it was such fun to watch you try to buy popularity. We all got a good chuckle about it."

Guy's smile fell as he towered over Tilly, but she refused to shrink back. Six years ago, she'd been too timid to say or do anything. Even a year ago she would have been. However, Parker changed that. His family changed that. She wasn't a timid, shy little girl anymore. She wasn't weak. She was strong, smart, and a woman who had something worth fighting for—love.

"Now, what am I doing here? I see you need someone else to help you, again. You couldn't just find my father?" Tilly rolled her eyes and could hear the anger in the way Guy ground his teeth together.

"I don't need anyone's help."

Tilly blinked. "Really? Then why are my mother and I visiting you right now?" Tilly waited for a second and when he didn't answer she huffed, "If Mother is even here."

Guy jerked his chin to the gunman, who left the room. Tilly put her best bored face on as she looked at her nails. Just because she was something other than another spoiled socialite didn't mean she didn't know how to play one. And that was exactly what she was going to do because then Guy wouldn't think twice about leaving them alone again. Plus, it would buy her time to think and plan an escape.

The door opened and her mother was shoved into the room. Tilly wanted to race to her and shove the asshole who was manhandling her, but she didn't. Instead, she stood and in her best stiff-upper-lip way, smiled and said, "Hello, Mummy. I see Guy's hospitality hasn't improved over time. You're lucky you missed his parties. He never knew how to treat his guests."

Shock registered on her mother's mascara-smeared face before she, too, carefully disguised her feelings behind a mask of cool indifference. She'd tried to teach Tilly the old ways of cool sophistication, but that had never been Tilly.

She was warm and caring. Not disconnected from people and their feelings.

"Come, Mummy," Tilly said, patting the sofa next to her. She turned to Guy and with a look of pure snobbery said, "I don't suppose you have any good tea?"

"Of course, I have good tea," Guy ground out.

"Oh," Tilly said, sounding surprised. "Excellent. We'll both take a cup. Sugar and milk, too, thank you. Now if you'll give us a minute to have our tea and catch up, we'll be right with you."

"You're kicking me out of my room?" Guy laughed.

Tilly blinked innocently as if she couldn't understand the issue. "Yes, I am. If you want our cooperation—and trust me, you'll need it to get to my father—we require a moment to chat and some hot tea to calm me after that manhandling of a welcome your man gave me."

Tilly sat back down and her mother silently sat next to her, staring at her as if she had two heads.

"Fine, ten minutes," Guy said before nodding to the sniper to get their tea.

The second the door closed Tilly threw her cuffed arms around her mother. "Are you all right? Did he hurt you?"

"Me? Who are you and what have you done to my daughter?" Celina Bradford asked in wonder.

"I've fallen in love, learned how to kill someone with a spoon, and am ready to break us out of here."

If her mother had been Gemma, she'd be asking about a wedding by now. The thought made Tilly smile as she glanced around. There were windows, but they were too high up to jump out.

"Did you hit your head?" her mother asked instead. "Oh no. Please tell me you didn't fall in love with Callum and he hit you on the head. Your father has had him in mind for you as a husband since you were five. That idiot boy is a twat and I refuse to let you marry him."

"Wait, you don't like Callum? Then why did you push me to be friends with that group?"

Her mother shrugged. "They're good society. That doesn't mean I want you to marry him. I always thought you'd do well for royalty. You'd be the next Kate Middleton - a royal duchess and princess, eventually." Celina got a dreamy look in her eyes that Tilly needed to clear up right away.

"I fell in love with Parker Davies. He's a US Marshal and also the reason I'll be able to get us out of here." Tilly dropped her voice as the door opened and the gunman came in pushing a tea tray. The image almost made Tilly laugh. "Thank you, Sniper. You can leave us now."

"Sniper?" he asked in a deep voice, sounding a bit surprised. It was actually only the fourth word he'd ever spoken.

"What else am I to call you? You haven't introduced yourself or been particularly chatty. What should I call you then?"

"Sniper is good."

Then he turned around and left.

"Exactly how are you going to save us with a tea service?" her mother asked.

"You'll see," Tilly said with a smile as she got to work fixing her tea.

∾

Parker grabbed one of Dylan's satellite phones along with a duffle bag full of weapons. Dylan was upset he couldn't go with him, but Abby was due soon and Ahmed would kill him if he weren't there for it. Well, after Abby killed him for leaving her behind.

"Have you notified the US Marshals in New York City?" Ryan asked from the seat across from Parker on Sebastian's private jet.

"Yeah. You get in touch with the FBI?"

Ryan nodded. "Got us all cleared to work with you on the capture instead of the local office. However, they insist on being present. They'll be at the airport to hammer out the details."

"The Marshals weren't as understanding," Parker told him. "They didn't like that I was bringing my own FBI Hostage Rescue team with me. They're also meeting me at the airport where we'll be able to waste hours in a jurisdictional pissing contest."

"Don't worry about that," Greer said calmly. "You all just go get Tilly and her mother and I'll take care of the rest." The benefits of having a cousin who worked for the president and ran a secret black ops group just kept getting better and better. Unfortunately, said black ops group was in the rebuilding phase since Abby was out on maternity leave. However, that didn't hinder Greer's ability to get things done. And in this case, she would cut all that bureaucratic red tape with one glare.

Parker didn't listen to their exchange when he saw Theodore Bradford's satellite phone number pop up on his phone. "Bradford. This is Davies."

"I got your text about my wife and daughter." The man sounded distraught. Good, he should be. He had put them in danger. "Who has them? What do you need me to do?"

"Are you willing to turn yourself in?"

"Will it save my family?" Bradford asked.

"Depends on where you are right now."

"New York City," Bradford said after a pause.

"Then yes, it will. I'm going to use you as a distraction to rescue your family."

"Who has them if not you?"

Parker let out a sigh. "Look, Bradford. I'm going to be honest. I love your daughter and I am going to marry her if she says yes. For Tilly's sake, I'm going to say this one time. You need to call an attorney named Isabelle Perez in Miami right now. Then you need her to call my boss to tell him that you'll testify against every single person you gave money to and get the best deal you can. Isabelle has his number. Once that's signed and in place, I'll tell you everything so you can help me save your wife and daughter."

"I need my books."

"We have them."

"Both of them?" Bradford asked.

"Yes. And we've been able to partially decode them as well. However, the cipher would be handy. I'm assuming the Panther helped you with it."

"How did you know that? And we still need to discuss your marrying my daughter."

"In New York. Now, call Isabelle and then call me back when it's all done. Tell her she has forty-three minutes to get this deal done."

Parker hung up, closed his eyes. "So, you're going to marry Tilly." Parker could hear the smile in Ryan's voice as suddenly every cell phone on the plane went bonkers with bets being placed on the Blossom Café Betting App. Yeah, maybe Parker should have talked to Bradford in private, but he wasn't ashamed of his feelings. He was going to marry Tilly and he'd be damned if he let Guy hurt one hair on her head and live.

. . .

It only took Isabelle twenty-seven minutes to work out a deal. When Bradford called back, Isabelle was on the call, too. "Hello, Marshal Davies. I hear a wedding may be in your future and that I have you to thank for another client."

"What can I say? I like you, Ms. Perez. Now, what were you able to get done?"

"Just tell my client when and where to meet you and he will turn himself over to you and you alone. After you save his wife and daughter, my client will turn the cipher over to you and testify about every single criminal and criminal organization he has worked with, but with one exception."

"Which is?" Parker asked.

"The Panther. He will not testify or give any information regarding that person. For that and for his role in funding organized crime, he's agreed to spend five years in a minimum-security federal prison, with the possibility of parole after three years. The deal has been signed by all parties and I've emailed you a copy. I believe my part in this is done. I expect a wedding invitation," Isabelle said before saying her goodbyes and disconnecting from the call.

"Who has my wife and daughter?" Bradford asked when Isabelle hung up.

"There's going to be a jurisdictional showdown at the airport. I'll fill you in at SA Tech's headquarters. Meet me in the lobby in thirty minutes."

"SA Tech? What does Sebastian Abel have to do with this?"

"He's my cousin-in-law and I'm using his plane. I assume you know the place?"

"I know it. I'll see you there, Davies. And I haven't forgotten that you want to marry my daughter."

"And I haven't forgotten she wouldn't be in danger if not for your criminal activities."

Parker hung up and saw Jackson, the middle sibling between Ryan and Greer, shaking his head. He was in charge of his FBI Hostage Rescue team. Talon and Lucas, the other members of the team, were shaking their heads, too.

"What?" Parker asked.

"Way to get in with your father-in-law," Jackson said with a snicker.

"Yeah, well, I think the fact I'm putting him in jail is already a strike against me. I'm not going to be buddy-buddy with him when he's the reason the woman I love is in danger."

"Still, he's going to get out and then you'll have an old man who's been in the slammer learning how to make shivs at your Christmas dinner," Talon said.

"First, I rescue Tilly and her mother. Then I'll work on getting on his good side if he holds up his end of the bargain. Really, you think they make shivs in a country club prison?"

"That sounds reasonable," Lucas said. "Of course, where I'm from we just strip down, cut through the ice, and jump in the water. Whoever lasts the longest is the winner and then you're too damn cold to continue fighting."

"Northern Alaska is a very interesting place," Parker said, trying not to laugh. The man's best friend was a polar bear named Bertha. So freezing your nuts off to determine the winner of an argument didn't seem like a far stretch.

"Oh, look. They're waiting with their lights on," Greer said as she looked out the window. The plane was about to touch down. When Parker looked out he saw more black SUVs with flashing lights than he could count. "There are the Marshals. They're the ones in the jeans. Then over there's the FBI. They're the ones dressed like morticians."

Ryan looked down at himself in jeans, cowboy boots, and a blue shirt with Keeneston High School Football written across it in white. "I guess I should have put on my uniform."

"Oh, goodie," Greer said with a smirk. "That SUV is Homeland and the other is the Department of Justice. The DOJ is the Marshals' daddy agency."

"Sweetheart," Sebastian said as they landed. "Play nice."

"Like you're playing nice in that corporate takeover you're working on?"

"Point taken. Have fun annihilating them. It is very sexy when you make federal agents cry."

Greer turned to Parker with a big smile. "I'll go out first. As soon as you see me call them all around, I want you to walk straight for the SUV nearest the exit and go. Don't stop if they call you. Don't even acknowledge them. Sebastian will escort you to his building and I'll meet you there when you're all done. Don't wait for me. Rescue Tilly the second you can."

"Thank you, Greer," Parker said to his cousin. He'd remembered not that long ago when she's felt adrift in her life, not wanting to stay in the FBI but not knowing what to do instead. Now she had fully come into herself working directly for the president and running his black ops group while happily married to one of the richest, powerful, and ruthless businessmen in the world—who just happened to be a big teddy bear for Greer.

25

Theodore Bradford was everything Parker had expected. He sat in the lobby of SA Tech as if he owned it and wasn't a criminal on the run. He wore a three-piece suit and a bow tie. His loafers were Italian leather and handmade. The only things that stood out were the fine lines around his lips where he was pressing them together with worry.

"Bradford. I'm US Marshal Parker Davies." Parker said, looking down at the man sitting in the chair.

Bradford stood and looked way up into Parker's face, but he didn't flinch back at the cold stare Parker gave him. Instead, he held out his hand. "So, you're going to be my son-in-law."

"Sorry it's not that jackass Callum, but I at least love your daughter."

"I guessed that when you gave me Isabelle's information." Bradford turned and shook Sebastian's hand next. "Sebastian. It's good to see you again."

"Bradford," was all Sebastian said before turning to Parker. "Call me if you need anything. My plane is at your disposal."

"Thank you." When Sebastian walked away, Parker turned to Ryan, Jackson, Talon, and Lucas to introduce them to Bradford.

"FBI? I thought you were a Marshal?" Bradford asked, looking around to see if Marshals were about to pop out and surround them.

"I am. Ryan is the head of the Lexington FBI office and my cousin. Jackson is his brother and the leader of HRT. Their sister, Greer, is married to Sebastian Abel."

Bradford's eyebrows rose. "Well, this certainly isn't the family I saw my little girl marrying into, but at least she'll be safe."

"No thanks to you." Parker couldn't stop the snide remark from coming out.

Bradford seemed to deflate in front of him. "You're right. I should have just sold an estate and cut back on spending, but I didn't. I didn't mean to become what I am. I thought I could just do it once, but the money was so good I kept coming back, and now, here we are. Now, who has my daughter?"

"Guy Fausto," Parker said. He understood how Bradford got into this position. Corruption, crime, and addiction always start with giving in only one time. Then just one more time, and then again, and again until you were fully corrupt, a criminal, or an addict. But no matter how it came to be, it was still illegal.

"That bastard. I knew it had to be him. He's wanted everything I have since I met him. He hit on my wife, hit on my daughter, stole my chef, my secretary, the list goes on. I continued to work with him because the money was so good. He brought in A-list clients who were more than happy to keep coming back to him, but he's an illusion. He doesn't have the money, he gets it from me. Now he's looking to cut me out, take my money, my system, and my family. What do you want me to do?" Bradford asked.

"I want you to knock on his front door, punch him in the face, and get him talking. You'll be wearing a wire and I want an airtight confession from him."

"What will you be doing while I do your job for you?"

Parker smirked, but it wasn't a funny smirk. It was the kind that made Bradford take a step back with fear. "I'll be saving your family." Parker towered over Bradford using the full force of his height and strength to intimidate him. "Remember this: I love your daughter. I don't love you. You turn on us and I'll kill you and Guy without thinking twice about it."

Bradford gulped, but nodded. "I'll do anything to save my daughter. But that doesn't mean I'll approve of your marriage. She deserves better."

"Maybe, but she deserves love and I can give her that. Now, let's get you wired up."

Tilly held the bowl of the spoon to the edge of a granite-topped table and then smashed her shoe down on the handle. The silver snapped and Tilly smiled triumphantly. The tea was hot, the spoon was now sharp, and a heavy candlestick was now resting between the silk cushions.

"What are you going to do with that?" her mother asked as if it weren't obvious.

"I'm going to kill the next man who comes into this room," Tilly said with a smile as she palmed the spoon and sat down next to her mother. "You hit them with the candlestick if I miss."

"I will do no such thing."

Tilly turned to her mother with disbelief. "Do you want to die? Because you have to know that's what Guy is going to do. He's going to kill us, Mother. Otherwise, he would have stayed hidden and never let us know that he was behind our abductions. He's going to use us to get Dad here and then kill all of us after getting the information he needs."

Deep from within the house the doorbell rang. Tilly looked at her mother and then to the door. Footsteps were coming down the long hallway. Tilly tightened her grip on her sterling silver shiv and waited.

Parker heard Bradford's conversation with Guy through the earpiece he wore as he, Ryan, Jackson, Talon, and Lucas crawled silently from the water at the back of the island. Bradford had driven the boat and dropped them near the back before docking and boldly walking up to the front door.

"I heard you've been looking for me," Bradford said as Parker slipped up to the back door of the mansion. Jackson, Lucas, and Talon had silently split off into the night. Ryan was by Parker's side as he kept an eye on his cell phone.

"Okay," Ryan whispered into his coms. "Security system is offline. Go."

Parker silently thanked Kale as he jimmied the lock and opened the French doors. Together, they silently slid into a dark library.

"Where are my girls?" Bradford was asking Guy.

"Just having some tea in the upstairs salon. Why don't we go to my office and talk business?" It was stated as an order instead of a question.

"We need to move," Ryan whispered as they hurried from the room and into a hall. "Where's the salon?"

"I see them," Talon whispered in his slight Aussie accent. "Third floor, north corner room. I have eyes. They're sitting on a couch in the middle of the room. The door just opened and an armed man is now in the room, but I don't have a shot. The women are in the way."

"Going up the south stairwell," Jackson's voice was clear but quiet.

"I'm covering the second floor," Lucas's voice came through softly.

"Heading up the north stairwell," Parker told them.

"You and Jackson get Tilly and her mother. I'll stay here and keep the exit clear," Ryan whispered.

Parker nodded and raced up the stairs without making a sound. Every lesson his father had ever taught him surged forward on its own. It was as if spy muscle memory was a thing as his footfalls became silent, his hand didn't shake on the trigger, his breathing was slow and steady, and the fear he had was shoved aside and used to fuel him instead of hinder him.

"At the third-floor stairwell door," Jackson whispered into the comms.

"Moving into position," Parker answered as he reached out with his left hand to take hold of the doorknob. "Ready."

"Go," Jackson answered as Bradford continued to gather all the evidence Parker would need to take Guy down.

"Damn," Lucas whispered. "We have hostiles on the second floor. Five men, armed, just ran out of a room for the north stairwell. You have fifteen seconds."

Tilly knew something was happening. Sniper put his finger to his ear and then his eyes went straight to hers. Tilly tried not to react as she kept the bored debutante look on her face.

"Go close the drapes," Sniper ordered her.

Tilly sighed audibly and stood. When she walked toward the main bank of windows, she let the spoon handle drop from her sleeve and into her hand. She approached the window with trepidation. Something or someone was out there. She just didn't know if it was good or bad. Would Parker have already found her?

The second Tilly closed the drapes, Sniper made his move. He was behind her with his forearm across her throat and the gun to her head before she had time to turn around.

"Don't make a sound," he whispered in her ear as he marched her toward her mother. He stopped when they were facing the door and shoved Tilly down onto the couch next to her mother.

Suddenly gunshots erupted and fear unlike anything Tilly had ever known filled her. Had they just killed her rescue? Her love? Her Parker?

26

Parker and Jackson moved as one. Their parents had been training them together since they were children. At the time, they had thought they were just funny games to play but no matter which cousin Parker was partnered with, they all moved the same. They all knew the hand signals. They all knew the different attack strategies. And they all knew how to put ego aside and do what needed to be done. Which was exactly why Parker fell to back up Jackson as he began to issue orders for when they entered the hall.

They met at the door leading to the room that held Tilly and her mother. Two large marble statues of naked women sat on each side of the door.

"Use them for cover. High or low?" Jackson whispered.

"Low," Parker said, not needing Jackson to explain what he meant. Parker dropped to his knee and aimed for the stairwell door.

Jackson was behind him standing with his gun aimed as they both leaned around the statue. "We take out the backup and then bust in. It's no longer a surprise. You go in low. I'll go in high. Take any shot you have."

"Got it." Parker aimed and waited.

He didn't have to wait long. The door was thrown open and the men came out in a two-by-two formation. Jackson fired at the same time Parker did and the men dropped.

"Incoming up the south stairwell," Parker heard Lucas calmly say over the comms.

"Clear the second floor and follow them so we can trap them," Jackson ordered.

"You got it," Lucas said before comms went silent.

Parker waited; his gun unwavering. He listened to Bradford's voice rise. He heard Guy Fausto spill all the information and evidence they would need to put him in jail forever. But then Bradford's conversation suddenly stopped after the sound of a gunshot. "Ryan, get Fausto," Parker spoke as the door handle at the stairwell began to slowly turn.

"On it," Ryan replied.

Parker pushed down the fear and adrenaline racing through his body as they shifted cover to the south. His eyes didn't leave the stairwell door as his finger gently rested on the trigger. He slowed his breathing and then he was firing as masked men with assault rifles raced through the door.

Tilly's eyes didn't leave the door when the shots started, so she was caught off guard when Sniper grabbed her by the hair and yanked her off the couch. Her mother screamed and lunged for her, but Sniper kicked her in the chest, sending her sprawling backward.

"Come here," he growled as pain ripped through her scalp.

Tilly scrambled on her hands and knees as he positioned himself with both women in front of him. Her mother was sobbing on the couch to his left. Tilly was at his feet with a gun to her head and his hand in her hair.

Tears streamed down her cheeks as the shooting continued outside the door. Her brain didn't know who was out there, but her heart did. Parker had come for her.

"Get up," the man ordered as he yanked her head upward to force her onto her knees and then to her feet a moment before the door was kicked in.

"Parker!" Tilly shouted the second she saw the two men in head-to-toe black and gray camouflage. It was as if she knew instantly which one was Parker. The trouble was Parker and whoever the other man was were sitting ducks as the door framed them. They had no cover to hide behind, but they didn't seem too worried as they kept their weapons aimed right at her because Sniper was using her as a human shield.

"It's okay, sweetheart. Don't worry." Parker's eyes never left the point over her shoulder where Sniper's head was. "Let them go and we'll let you walk out of here, which is more than we did for your backup."

"Like hell you will."

"Sweetheart, do you remember family dinner?" Parker asked. Tilly gulped in a breath and focused on his words. Family dinner? What was he getting at?

"What does family dinner have to do with anything? Drop your weapons and get out or I'll kill you both and then her," Sniper ordered.

"Layne just loved you and I can't wait for her to see you again," Parker said, ignoring Sniper.

Tilly felt her brows furrow, but then reality came snapping back into hyperfocus. Parker had spotted the silver spoon handle in her hand. Tilly tightened her grip on it. She kept her eyes on Parker, and when he gave the slightest of nods, she stabbed the broken handle as hard as she could into Sniper's thigh.

Sniper screamed and Tilly fell to the ground at the same time two shots echoed in the room.

"You. Son. Of. A. Bitch." Tilly uncovered her hands from her head to find her mother beating the dead sniper with a candlestick.

Parker was racing toward Tilly and all she could think about was getting to him.

"Are you hurt?" they both asked at the same time while running their hands over each other, looking for injuries.

"Ma'am," the other man in camo said, coming up to Tilly's mother. "I think you got him."

"I want him to feel this as he goes to hell."

"Mother!" Tilly gasped. This was not like her mother at all.

The man standing next to her mother grinned. "Ma'am, you're going to love visiting Keeneston. I'm Parker's cousin Jackson."

"Wow, she's really going at 'im," another man in camo said from the door. "Reminds me of when my Bertha gets a seal."

"And that's my teammate, Lucas. Excuse him. He's from Northern Alaska," Jackson said as Parker held Tilly tight.

Her mother stopped beating the man and blew out a puff of air to push back her normally perfect hair from her eyes. "Celina Bradford. It's a pleasure to meet you both." And there was her mother. Her perfectly perfect manners were back in place as she smoothed down her expensive designer dress. "I assume the man holding my daughter is the man she loves?"

Parker didn't let go of Tilly as he stood, bringing her up to her feet with him. His arm was around her and her face was half buried in his chest as she clung to him. Even in the middle of the chaos and danger, she'd never felt safer.

"Thank you for rescuing me."

"You were doing a fine job of it yourself, but I'm happy to be your backup any day." Parker kissed the top of her head and Tilly was ready to curl up in this lap and kiss him into next week. "Mrs. Bradford, I'm Parker Davies, Tilly's boyfriend. It's a pleasure to meet you and I'd love to spend all day telling you how special your daughter is, but we have to get moving. Your husband is downstairs and has been shot."

Parker had wanted to cry out in relief when Tilly dropped to the ground and he'd shot the man holding a gun to her head. However, seconds later Ryan had come onto the comms and said that Guy was in custody and Bradford had been shot. Ryan had Guy in hand and Talon was working to save Bradford's life.

"Theo!" Mrs. Bradford cried as she pushed past Parker and raced out the door.

"Follow me, ma'am," Lucas called out, directing her down the south stairwell.

Tilly similarly tried to sprint to her father, but Parker held her hand. "It's not good. Be prepared." Tilly nodded and Parker took off running, still holding her hand.

They caught up with Lucas and Mrs. Bradford in the stairwell and followed them into the study. Guy was on his stomach on the floor with his hands behind him in cuffs. Bradford was on his back on the floor with Talon hovering over him pressing a bloody cloth onto the man's chest.

"Theo!" Tilly's mother cried as she dropped to her knees beside her husband. His eyes fluttered open as Tilly pulled her hand from Parker and dropped to the floor next to her mother.

"He saved you then?" Her father struggled to say between gasps of air. He was having great difficulty breathing and Parker saw he was turning blue. Tilly nodded as she tried not to cry. Parker saw her resolve fail as tears began to flow. "I guess I'll have to give him my approval to marry you then."

Parker would have celebrated, but Talon looked at him with worry on his face. "His heart rate is through the roof. EMTs have been called, but it will take ten minutes for them to fly here."

Parker stepped out into the hall and video-called his cousin Jace. "Paramedics are ten minutes out and I don't think he has time. Can you tell me what to do?"

"Let me see him," Jace said, moving closer to the camera so he could get a good look at Bradford's injuries as Parker walked back inside the study.

"He was shot once in the chest before Ryan got to them and took the shooter down," Talon was saying as Parker showed the gunshot wound. "His heart rate is fast, he's struggling to breathe, and he has a cough."

"Mr. Bradford," Jace said loudly, forcing Bradford's eyes open. "Does your chest hurt when you take a breath?"

"Y-Yes," Bradford struggled to say.

"Parker, he has a pneumothorax caused by the gunshot wound. A rib could have punctured it or the bullet itself. However, there's air trapped around his lungs. You need to release it or he'll die," Jace told him as calmly as he would tell him what the special was at the Blossom Café.

"Okay, what do I do?" Parker asked, handing the phone to Lucas.

"Look for a first aid kit and a needle of some kind. If that fails, a knife and a straw will work. Especially those reusable metal ones," Jace said.

"Where's your first aid kit?" Ryan asked Guy.

Guy refused to respond. Instead, he looked away from Ryan.

Suddenly, Mrs. Bradford leaped up, candlestick still in hand, and smashed the silver square base against Guy's back. "Tell me where everything is, or I will bash your head in!" she growled as she swung the candlestick with progressively more force.

"Ow! Someone stop her!" Guy shouted between grunts.

"Stop what?" Ryan asked. "I don't see anything. I'd just answer the nice lady's question."

"Fine! In the butler's pantry off the kitchen. Make her stop!"

"Hmm, sorry, I can't hear you," Ryan said before he took off running for the butler's pantry.

"Parker," Bradford gasped. "Cipher. Celina has it."

"A cipher? What are you talking about Theo?" Celina asked as she rushed back to her husband.

"Your necklace, love. Give it to Parker."

"I don't understand," she said even as she unclasped it and handed it to him.

"I was involved in something illegal. This is it. That is what I deserve. Your necklace is the key. It's why I made you swear you'd never take it off."

"But it's nothing but a gold chain," she said.

"It's much more than that. It's code." That was the last Bradford said before he passed out.

"Found it!" Ryan yelled as he ran back into the room and shoved a red tackle box with a white cross on it to Parker. Parker put the necklace in his pocket and got to work saving Bradford.

"Okay, Jace. What do I do?" Parker opened the box and Lucas showed Jace what was inside.

"Put on a pair of gloves. Cut his shirt off," Jace instructed and then waited while Parker followed the instructions. "Place your hands on each side of his ribcage and feel which side is expanding and which isn't."

"The left isn't. It's where the gunshot is," Parker told him.

"Good. Get some pillows and prop him slightly up. Then I want you to clean the area with either rubbing alcohol or iodine, whichever is in the kit." Jace waited while Parker followed his instructions. "Now feel for his collarbone and count the ribs down. You want to place the needle into the second intercostal space," Jace calmly explained.

Parker froze. "A little less medical speak," Parker requested.

"You're going to insert the needle through the skin and muscle right about the third rib, which will feel like the second rib because of the collarbone being in the way of the first rib. Understand?"

"Got it." Parker didn't have it. He theoretically knew what Jace was saying, but it was very different sitting there, holding a needle, and pressing it through the skin, and then shoving it hard past the pectoral muscle.

Hisssss.

"That's it. You got it. That will hold him until paramedics arrive. Good job, Parker," Jace said.

"I'm sorry," Bradford said to his wife the second he came around. "I'm going to go to prison for a little while, but I'll be back and we'll be together again."

"Prison?" Tilly asked and by the accusatory glare she was giving Parker, he worried it might cause a permanent rift between them. "You're arresting my father?"

"I have to. Tilly, it's my job and he's a fugitive." Parker at least didn't say criminal, but it didn't seem to matter by the matching glare mother and daughter were now giving him.

"My dears," Bradford said with a little cough followed by a groan as Talon kept pressure on the gunshot wound that was still bleeding. "I'm guilty. I broke the law. But Parker helped me get the best deal I could. He could have forced me here and arrested me. But before we even talked, he got me a lawyer and told me to make a deal. I won't be in prison too long, just a couple of years. He promised to keep you safe and I promised I'd turn over my evidence. He lived up to his promise, although seeing my wife beat a man with a candlestick will keep me in line from now on."

Bradford tried to laugh but ended up coughing instead.

"Tilly," Bradford said once he caught his breath. "Parker is a good man. He loves you very much. I'm happy you found what I have with your mother."

"You're assuming I'm waiting for you to get out of prison. Do you have any idea how furious I am with you right now?" his wife interrupted.

"I'm sorry, my dear. I just wanted to keep you in the lifestyle you were accustomed to."

"And I just want you, Theo. I'm sorry I didn't realize we needed to tighten our belts, but I will. By the time you get home, I won't be mad and we won't have financial issues either."

"Darling," Bradford began as EMTs, FBI, and US Marshals ran in. "What are you going to do?"

"Well, for one, I'm selling the Florida estate and moving to Kentucky where our daughter, son, and grandchildren will be. I can think of a couple of other properties we don't need either. Don't worry, dear. I'll have everything taken care of by the time you come home. Now," Mrs. Bradford said, keeping her husband's attention on her while the

EMTs took over. "I expect you to get buff in prison so you can make up the next couple of years to me. Plus, we'll need to keep up with the grandchildren. By the way these two look at each other, you're going to be a grandfather sooner rather than later."

A happy smile came over his face as he grabbed Tilly's hand. "Say yes when the time comes. I'm sorry, Til. I'll make it up to you by being the best grandpapa you've ever seen. Parker, take care of my ladies."

Parker hadn't wanted Bradford's approval. But now that he had it, he knew it was important. Parker moved around the gurney Bradford was placed on and put his arm around Tilly. "I will. However, sir, I saw your wife with the candlestick and your daughter stab someone with a spoon. I don't think they need me."

"No," Ryan groaned as Guy was hauled off. "Not a spoon. It was bad enough when Porter did it, but another one? Miles and Layne will never shut up about it now."

Tilly smiled as she held her father's hand in one of hers and Parker's in the other. Parker. "I love you, Dad," Tilly said, leaning down and kissing his cheek.

"Let his wife go with him," Parker ordered. There were grumblings from the variety of government agencies present, but whatever Greer had said worked. They listened as they let Celina accompany Theo in the ambulance.

"Tilly," Parker said. There was so much to say. So many emotions to untangle. The fear, the love, the desire to lock her in his bedroom and never let her leave again.

"Marshal Davies, we need a word," someone in a suit demanded.

"Til," Parker said, begging her to understand what he was feeling with just a look.

"I know." Tilly's tears were slowing as she hugged him

hard. He cupped her head with his hands and held her tight against his chest and just breathed her in.

"Now, Davies," the man snapped.

"And who the hell do you think you are?" Ryan snapped back with Jackson, Talon, and Lucas backing him up.

"Go," Tilly said softly as she pulled away from him. "I'll be here when you're done. I love you, Parker."

Parker didn't want to leave her, but his cousins were dangerously close to punching out the governor of New York. Parker leaned over and kissed her quickly on the lips. "I love you, too."

Parker strode into the shitstorm with a smile. Their relationship started with handcuffs, but luckily didn't end because of them.

27

One week later . . .

It was over. Tilly had sat with her mother as her father finished his official testimony that afternoon in New York City. It turned out her father hadn't knowingly funded all of the criminals. It had started out with a loan as a favor to Guy Fausto and grown from there. By the time Mr. Bradford figured out what was going on, he was in it too deep to get out. So, he began to keep journals in the event he was arrested. With the help of The Panther, he'd traced all the money Fausto had loaned out. The main wallet and account the government had assumed was her father's had actually been Fausto's. But, it had been her father who loaned the money to Fausto in the first place, so he was involved from the very beginning. All the names, orders, money, and every shred of evidence, had been turned over to the government. Parker and half his family had already headed up the raids arresting the criminals her father had funded within twenty-four hours of returning to Keeneston.

The links of her mother's necklace had held the computer binary code needed to decipher the books. They hadn't waited for her father's testimony. They'd organized the raids starting with the most dangerous and working their way out to the shallow ends of the criminal pool.

While Parker was finishing up the raids, Isabelle had worked to clear Tilly and Celina. As a result, mother and daughter had been fully cleared of all criminal charges. Tilly's charity account had been unfrozen, along with her trust fund. Some of her parents' joint accounts had been confiscated by the government, but her mother had already come up with a plan. It was strange to say, but this had brought them together.

"Thank you again for the ride," her mother said to Sebastian Abel as they got onto his plane after saying goodbye to her father. They had decided to visit him every month after he was medically cleared and settled in prison.

"It's no problem, Mrs. Bradford."

"I also appreciate you helping me sell my plane." Sebastian nodded his head as if to say "You're welcome" before getting back to work.

"How are the rest of the sales going?" Tilly asked once they were in the air. When they'd been given the legal all-clear three days earlier, Tilly and her mother had gone through all their assets and her mother began a clearance sale of all the things she didn't want, need, or value.

"The plane was sold this morning. I have a buyer for the yacht and it will close next week. I've also found some buyers for a couple of the paintings I've always hated but your father insisted on buying. I figured getting rid of them would be my own little payback for his stupidity. The houses in Florida, Los Angeles, Hawaii, Vanuatu, and the Emirates are going to be listed next week. I've listed which personal items are to be shipped to Kentucky and which are to be sold with the houses. The funds from those sales should refill the trust funds, especially without having to pay for the houses' upkeep. Also, per your suggestion, I'm setting aside a part of the money for Mrs. Barrow so she can retire. I also made sure Joel got a large bonus and the best recommendation I've ever written. However, it turned out I didn't need to write it after all."

"Did Joel get a new job?" Tilly asked.

"Job, yes. New, no. They decided to move to the house I'm buying in Kentucky this summer. His wife got a job at the hospital as a nurse and they've already registered their daughter for school in Lexington starting this fall."

"Oh, what wonderful news." Joel was part of their family and it was nice to see her mother realize that, too. This week had been a lot for both of them, but more so for her mother. "I'm sorry you're having to go through all this."

Her mother shook her head. "Don't be. It's my fault. I should have had an equal say in our finances. Instead, I just went on spending and thinking nothing of it. It was just as selfish of me as it was stupid of your father to resort to criminal money lending instead of telling me to cut back, trim the sails financially. But what about you and your horses? Where will they go when we sell the farm?"

"Willa is building a state-of-the-art equestrian facility and she said I can board my horses there. In the meantime, Reagan has flown my stable from Florida to Keeneston. My babies are safe in Porter's rodeo barns right now."

Her mother reached out and took Tilly's hand in hers. "Does he make you happy?"

There was no question of who "he" was. "Yes. Parker makes me very happy, Mother."

"I'm glad some good could come from all of this. He's a very fine man, Tilly."

Her mother closed her eyes and Tilly turned to look out over the clouds in the sky. It was over, but now everything seemed up in the air. What was in her and Parker's future and how would it be now that the case was over?

"Are you sure you got everything?" Parker asked his cousin Landon for the hundredth time.

"Yes. I have all her favorites made. They will be in the warmer by the fire when you two get here." Landon had graciously volunteered to make a very special dinner for Parker and Tilly tonight. Well, after Parker begged, that is. But Landon was a good guy. He wouldn't hold that over Parker for a decade like his brother would have. "It'll be perfect. Don't worry."

"Thanks, man. And thanks for not telling anyone."

"Who would I tell?" Landon asked innocently.

"You didn't," Parker gasped. "You told someone."

"I didn't. I swear. But"—Landon grimaced —"DeAndre was picking up an order when you called. He saw your name on my phone before I could hide it and you know how he just *knows* things. It's freaky."

Parker cursed. "I wonder how much time I have."

"I'll hold them off as long as I can. Want me to block the road with my car?" Landon asked. "Bribe them with food? What do you need me to do?"

"You're a good cousin, Landon. And I'll take you up on that offer. Just give me until dark."

"You got it. Good luck."

. . .

Parker leaned against the door of his SUV, arms folded across his chest as he waited for Sebastian's plane to land. The engagement ring felt heavy in his pocket. He kept touching it, worried it would spontaneously combust and he'd be left with no ring.

It has been a hard week, but there was never any doubt of his feelings for Tilly. Every day he loved her more and more. She carried herself with dignity, grace, and unshakable poise when the press descended on her. On the nights they were together, he'd held her as she slept after making love and knew this was their darkest time and yet their love thrived. Every mission he went on, it was Tilly who brought him home.

His parents had backed off the whole marriage thing. Instead they focused on supporting Mrs. Bradford and Tilly as if they were already family. In Parker's mind, and apparently all of Keeneston's, they already were. Tonight, he'd make it official. He'd waited and waited to make Tilly his. And now that she was, he was never going to let her go.

The plane appeared and landed smoothly before rolling to a stop in the private section of the airport. Mrs. Bradford appeared first on Sebastian's arm. He escorted her off the plane with Tilly right behind.

Mrs. Bradford smiled at him and, he saw approval even through the exhaustion on her face. "I found a lovely place outside of Lexington. Don't worry. Your mother-in-law won't be too near."

"And she only has a candlestick. My mother-in-law has a rifle," Sebastian muttered as he held the door to the private car service open for Mrs. Bradford.

Mrs. Bradford looked out and winked before giving the address of her hotel.

"Good luck tonight," Sebastian whispered as Tilly hugged her mother goodbye.

"How do you know?"

"DeAndre. He knows everything. I'm not one to be fanciful, but I think he has ESP and can read minds."

As Sebastian got into the car, Parker shot off a text to Landon for help speeding up the plan and maybe borrowing a combine or some large tractor to block the entrance.

"I missed you."

Parker shoved his phone into his back pocket and kissed his hopefully soon-to-be-fiancée. "I missed you, too. I'm sorry I couldn't be there today. I had the last few arrests to oversee. How did it go?"

Tilly let out a long breath as she climbed into the SUV. Parker hurried around to the driver's side and began the drive to their surprise evening.

"It went well. He's feeling a lot better but will still be in the hospital and then rehab for quite a while. Isabelle already has the clock started and he'll have his first parole hearing in two years. He said it was a relief to testify."

"And how are you doing?" Parker asked. Plan or no plan, if she weren't in the right headspace, he'd hold off on the proposal.

Tilly took a deep breath and smiled. "I'm good. In a strange way, it's brought my family closer together. I also feel ready to start a new life. I don't feel the pressure of my name anymore. I was always so scared I would be a disappointment to the Bradford legacy, but in a strange way it's a relief that my father did this. At least it's come out that while he was a criminal, he wasn't a malicious one like Guy. I'm free now, if that makes sense."

"It does. Plus, you could never be a disappointment. If

you talk to Cady at the distillery, she believes you're her guardian angel."

Tilly blushed and Parker reached out for her hand. He held it as they drove through Lexington and onto the winding country roads leading to Keeneston.

"Where are we going?" Tilly asked as they passed the driveway to the house.

"Someplace special for tonight."

Tilly smiled but didn't ask. She knew he wouldn't tell her. But when he pulled into the field with the water tower leading to the cabin, she laughed. "Where our romance finally began."

"*Finally* being the keyword," Parker said even as he caught Landon ducking behind a huge tractor with a hay baler attached. Landon just moved up to favorite cousin status.

"Oh, Parker!" Tilly gasped as they drove into the clearing.

Yup, favorite cousin for sure. Landon had a table set with a white tablecloth and fancy plate settings. Champagne was chilling in a silver stand. There was a fire in the firepit and lanterns lined the entire outdoor space.

"I wanted to do something special for you."

Happy tears filled her eyes as she turned to him. "This is definitely special. Our poor cabin though!"

"I've been working on cleaning it up. Don't worry, sweetheart. It'll be ready for a weekend visit very soon."

Parker opened her door and escorted her to the table. He helped Tilly onto her chair and popped the champagne. His hands began to shake from nerves as he opened the travel box that Landon had stored to keep all their food hot.

The plan was to eat dinner, laugh, and generally be in love and then propose over Tilly's favorite dessert. However,

Parker was having a very hard time focusing on food or even the conversation.

"Parker? Are you all right? You look a little pale."

Parker gulped. He hunted the most dangerous criminals in the world. He could ask the woman he loved to marry him. What he couldn't do was wait.

"I'm sorry, Til. I had this all planned out, but I just can't wait another minute." Parker rose from his chair, took a step around the table, and went down on one knee. "I can't wait another minute to tell you I love you with every breath I take. I love that you give me hell. I love that you give me a taste of heaven. I love that you're kind. I love that you're loyal. I love that you're you," Parker said, remembering to pull the ring from his pocket. "I can't wait another moment to ask you. Tilly, will you marry me?"

Parker held his breath, but when Tilly smiled, he didn't need to hear her answer. It told him everything he needed to know.

"Yes. I'd be honored to marry you, Parker." Tears, these of joy, rolled down her cheeks. But it was her smile that Parker couldn't stop looking at as he slid the ring onto her finger.

28

Tilly felt as if she were dancing in the night sky among the stars as she kissed Parker, her fiancé.

"I held them off as long as I could!" Tilly and Parker broke from their kiss as Landon ran into the clearing. "Your father hotwired the tractor and moved it."

Parker laughed as he held her tight against his chest—her favorite place to be. "Don't worry, Landon. I couldn't wait until dessert to ask."

"Oh, thank goodness." Landon grabbed the champagne bottle and took a deep drink straight from the bottle. "That was so stressful. But I get to be the first. Congratulations!"

Tilly laughed as family and friends descended on them. Cars circled the clearing and parked down the narrow drive. Music played. More food appeared. And the hugs. She hugged everyone in Keeneston.

"Congratulations, honey!"

"Mom?" Tilly cried, realizing how good it felt to have her mom there to celebrate with her. "What are you doing here?"

"Willa called me just as I was leaving the airport and had me go directly to their house." Then she was in her mother's arms and Tilly felt as if she could finally be the real Tilly she'd always been deep down inside. Not Matilda Bradford, blueblood socialite, poor little rich girl. But now she was free to be Tilly Davies, small business entrepreneur and small-town girl. "I'm so happy for you. You're glowing!"

"And she'll be glowing even more when she's a bride!" Gemma said, joining them.

"Oh yes. I can see it now. An orchestra. Candles. Doves." Her mother had stars in her eyes as she and Gemma went off to plan a grand wedding and Tilly's smile slipped a little.

"What is it?" Parker asked quietly as the party got into full swing.

"What our moms are talking about. That's what I used to want when I was younger. The huge, over-the-top wedding," Tilly admitted.

"What do you want now?" Parker asked. "Your wish is my command. All I want is you, Tilly. Everything else is just ... everything else."

"Really?" Tilly nibbled on her lip, worrying if she should say what she really wanted.

"Til, I'm going to be your husband. You should always tell me what you want." Parker leaned forward and placed his lips near her ear. "Or how you want it."

Parker was right. He gave her the confidence and courage to be honest about who she was and what she wanted. That's how she found herself rising onto her tiptoes and whispering into Parker's ear.

"Well, that's a first."

Tilly worried her lip. "Too much?"

"No. It's perfect."

"Really?" Tilly felt so excited she was about to burst.

"Really. It's us."

Parker kissed her and everyone around them cheered.

Poppy shoved her phone into her back pocket before her older sister, Zinnia, saw the email. She put some leftovers into a container and then called to her sister. "Father Ben called in a late order. I told him I'd run it down to him real quick."

"Take your time," Zinnia called from where she was wiping down the empty tables. "Everyone is at the engagement party so I'm going to close early tonight."

"I'll be back to help you close up."

"Sounds good. Tell Ben 'hi' for me and see how he likes the fried chicken. I added a little something to the breading," Zinnia called out as Poppy was walking out the back door.

They'd been in Keeneston so long it had begun to feel safe, but then the letters and emails started to arrive. Tears threatened as she quickly walked to the church. She turned and walked through the parking lot to the small house behind the church and knocked.

The door opened and Father Ben looked out with surprise. "Poppy, what are you doing here? Is everything alright?"

Poppy put on a fake smile and held up her bag. "Zinnia tried something new with the chicken and wants your opinion."

"Thank you. Come in." Ben held open the door and Poppy walked inside. "Are you going to the engagement party?"

Poppy nodded. "In just a bit. We're closing up early."

"Good." Ben pulled out the second chair to the two-person kitchen table for her. "Now, tell me why you're really here."

Poppy took a shaky breath. "I need you to hear my confession."

"Of course, but why now?"

"Because I don't know how much time I have left."

"Are you sure? I know it's what I want, but—" Tilly asked as they parked the car. The engagement party was still going on, but Parker had snuck Tilly out through the woods to the water tower. And while Landon didn't know it yet, he'd let Parker borrow his car.

"I'm sure, Tilly. There's nothing I want more."

Parker took her hand and walked up the steps before knocking on the door.

"Looks like I'm hosting a party."

"Sorry to bother you so late at night," Parker said, catching someone else in the small house. "Hi, Poppy. Are we interrupting?" Parker frowned as he noticed the tear-stained face Poppy was trying to hide.

"No! Not at all," she said with fake cheerfulness. "Let me just put this to-go order in the kitchen."

"Congratulations," Father Ben said, smiling at them both. "Want me to grab my calendar to reserve a date? Your mothers and grandmother have already texted me their suggestions."

"No," Tilly said nervously.

"No? Okay, then. You don't have to pick a date now," Father Ben said.

"We have a date," Parker said as he grinned down at Tilly. She saw him smiling and her nerves vanished as she smiled up at him.

"Oh, when?" Ben asked, pulling out his phone to put it on the calendar.

"Now," Parker and Tilly said together.

Poppy gasped from inside the small house and Ben went a little pale.

"I'm sorry," he said slowly. "Did you say now?"

"You're eloping?" Poppy asked. The tears in her eyes had been replaced with excitement. "And I know about it before anyone else?"

"Um," Ben said, clearly looking worried. "You need a license."

Parker reached into his pocket and pulled it out. "Good thing my mother and grandmother are obsessed with getting us married quickly and have all the paperwork done for us. Remember, you dropped it off our first night in Keeneston?"

Parker thought he heard the priest curse under his breath. "Is this what you both really want?" Father Ben asked.

"More than anything," Tilly said, squeezing his hand as she smiled up at him.

"Okay then. We'll need two witnesses and another priest to bury me after your family kills me."

"Stop being so dramatic," Poppy said with a roll of her eyes. "I'll call Zinnia. She and I can be your witnesses."

"Then let's go to the church." Ben took a fortifying breath as he grabbed his collar from where it sat on the side table and slipped it around his neck. "Or do you want me to change fully first?"

Parker took in Ben's jeans and black T-shirt with the

white clerical collar around his neck and grinned. "Nope. It's perfect," Parker said as he gestured to his own outfit of jeans and a white button-down shirt.

Tilly was practically bouncing with excitement next to him in a simple white floor-length maxi dress she pulled from the closet. She was the most beautiful bride Parker had ever seen.

Ben turned on the lights to the church and the room glowed to life. Ben turned on his phone and seconds later, beautiful instrumental music filled the church. The doors were flung open and Poppy and Zinnia rushed in, both wearing huge smiles.

"We picked these on the way," Zinnia said, holding out a bouquet of flowers.

"Just don't mention some of the planters along Main Street looking a little bare," Poppy said, trying not to laugh.

"Thank you," Tilly told them. "They're perfect. Thanks for being here with us."

Poppy and Zinnia got into place and in the warm glow of the lights, the history of the church, and the company of three friends, Parker married the woman of his dreams.

"You may now kiss the bride," Ben said with a smile, his fear of Gemma and Marcy temporarily pushed aside.

Parker slid his hand against Tilly's cheek and into her unbound hair. "I'll love you forever," he whispered to her before sealing their future with a kiss.

Poppy and Zinnia cheered as Ben sent them off as Parker and Tilly Davies. Tilly was laughing, Parker couldn't stop smiling, and then they were on their way.

"Any idea on where we can honeymoon?" Tilly asked.

"Well, I spoke to my boss to get some time off and we can take a US Marshals plane leaving Lexington for Los Angeles in thirty minutes. I was thinking Hawaii."

"You know, my family still has that house in the Maldives. I bet we could get a flight there from L.A." Tilly was already looking for tickets on her phone.

"I have a better idea. I want one week where no one knows where we are so I can do nothing but celebrate that a country boy like me was lucky enough to marry a woman like you."

"You mean a woman who can outride and outshoot you?"

Parker laughed as he made a call. "You bet I do," he said as the phone rang. "Hello, Addie. Sorry, Your Royal Highness, Queen Addison of Bermalia," he said with a chuckle, knowing she was probably rolling her eyes at him. "I have a favor to ask. Do you happen to have any diplomatic planes in L.A.?"

~

It took almost twenty-four hours of travel, but Parker thought it was worth every minute. They had their own private island paradise for the next eight days. Addison came through and redirected them to New York where she and Draven had just arrived for a meeting with the United Nations. Parker's boss had been amazing and held up a prisoner transport at the airport long enough for Parker and Tilly to jump on it to New York.

The flight to New York was short. The flight on the king and queen's private jet to Maldives was very long. However, it had been perfect. The crew had been apprised of the situation. Chilled champagne and a mini wedding cake greeted them. A guest room had been covered in rose petals where a gold royal member festooned with a fancy bow sat in the middle of the bed.

They hardly left their bedroom the entire flight. But now they were standing in the open-air living room looking out at a pristine white sand beach and the bluest water Parker had ever seen.

"Ready to go swimming?" Tilly asked.

Parker's breath caught as his wife strode out wearing nothing at all. "Funny," Parker said, shoving down his swim trunks and throwing them inside. "We're wearing the same thing."

"Hopefully you'll be wearing me, if you can catch me." Tilly gave him a wink and took off running for the ocean.

Parker laughed and chased after her. Life with Tilly was never going to be boring. He caught up to her in the clear water and pulled her against him. "I caught you, wife."

"I'll let you in on a little secret, husband," Tilly said with a mischievous twinkle in her eye as the water lapped against her bare breasts. "I'll always let you catch me."

Tilly reached up and laced her fingers around Parker's neck and pulled him down to her. Parker kissed her with all the love he had. His hands came out of the water to caress her breasts before he pulled her legs around his hips.

"I love that we're out here alone and no one knows where we are," Tilly said against his lips. "It makes me want to do very, very naughty things."

"Really? Like what?"

"Like making love in the middle of an ocean, on the beach, against the palm tree, on that swing over the water."

"How about I start checking some of those places off your sex bucket list," Parker told her, as he pressed against her with his hips.

"I love you," Tilly said, looking into his eyes as she slid onto him. It was the most erotic moment of his life, well, at least until they tried the swing.

.   .   .

Hours later, Parker and Tilly lay naked on the patio, holding hands when a boat came into view.

"Who's that?" Parker asked, shielding his eyes from the late afternoon sun. They'd made love three times today so far, but that palm tree was still calling their names.

"Oh, that's the delivery boat. I ordered us some groceries and some things we forgot to pack." Tilly grabbed a cotton dress and threw it on while he stepped into his swim trunks and went to greet the speedboat.

"Hello, Miss Bradford!"

"Hello, Samar!" Tilly called out. "But it's Mrs. Davies now. I just got married. This is my husband, Parker. Parker, this is Samar."

Parker shook his hand and grabbed a bag of groceries. "Nice to meet you. Let me help you."

"Thank you," Samar said, handing some bags to Parker.

Parker noticed that Tilly reached in and took some as well. "My, isn't that palm tree big? I haven't noticed how big it was before. Very sturdy-looking."

Parker was going to get her back for this. "Yes, it is. I imagine it's very hard and lasts a very long time. You could probably pound at it over and over again and it wouldn't come . . . out of the ground."

Tilly turned pink and shot an embarrassed look to Samar, who was luckily ahead of them. "Point, team husband," Parker said with a wink before hurrying to catch up with Samar.

"Well, that's everything," Samar said, setting down a large box he was carrying. "Best wishes for a blessed marriage."

"Thank you, Samar." Tilly waved him off from the patio.

Parker's nose twitched. "Do you smell that?"

"Smell what?"

Parker pulled open the box and stared in disbelief. There was his grandmother's apple pie and an envelope.

"Is that . . .?"

"It is. My grandmother not only found us but somehow got one of her apple pies delivered!" Parker opened the envelope and pulled out a handwritten note.

Congratulations to the new Mr. and Mrs. Davies. I couldn't be happier for you both. Enclosed is a pie for you to enjoy on your honeymoon. Don't worry, we'll have the reception all ready for you when you return next week.

"She even has the time of our arrival flight and organized someone to pick us up at the airport to bring us to our reception," Tilly said in wonder. "Are you sure it wasn't your grandmother in the CIA and not your dad?"

"I've also enclosed some photographs for you. Every couple should have pictures from their wedding day." Parker read out loud. "Congratulations. I expect a honeymoon baby so that I can die happy."

"We didn't take any photos on our wedding day," Tilly said as Parker emptied the large envelope. Out came picture after picture of their wedding. "What? How?"

"I think you may be right. She had to be CIA."

"Oh, Parker, look at this one." Tilly held up a picture of their first kiss as man and wife. Then there was another one of them looking lovingly into each other's eyes as they held hands and repeated their vows. "I'm so glad she got these, however she did."

"Father Ben sold us out. That's how she got them."

"Then I'm glad he did. They're beautiful."

"Not as beautiful as my wife. Look at that," Parker said, pointing to the palm tree.

When Tilly looked, he grabbed the pie and made a run for it.

"Parker!" Tilly called out with mock anger before running after him, laughter filling the island and their clothes littering the sand.

EPILOGUE

One week later
  Keeneston . . .

The night was perfect. Music filled the farm as everyone danced. A temporary dance floor had been laid under lights that had been strung at the farm Parker shared with his family. Tables filled with flowers and candles encircled the dance floor as people talked, laughed, and celebrated together.

Parker held his wife in his arms as they endured good-natured ribbing for depriving the town of a wedding. However, they were making up for it with the reception party their mothers had planned.

"How bad has it been for you?" Parker asked Father Ben when the Rose sisters went to sit down with his Grandma Marcy.

"I didn't get a single baked good after church last week. I would have starved to death if it hadn't been for Poppy and

Zinnia. They've been bragging all week that they were the only witnesses."

"Not the only ones. Thanks for selling us out to my grandma," Parker joked.

Ben's brow creased in confusion. "What are you talking about?"

"You telling my grandma that we were getting married so she could take pictures of the ceremony." Parker would have rolled his eyes except for the look on Ben's face clearly said the priest had no idea what Parker was talking about. "You didn't tell my grandma, did you?"

"Told you, CIA super spy," Tilly whispered to them as they all turned to look at Grandma Marcy sitting with the Rose sisters.

～

"And with that, ladies, I am out!" Gemma held up a bottle of champagne and drank straight from it. "This one was a doozy, but all four kids are finally married to their true loves."

"I'm never going to see that happen," Tammy groaned. "Cassidy is just coming into her own and then Cricket—" The table of moms turned to see Dylan swinging his little sister around on the dance floor. A menopause baby had drastically changed her timeline, but Tammy wouldn't trade it for the world as she watched her family make Cricket squeal with laughter.

"I'm right there with you, Tammy," Annie said with a sigh. "And I don't have the excuse of having a child in preschool. My two boys are just blind to love."

"What about Colton? He's getting settled with running

the Keeneston Fire Department and heading up the emergency response team for this area," Kenna asked about Annie's eldest son.

"And taking full advantage of the perks of being a sex object. He's doing that stupid firefighter calendar for the Keeneston Belles. I swear, his social media is filled with tags from every woman in Lexington. He's never going to settle down."

"That's how Kale is," Bridget sighed. "I'm stuck at fifty percent. I can't believe Abby is married and having a baby before Kale is settled down. Kale complained about working out at the farm with Ahmed until I couldn't stand it anymore. Well, he's not complaining now."

Bridget turned to look at her son. Gone was the gangly youth and in his place was a man. "How did they grow up so fast? When did he get all those muscles and start looking like my husband? He even has Ahmed's glare. After the baby is born, Kale is going to serve his time in the Rahmi army. He doesn't have to since he's also American, but suddenly he wants to. He said it will make him well rounded and balance out his nerd side."

"Nerds are sexy," Tammy said with a giggle. Her husband, Pierce, was the nerd of the Davies brothers and in turn had invented a crazy number of things designed to help agriculture.

"Yeah, well, mix sexy computer guy with ripped soldier and what do you get?" Bridget asked.

"A man nowhere near getting married," Dani said with a sigh as she looked at their matchmaking book. "Which means that leaves only one option for who is next."

"Landon," they all said, turning to look at Annie and Cade's youngest son.

"Every woman likes a man who can cook," Morgan said with a nod.

"I daresay, will this one be easy?" Paige asked.

"Don't jinx it!" Katelyn said, knocking on the wood table just to make sure.

"But who can we set Landon up with?" Annie asked of her son. "He has quietly dated a few women, but they never lasted that long with his crazy schedule as he gets his restaurant up and running."

"So, we need someone independent, yet supportive," Kenna said as she looked around. "Tandy? She's busy prosecuting Mr. Chapman almost monthly. As an attorney she knows all about long hours."

"Or maybe Cady Woodson?" Paige suggested. "She runs the distillery, and as one of the few woman distillers, she knows about starting a company like Landon's. Plus, food and bourbon go hand in hand."

"I don't know," Annie said, looking at her son. Landon was dancing with the bride. Cady was dancing with Cody, the sheriff's deputy. Neither seemed to care where the other was on the dance floor. "I think I would see a spark by now if there was something between them."

"But they work together, right?" Katelyn asked.

"Kind of. She provides the bourbon for his restaurant, which means they spend time together. So if there were something between them, I would think I would have seen it by now," Annie said and then sighed. "I'm never going to get my boys married. Cricket will be married before they are."

"Don't lose faith," Dani said sympathetically.

"We will find the perfect person for Landon. We haven't failed yet," Morgan said supportively.

"Okay, then." Dani picked up her pen and wrote Landon's name in the book and placed a question mark next to it. "Landon's up. Ladies, be on the lookout for the perfect woman for him."

"Well, at least they realized Cady wasn't right for Landon. They're finally learning," Miss Lily said as she, her sisters, and Marcy turned their hearing aids back down.

"Landon, dear," Miss Lily called out to where Landon was walking off the dance floor. "Can you help us for a moment?"

Landon wore his easy smile as he joined them. "Anything for a tableful of beautiful women. How can I be of service?"

"Can you open this bottle of champagne?" Miss Lily asked.

"So many pretty ladies here tonight," Miss Daisy hedged, but she saw the flicker of amusement in Landon's eyes. He knew what they were up to.

"Sorry to disappoint, ladies, but I'm not interested in any of them. They're my friends and that's all. Plus, I'm so busy at the restaurant it's hard to find time to date or find someone who understands my busy schedule."

"Oh, you're not a disappointment," Marcy said, smiling up at her grandson. "We're out of the matchmaking business anyway. The right woman will come along and you'll know it the second she does."

"Thanks, Grandma," Landon said as he poured the champagne.

"Landon, I know how busy you are, but I thought I could

show you one of my specialties. You might be able to put your twist on it for your menu," Miss Violet told him. "Anton has some recipes to pass down, too, and we couldn't think of anyone we trust more than you with them."

"I'd love to learn to cook any of your or your husband's recipes. You know it was you who inspired me to be a chef," Landon said eagerly, just as Miss Violet planned.

"You're such a sweet young man. How about tomorrow morning?" Miss Violet asked as they set up a plan to meet.

"And what about your apple pie recipe, Grandma? When are you going to give that to me?" Landon asked as everyone laughed.

"You can have it when I've died happy and I can't do that until everyone is happily married and have given me my great-grandchildren." Marcy teased, only it wasn't a tease. She was determined to live that long and then, and only then, would Landon get the recipe. Or maybe her granddaughters, too, so that they could ensure the next generation was happily married. You never knew when a good pie was needed to bribe someone. Speaking of which . . . "Now, go dance and enjoy your night."

"Yes, ma'am." Landon kissed her cheek and went to join a bunch of his cousins by the bar.

"You ladies are looking lovely this evening," Ahmed's deep voice rumbled over them. Marcy might be old, but she wasn't dead. This was the best pie she'd ever made. She might have to find more ways for Ahmed to help her in the future.

"The pie is in the bag," Marcy said to him as he bent down and kissed her cheek. "Thank you for letting me borrow your drone."

"You are very welcome and the pie is very appreciated.

Call me anytime you want to use one of my toys to spy."
Ahmed winked and Marcy wondered if she needed to take
some of her blood pressure medicine.

"Now, Ahmed. It's not spying. It's just watching out for
our loved ones."

"Speaking of which, my daughter should not be dancing
this close to her due date. Excuse me, ladies."

"I have a twenty on him fainting when Abby goes into
labor," Miss Lily said.

"Make that fifty," Miss Daisy added.

"I don't bet on sure things," Miss Violet said with a
laugh.

Marcy looked down at her phone. "Hmm, this is
interesting. What do you ladies think?" She turned her
phone so they could see it.

"That is interesting," Miss Lily agreed.

"Maybe she needs a welcome pie," Miss Daisy suggested.

"That's just the thing. We have to be neighborly after
all." Marcy smiled and looked at Landon. Bless his heart, he
had no idea that love was about to find him.

Landon laughed with his cousins and friends as they shared
a drink. He glanced at the dance floor during a slow song
and saw his cousins happily dancing with their spouses.
He'd like that someday. He just didn't know how to find a
woman to date when he was at the restaurant almost every
night.

"It just hit the news, so I can finally say something,"
Knox Everett said to the group of single guys not slow
dancing with their wives. "We got a new passing game

coordinator. I'll be working with her directly before and during game."

"Her?" Landon asked.

Knox nodded. "Yup. Kate Ellington. First woman in history to be at that level for a pro football team."

"How do you and the receivers feel about her?" Kale asked.

"I really like her. We met with the finalists a couple of weeks ago and I told my dad she was my pick. My receivers like her, too, but are a little more hesitant. They're a little worried since she's young for the position, but she knows her stuff. Her mind is freaking fast at picking up patterns and running through a variety of situations. Plus, she's earned it. She was a passing coordinator for the collegiate national champions. She was with them for only two years and revamped their whole program. However, we're aware she's never had a position at this level. No matter what college thinks, they're not the pros."

"I read about her," Landon said, remembering the article that had come out right before the championship game. "When does she start?",

"Monday. The front office is scrambling to find her housing and get her moved. I'm sure you'll meet her at the next coaches' dinner," Knox said about the weekly dinners the coaches held at his restaurant.

"I look forward to it," Landon said, meaning it. The article on Kate Ellington had been fascinating.

The music slowed to a stop and Landon turned his attention to the dance floor where Parker and Tilly were getting ready to cut the cake he'd made. In the silence, there was a gasp.

"Abby?" Dylan asked as Ahmed shoved through the crowd.

"What is it? Your heart rate is elevated?" Ahmed asked.

Abby's hand was on her stomach and her face with a little pale. "Ow." She twisted a bit as if stretching.

"You're in labor. Code green! Code green!" Ahmed yelled as he began spinning around looking slightly lost.

"Did you just steal my grandchild labor codes?" Uncle Miles asked.

"I improved them," Ahmed said as he called for the armored car.

Dylan was rubbing his wife's back as she took a deep breath. Jace was talking to her, and as she took some deep breaths, color raced back to her face and Landon could see her shoulders relax. "False alarm. I'm good, but the baby really wants some cake," Abby called out. "Sorry for the interruption. Bunbun got all excited about the cake and kicked. Hard."

Landon would have told Ahmed he could call off the military escort, but he was already running from the tent organizing a possible air evacuation. He'd figure it out soon enough.

Landon pulled out his phone after clapping for the happy couple and saw the news notification announcing Kate Ellington as a coordinator for the Lexington Thoroughbreds. She was young. The same age as Landon was, in fact. She'd accomplished a lot in life for just twenty-nine. While some headlines were excited for her to join the pros, most were casting doubt on her ability. Landon knew how that felt. Try starting a restaurant when you know eighty percent close within the first five years. Landon paused on her picture that was so different from the other coaches on the team.

Trey Everett always smiled around Keeneston, but he was straight-faced and serious in his picture. Same for Will

Ashton, the owner and former pro QB. In fact, Kate was not only the only woman in the lineup, she was the only one smiling. She was beautiful, too. He was sure the sportscasters would make the story of her hiring about looks as opposed to her ability. That always seemed to happen to women. His sister, Sophie, complained about it all the time. Well, Landon was looking forward to meeting Kate at the next dinner no matter what the press said.

Landon stepped away from the dancing and walked over to a giant tree hidden in the shadows. When he looked up Kate, he'd noticed he had two emails about work. They were low on the onions he wanted and could only ship half of the quantity he needed, so he'd either have to find another vendor or change this week's menu. The other was that his supplier was out of the kind of wine he had ordered. It was always something when you owned your own business.

Landon leaned against the tree to reply to the emails when something brushed his forehead. Not looking up from his phone, Landon brushed it aside. Oddly, what he'd assumed was a leaf felt like silk. Landon looked up and right into a pair of silk panties hanging from the lower limb. The panty droppers had struck again.

Parker kissed his wife and laughed when his friends and family cheered. He'd never been happier than he was right then. Tilly giggled as he broke from the kiss and spun her on the dance floor. This cowboy had moves.

"I love you, Tilly," Parker said once the dance slowed and other couples joined them on the dance floor. Parker held his wife close, rubbing his thumb against her back as they danced. He couldn't wait to get her home alone and show her how much he loved her, too.

"I love you, too. Now, how about we steal Ahmed's armored car and get out of here?"

Parker laughed, but grabbed her hand as they made a run toward their happily ever after.

THE END

Bluegrass Series

Bluegrass State of Mind

Risky Shot

Dead Heat

Bluegrass Brothers

Bluegrass Undercover

Rising Storm

Secret Santa: A Bluegrass Series Novella

Acquiring Trouble

Relentless Pursuit

Secrets Collide

Final Vow

Bluegrass Singles

All Hung Up

Bluegrass Dawn

The Perfect Gift

The Keeneston Roses

Forever Bluegrass Series

Forever Entangled

Forever Hidden

Forever Betrayed

Forever Driven

Forever Secret

Forever Surprised

Forever Concealed

Forever Devoted

Forever Hunted

Forever Guarded

Forever Notorious

Forever Ventured

Forever Freed

Forever Saved

Forever Bold

Forever Thrown

Forever Lies

Forever Protected

Forever Paired

Shadows Landing Series

Saving Shadows

Sunken Shadows

Lasting Shadows

Fierce Shadows

Broken Shadows

Framed Shadows

Endless Shadows

Fading Shadows

Damaged Shadows (coming Oct 2022)

Women of Power Series

Chosen for Power

Built for Power

Fashioned for Power

Destined for Power

Web of Lies Series

Whispered Lies

Rogue Lies

Shattered Lies

Moonshine Hollow Series

Moonshine & Murder

Moonshine & Malice

Moonshine & Mayhem

Moonshine & Mischief

Moonshine & Menace

Moonshine & Masquerades

ABOUT THE AUTHOR

Kathleen Brooks is a New York Times, Wall Street Journal, and USA Today bestselling author. Kathleen's stories are romantic suspense featuring strong female heroines, humor, and happily-ever-afters. Her Bluegrass Series and follow-up Bluegrass Brothers Series feature small town charm with quirky characters that have captured the hearts of readers around the world.

Kathleen is an animal lover who supports rescue organizations and other non-profit organizations such as Friends and Vets Helping Pets whose goals are to protect and save our four-legged family members.

Email Notice of New Releases

https://kathleen-brooks.com/new-release-notifications

Kathleen's Website
www.kathleen-brooks.com
Facebook Page
www.facebook.com/KathleenBrooksAuthor
Twitter
www.twitter.com/BluegrassBrooks
Goodreads
www.goodreads.com

Made in the USA
Monee, IL
30 August 2022

12751649R00173